The Lethal Elixir kept me intrigued from start to finish. It is just the right mix of great characters, romance and science. It is great to see a smart female physician try to figure out a complex medical/bioterrorism puzzle much like it is done in the real world.

Margaret Hagan, M.D.
Infectious Disease Physician
Director: Infection Prevention, Ascension Via Christi Hospitals
Wichita, KS

Dr. Ross has once again combined a medical thriller with mystery, intrigue and a storyline that is full of cliffhangers and plot twists with such a sexy edge! It's full of suspenseful magic!

Tina Eddy
Regional Vice President
Fresenius Medical Care North America

WARNING: You will not be able to put this book down! It grabs you from the first page and takes you on a wild roller coaster ride until the very end. The unexpected twists and turns will leave you breathless.

Sierra Scott
TV News Anchor & Ms. America 2020

THE
LETHAL
ELIXIR

DENNIS ROSS

ARCHWAY
PUBLISHING

Archway Publishing books may be ordered
through booksellers or by contacting:

Archway Publishing
1663 Liberty Drive
Bloomington, IN 47403
www.archwaypublishing.com
844-669-3957

ISBN: 978-1-6657-0475-5 (sc)
ISBN: 978-1-6657-0473-1 (hc)
ISBN: 978-1-6657-0474-8 (e)

Library of Congress Control Number: 2021906083

Print information available on the last page.

Archway Publishing rev. date: 08/03/2021

I wish to thank Dr. Angela Hewlett and Dr. Margaret Hagan for their invaluable recommendations and suggestions in writing this book. I would also like to thank my wife Ann and children Amy, Mindy, Kristy and Aaron for their unconditional support and love. Finally, I would like to recognize all those who have suffered in the viral pandemic either experiencing the disease or losing loved ones.

PROLOGUE

Jason Turley entered Mickey's Bar and Grill not far from his apartment. It was a Thursday night in September. The holidays were around the corner, but since he'd moved to Chicago, his life had been miserable. He had no plans to go home this year. No friends. Other than work, there was little that gave him any pleasure.

He knew very few people, mostly because he kept to himself. His previous encounters with women hadn't been all that successful, and he wasn't particularly close to his family.

He entered the poorly lit establishment and found a small table in one corner of the room. The place was smoky, which made his eyes water slightly, but he didn't mind. He just wanted a stiff drink to take his mind off of his existence.

There were very few people in the bar, which was fine with him. He wasn't in much of a mood to talk to anyone.

A waitress in a very short outfit came to his table and asked him for his order. As he glanced up, he subtly studied her figure. He hadn't had much contact with women lately, and seeing this attractive waitress made him realize that he missed having a girlfriend.

1

"I'm Sheila," she said. "Is there something you would like from the bar?"

"Sure, how about an old-fashioned?"

"Any particular whisky?" she asked.

"I like Templeton Rye. Do you have that?"

"I'm sure we do. On the rocks?"

"Perfect."

As he was snacking on the nuts and pretzels, he caught sight, out of the corner of his eye, of an attractive Asian woman by herself. He hadn't noticed her when he first came in, probably because of the dim lighting and smoke. She seemed lonely, simply staring ahead—but then she turned, looked directly at him, and smiled.

She had her legs crossed, and they seemed perfectly proportioned. Her low-cut red dress set off a figure that was equally desirable. He was taken aback initially by the attention she seemed to show him, but he cordially returned her smile. She had ordered a gin and tonic, and as it was delivered to her table, she whispered something to the same waitress who had waited on him.

A few minutes later, Sheila walked over and told him, "That lady over there asked if she could join you. She's here alone, and she thought that the two of you could get to know each other."

"Sure, why not. Have her bring her drink over."

A few minutes later, the lady in red joined him and extended her hand as she sat down.

"Susan, Susan Lee. You looked a little lonely over here, so I thought we could get acquainted. Maybe we could commiserate together."

"Jason Turley. So I guess you have something that you're unhappy about?"

"It's called a husband," she replied with a grimace. "Frank

and I aren't exactly getting along. I'm not sure that we ever will. It was never a great fit from the beginning. He's horrible to be around. He cares very little about me; gone all the time and not very friendly. We've been married for five years, but I can't imagine being married to him for five more."

"I'm sorry to hear that," said Jason. "Maybe it's why I've never gotten married. I've always been concerned that after the honeymoon, I would look at her and say *What have I done?*"

"Here's some advice," Susan replied. "Take your time and make sure before taking the big plunge."

"Do you have any children?" he asked.

"No, thank goodness. That would really complicate things."

"So, where's your husband tonight?"

"Gone away on business as usual," she said. "I kind of wonder if there's some other woman in his life. Can't prove it, however. So, what about you? What do you do? Are you connected with someone?"

"I just moved here from Washington, DC," he told her. "I worked for the government there, and at times I miss the job I had. Now I'm in finance, which quite frankly is boring. In DC, there was always something exciting going on. And no, no one special in my life."

"So, no girlfriends? I would have thought a good-looking guy like you would have three or four."

"No, not exactly like that. I've had few, but none that I really fell for."

"What was your government job?"

"I worked at the Pentagon. I was in the area of bioweapons research. I know it seems crazy, since I'm a financial analyst, but they needed someone to crunch numbers."

He added, "You know, it's a crazy world out there. We

were looking at all the nontraditional weapons that could be used in war. Now I work as a financial analyst for an investment bank. Substantially different in many ways from what I did before, but numbers are numbers. I think I'm pretty good at what I do, and the investment bank likes the research I conduct for them."

"Your old job sounds much more interesting. New weaponry sounds very exciting—like James Bond," she said, smiling.

He smiled back. "Not really. Besides the usual bombs and bullets, there's gas warfare and germ warfare. You probably know that gas warfare is banned, but it seems to still crop up in Third World nations. Germ warfare, that's a little newer. With the broad use of antibiotics in the world, bacteria and viruses are becoming more difficult to treat. Now, if you modify them in a lab, you can make them very lethal."

"Interesting, but very scary, if you ask me."

"Now that's an understatement," he said. "Germ warfare could wipe out millions without firing a shot, and no loss of life on your side. That is, unless it would get out of control. If you have the germ weapon, you better be sure you also have the treatment for it."

"I can see that. What an interesting profession. So why did you leave?"

"I suppose I was getting a little restless," he said. "No social life, and I thought that a move to another city might help that. So far, I'd say life is boring."

Staring directly at him, she said, "Maybe I can help that?"

"Maybe you can. It sounds like you're a woman with experience," he said as he placed his hand on her leg.

"Some, I suppose, but I'm guessing you could teach me more."

"Why don't we finish our drinks, and you can come over to my apartment?" he suggested. "It's not far from here."

"I'd love to."

They both finished their drinks at about the same time, and Susan followed Jason out to his car.

"Should I leave my car here or follow you?" she asked.

"How about you drive your car, and I'll leave mine here," he suggested. "I can always come back and get it later."

Susan got into the driver's seat, and Jason jumped into the passenger seat. He directed her to turn right, go about six blocks, and make a left. As she was driving, he let his hand slide up her skirt so he could feel her more intimately.

Susan groaned as he explored her. "You don't like to waste any time," she said. "I like a guy who takes control."

"I'm planning on taking more control when we arrive at my apartment."

They took the elevator to his tenth-floor apartment, and he opened the door. It was very well appointed, with contemporary furniture, a big-screen TV, and a desk with a computer. In one corner was a minibar, so Jason went immediately there to fix Susan a cocktail.

"So, another gin and tonic?" he asked.

"How about I have what you have?"

"Well, I'm not sure that you would like whisky or bourbon, but I'm having an old-fashioned. I've grown to like these, but it's strong."

"Strong sounds perfect at this time."

After completing his bartending, he handed her the drink first.

"Cheers. To a new relationship."

"Cheers," she responded.

After taking one sip, she set the glass down and proceeded to give Jason a very passionate kiss. He reciprocated by exploring her body. He found the zipper on the back of her dress and carefully slipped it down allowing the red dress to slide off of her shoulders. He unsnapped her bra, removing it. She was well developed, and it was obvious to him that she was very familiar with what she was doing.

She unbuckled his belt and slid his pants down. Soon they were both naked and in bed. Jason hadn't experienced such a sexual encounter in his life, and it didn't stop with one climax. After several hours, they both fell asleep.

When he awakened in the morning, he had a splitting headache. Susan lay beside him and began to wake as well.

"Well, what a night, Tiger," she said. "You're a monster in bed, and I loved it. It hasn't felt that good in a long time."

"I felt the same way. Can we meet again?"

"Of course," she said. "I want to hear more about your job. How interesting! But I have to go now. Frank will be coming home this afternoon."

After she left, Jason lay staring at the ceiling. *I know that I need to get up and go to work, but suddenly life has taken on a new perspective. It isn't just my job I have to think about. Now it's a new relationship that I would have never thought could have happened.*

He showered and dressed, grabbed a cup of coffee, and hurried off to his office.

Weeks passed, and he didn't hear from her. As Jason sat at his desk, his mind wandered. *I want to see her again,* he thought, *but maybe I'm getting myself into a mess. I haven't heard from her for more than a month. Maybe she's gotten back with her husband. She gave me her number, but I'm reluctant to call. I've got to get up my nerve and call her now.*

He lifted the receiver and slowly dialed. Susan answered after three rings.

"Susan, it's Jason. Can you talk now?"

"Yes," she said. "It's great timing. How have you been? I've been eager to hear from you and wondered if you had forgotten me."

"Are you kidding? I've wondered if you simply brushed me off after our one night together."

"How could I forget that night?" she exclaimed. "It was amazing."

"It was for me too, but I thought that you had likely reconnected with your husband. Has anything changed?"

"Are you kidding? Nothing will change with him," she said with disgust. "He's oblivious to me and what I do."

"In that case, is there a time we can see each other?"

"Tonight will work," she told him. "Frank's gone again."

"Fantastic. My place?"

"Sure, why not?"

"Come over about six thirty. I'll try to have something for us."

Jason couldn't concentrate on his work all day, thinking about seeing Susan again that night. He tried focusing on the tech stocks that he was to research, but today his mind would not stop wandering.

He thought, *what food should I prepare for tonight's dinner?* He decided to try a pasta dish with French bread and maybe white wine. He stopped on his way home to pick up the ingredients and a bottle of Chalk Hill Chardonnay. It was one of his favorites.

After preparing the food, he set up two plates on his small

table and lit two candles to set the mood. Promptly at six thirty, his doorbell rang.

"Susan, it is so great to see you again," he said as she came in. "You look stunning as always. I was so taken with you when we met for the first time in the bar. It was like something that was meant to be. But it's an issue that you're married."

"Married, yes, but I would same in name only. I'm not sure how much longer that is going to last. There isn't much of a relationship there." She frowned, then changed the subject. "I would rather hear more about you than talk about Frank. I want to hear about Washington, DC. The monuments, the federal buildings, the heart of our country's government—I've been told that it's beautiful. And you worked at the Pentagon. Wow. Only special people are there."

"Well, as I said before, DC was exciting. Besides the city, I had several interactions with JPEO. It's the Joint Program Executive Office for Chemical, Biological, Radiological, and Nuclear Defense. A lot easier to say JPEO. This agency is to combat these potential forces I mentioned."

"I'm curious," she said. "Are you developing new weapons or trying to find ways to suppress them?"

"Most of this I can't really talk about, but no, we're not developing them. It's a matter of controlling them. You see, if they were released here, we have to find a way to stop the spread, avoid fatalities and panic. These infections are brutal. Well, I would say horrible."

"So, what infections are we talking about?" she asked. "Tropical illnesses? Bacterial infections? Viruses?"

"All those," he told her. "We just don't know what our adversaries may be planning. There is intelligence that gives us some idea, but we still can't be sure. One thing that's evident: it would be easy to bring them into our country, and that's what scares us all."

"It's certainly admirable that you have helped investigate this," she said. "So, did you discover any cures or ways to stop them?"

"Look, I'm not the scientist, remember? But they have found some measures that will help. We are on the verge of being able to stop the spread of some of the more serious ones. Honestly, these are lethal diseases that aren't that easy to contain. I can't really say any more than this."

"I'm proud of you nevertheless," she said. "I'm sure you've contributed a great deal. With the American ingenuity, they'll find a treatment."

"I'm surprised at your interest in bioweapons," he remarked. "Every girl I ever dated could have cared less. But enough talk about work. You have to try my pasta with some wine."

"It looks delicious," she declared. "I'm amazed at how well you can cook."

"Being a bachelor, it's either cook or starve," he said with a chuckle. "Actually, I enjoy cooking."

"Wow, this is delicious," Susan said as she tasted the pasta and took a sip of the wine.

Jason had picked up a tiramisu from a local bakery for dessert. "Now don't tell me you made this," Susan said.

"No, not really," he admitted. "That I bought at this cute little bakery that makes the best pastries."

"Well, everything is just spectacular." She rose to go around the table and give him a kiss. "We could have some icing on the cake now. What do you think?"

"It's been six weeks, and I haven't forgotten our night together. I was hoping you would say that."

Moments later, they were in bed, making love. At the end,

Susan turned to him and said, "You have become so special to me. I haven't felt this way about anyone before. Let's not let our time apart go so long the next time."

"I won't now that I know you want to see me as much as I want to see you," Jason responded. "By the way," he added, "what is your Chinese name?"

"Huan Jiao," she said. "In China, women often keep their surname when they marry. But it's easier if you just call me Susan."

Two weeks passed. Jason had sent and received a few text messages back and forth with Susan. It always brightened his day. He wondered if this could be a problem if her husband were to discover them. He thought to himself, *Maybe it's better if I call more rather than text. It wouldn't be discoverable.* So, he dialed her number, hoping that he wouldn't reach her husband. Susan answered after a few rings, and she immediately recognized his voice.

"Susan," he said, "I'm tired of texting. How about we just meet face to face and do something."

"Sure, I'm all for that," she said. "How about a walk in the park? Clemson Park is near us."

"Perfect," he agreed. "I'll be leaving work in an hour. Should I meet you there?"

"Yes. I'll be by the fountain on the park bench. See you then."

Jason packed up the work that he had to take home for the evening and walked to his car. He knew exactly the park that Susan was talking about. He enjoyed walking around the lake, and although the weather was getting chilly, he thought it would be a good time to meet up. After stopping, he made his way to the bench. Susan was there overlooking the pond and the beautiful trees in their fall colors.

"Hey, gorgeous, you seem lost in thought," he said as he sat beside her.

"I am. It's so peaceful and quiet here. It's great to see you again. Let's go for a walk. It's a perfect day to be out here."

As they strolled along, Jason took hold of her hand, and she looked up at him and smiled.

"You know, when it's so beautiful and quiescent, you just wonder how the world could also be dangerous," she said. "I can't get out of my mind our discussion about the viruses and bacteria that you said could be released and infect millions. Why would anyone want to do that?"

"That's hard to understand," he admitted. "I guess they just have tremendous hatred or an overriding desire to cause destruction in order to change a society like ours."

"I suppose they're jealous of what we have here," she mused.

"That could be it. Who knows?"

"There is something I need to tell you," she said quietly. "I was supposed to have my period two weeks ago, and it hasn't happened. In the excitement of our night together, we didn't use any birth control. Basically, Frank and I don't have sex, so I just haven't been focused on that lately. I hope this doesn't mean something. I'm usually very regular."

"Oh my gosh," he exclaimed. "Are you kidding? Do you think that you might be pregnant?"

"I'm not sure," she said. "I've had a queasy stomach in the mornings, which has me concerned that I might be."

"How would we handle this?" he asked. "Let's get a test kit now and find out. I'll drive to the Walgreens that's nearby and pick up a kit. I have to know."

As they drove, there was no conversation. Finally, Jason

broke the silence. "I just hadn't thought about using protection. It was stupid of me. After I pick up the kit, let's go to my apartment and do the test."

He returned quickly from the drugstore and jumped in the car. They were close to his apartment, so it didn't take long before he was pulling into his parking spot. Susan went into the bathroom and passed urine to conduct the test. In a short time, she came out, and her face said it all.

"You're pregnant, aren't you?" asked Jason.

She nodded her head yes.

"Oh my God," he exclaimed. "What are we going to do?"

"I'll make sure that I have sex with Frank," she said, "and he'll think that this is his child. That's all we can do. In the meantime, we'll find time to be together."

As Jason stared at her in disbelief, he thought, *I can't believe I'm going to be a father.*

CHAPTER 1

Seven months later ...

The ambulance raced frantically to Deaconess Hospital through rush-hour traffic, with lights flashing and siren blaring. Its cargo, a male in his twenties, was writhing in pain, mumbling incoherent phrases and moving every extremity with no purposeful meaning. Dan Rutherford, the brawny paramedic driving the ambulance, gripped the steering wheel tightly as he weaved down Park Avenue. Turning his head over his right shoulder, he yelled to his fellow paramedic, "Tom, how's our patient?"

"Not good," Tom shouted back. "Blood pressure is 75/50, and he's totally delirious. Temperature is 103 degrees."

"Be sure to wear some protective gear," Dan advised. "We don't know what this guy may have."

"I've got on latex gloves, protective glasses, and a mask. I just noticed a pinkish fluid leaking through his clothing, so I'm going to take his shirt off and check it out," Tom responded. "Oh my gosh, he's covered with a rash, and some have blistered. Where they have ruptured is where the red fluid is coming from. It's likely bloody serum."

"Any history available?"

"His landlady discovered him on the floor of his apartment," Tom replied. "She mentioned that there was stool on the floor. Some of this appeared to be blood. Apparently, he hadn't been seen in several days. She couldn't tell me much other than he does have a girlfriend, but she wasn't sure of her name. She wasn't aware of any family."

"He needs IV fluids now," said Dan. "Give him a bolus of one thousand ccs normal saline. I'll let the emergency room know about his status. I'll tell them to get an isolation room available. Who knows what he's got?"

As the ambulance pulled into the overhanging portico of Deaconess ER, nurses and techs were there to help move the patient through the automatic doors. The area had been cleared of any other emergency-room traffic to ensure a quick entrance into a trauma room used at times for isolation. They knew they had a very sick patient to attend to. Dr. John Singer, a fourth-year surgical resident rotating on trauma, and a cadre of nursing staff stood draped in gowns, gloves, and masks. They had been warned of the potential infectious etiology.

"Wow, this guy is a mess," declared Singer. "How's his electrocardiogram?"

"Tachycardia," reported the charge nurse, "but no arrhythmias. Pressure's remained low and temp is still high. Should I keep the IV running fast?"

"Keep the rate at five hundred ccs an hour and get blood cultures, CBC, CMP, cardiac enzymes, viral PCR studies, and, if possible, a sample of this fluid leaking from the blisters to send for cultures," Singer responded. "Everyone needs protective gear. Oh, and who was in the back of the ambulance with the patient? I want that person taken to the decontamination room upstairs. He needs to shed his clothes and shower with the decontamination solution. I want him to wear scrubs, and we'll decide what to do with his clothing. May need to burn it."

James Singleton, a nurse technician, grumbled as he helped to undress the patient. "What a pain wearing all this gear!" he declared. "Do we really need protective gowns? These things are hot and miserable."

"Jack, listen to the doctor. We don't know what's going on here," warned his fellow tech.

"It's probably a simple virus, and we have to go through all this mess for nothing. I'm shedding this stuff as soon as possible. In fact, I'm getting rid of it now, since everyone's out of the room."

"Dr. Singer, we have the labs back. They don't look good," the charge nurse said. "Liver enzymes are very high, His creatinine is 5mg percent so his kidneys are shutting down, and he has a white blood cell count of thirty-five hundred. Interesting, isn't it? A low white count. Think it could be a virus?"

"Let's get an isolation bed in the medical intensive care," said Singer. "We'll use the new biocontainment unit. I think we should have Infectious Diseases see the patient as soon as possible. Whatever this guy has contracted, it isn't something ordinary, and we need help deciding on antibiotics. Get ahold of Maggie Hamilton. Oh, and we need Adam Foster and Eric Strong. He's likely going to need dialysis and a line."

Chest and abdominal X-rays were taken. Vasopressors were started to raise the patient's blood pressure, and once he appeared to stabilize, he was transferred using the service elevator to the special isolation room.

Deaconess had decided two years earlier that it wanted to be a leader in high-risk patients needing isolation, so a special area was set aside to isolate patients with contagious infections. The rooms were very sterile, with simple walls; no carpeting and no wallpaper; and a camera in the upper corner pointed at the bed to monitor the patient. There were windows to allow the patient to see outside and an air-filtration system that exchanged air without recirculating or exposing the remaining area to the air expelled. The air instead was sent outside through an elaborate air duct system.

For doctors and nurses to evaluate patients, they had to don special gowns with built-in fans to constantly force air away from them and into the room. They double-gloved their hands and fully covered the head and face.

Maggie Hamilton was the first of the specialists to arrive. Sitting at the control booth, she stared at the monitor, watching the patient thrash back and forth as a gowned nurse stood beside him to ensure he didn't injury himself. Maggie studied the vital signs and the lab work that had been collected in the emergency room.

She turned to the charge nurse and said, "So we don't

have much history here. I understand he was a loner except for possibly a girlfriend. Do you have his landlady's number? I want to give her call. Maybe she can give me some insight into what's gone on."

"The landlady's name is Gretchen Summers," the nurse replied. "She's the only contact we have. Here is her number, but EMS said she wasn't very helpful."

Maggie dialed the number, and a soft but pleasant voice answered after four rings.

"Ms. Summers, this is Dr. Hamilton," Maggie began. "I'm an infectious diseases specialist at Deaconess Hospital, and I'm seeing this young man who rents an apartment from you. You probably know he's very ill, but I wondered if you could give me some history."

"Well, Doctor, Alex keeps to himself. His full name is Alex Williamson. I never see him with friends, although occasionally there is a young woman who stops by. I believe she's his girlfriend. She's always been pleasant to me, but I don't remember her full name. I think she was Heidi something. Sorry, I can't remember."

"So how long has Alex lived in your apartment?"

"He has rented from me about two years," the landlady replied. "He's been a good renter. No parties. No damage to the apartment. No complaints from anyone."

"Any names of family?" Maggie asked.

"Sorry, he never gave me any emergency contact. Said there wasn't anyone, which I thought was rather sad, considering how young he was."

"Do you know where he worked?" Maggie pressed. "Maybe coworkers would have some information."

"I know that you will think this strange, but he always kept to himself, and although he was always pleasant, he never wanted to discuss his personal life with me at all. Since he paid his bills, I never pressed him on his employment."

"Had he complained to you about being ill at all?"

"No, not really," said the landlady. "In fact, he was a big exercise person. He worked out at the gym down the street. He often rode his bike there. I would see him come home being drenched. When I said to him that it must have been a big workout, he always said he liked to work up a sweat."

"Do you know the name of the gym?" asked Maggie.

"Oh, yeah, it was Rick's Gym and Fitness. Just a local place; not one of those chains, you know. Maybe someone there can give you more information."

"Do you know if he traveled outside of the country?"

"No, not that I'm aware of. As I said, he mainly just hung around his apartment."

"Thanks, Ms. Summers. If you think of something, page me through the hospital operator at Deaconess. This is probably the best way to reach me. By the way, keep his apartment locked and don't go in. I would like to arrange a special cleaning crew to avoid anyone getting this same illness."

Hanging up, Maggie mulled over where this young man could have contracted a serious infection. *He apparently didn't travel much, didn't have a lot of contact with others, was a loner, but somewhere he's gotten into something he shouldn't have, and whatever that was, it was serious. He's fighting for his life.*

Studying the lab results, she noted the low white blood cell count. *Could be overwhelming sepsis,* she thought. *Or perhaps a virus—but if a virus, this must be one hell of a virus.*

—◄▆▆▆►—

Maggie was staring straight ahead in deep thought as Adam Foster entered the control area.

"So, Maggie, what is it?" he asked. "You're so damn smart, I figured you would have the diagnosis by now."

"You're giving me too much credit. I just looked at the guy. Whatever it is, I'd say he has a fifty-fifty chance at best. I'm starting broad-spectrum antibiotics."

"Have you found anyone who can give you information on the patient?" Adam asked.

"No, not really. His landlady was very nice but also very unhelpful. She said he'd given her virtually no personal information, which seemed surprising to me. The only thing that could be helpful is that we know the name of the gym where he worked out. He has a girlfriend but no name. She didn't even know where he was employed."

"Really?" Adam said in surprise. "Didn't she need some assurance he could pay the rent?"

"I think she felt sorry for him. He must have been pretty reliable at paying and didn't cause her any trouble. I sense, in a way, she adopted him as a child. He supposedly didn't have any family."

"How are his vitals doing?" asked Adam.

"No worse. Norepinephrine and vasopressin to help his low blood pressure, and it's up to one hundred over seventy. No urine so far, so break out your dialysis machine."

"Eric should be here soon to put in the catheter to start him," Adam replied, "and he'll get you the intravenous access for your drugs and the pressers. Do you want me to call the gym and see if I can find out more information?"

"No," said Maggie, "I can do this. I started this, so let me give them a call."

Maggie grabbed the yellow pages and found Rick's Gym and Fitness. She wrote down the phone number, picked up a phone, and dialed the number. An enthusiastic male answered.

"Rick's Gym. How about joining our spinning class?"

"Actually, I could probably use that," said Maggie, "but I'm calling about one of your members who goes there regularly. My name is Dr. Margaret Hamilton, and Alex Williamson is a patient of mine here at Deaconess Hospital. He has been admitted to the intensive care unit and is very ill. I can't really give you more information, but we don't know much about him. He has no family, and it seems few friends, but his landlady says that he does work out in your gym four or five times a week. Supposedly he brings a girlfriend with him, but we don't know her name, and I was hoping that you could help me out. Any idea who she might be?"

"Oh, yeah, Alex. This guy is intense," said the voice on the phone. "You know, some people come to the gym, lean on the equipment, and flirt with girls or just talk for an hour. Not Alex. It is all business when he arrives. He goes from one piece of equipment to another, pumping the iron or doing something aerobic—and you're right, he has a cute girl with him. He always pays for her guest pass. Let me look through the sign-ins and see if I can find her name."

Maggie could hear papers shuffling as the man rummaged through the sign-in booklet. Soon, he came back on the line.

"Found it. Her name is Heidi Campton. You know, she is a lot like him. Doesn't say much. She focuses on working out and leaves sweating and pumped up. They usually ride the bike here."

"Do you have any contact information for her?" Maggie asked.

"We do make people sign a waiver and usually get other

contact information, but she only gave us an address: 110 Pine Street, Apartment 201. No phone number."

"Thank you," Maggie said. "This is very helpful. Oh, by the way, what's your name?"

"Sorry, I guess I never told you. It's Jake. Tell Alex we hope he gets better and comes back to inspire a few people here."

"I'll do that, and thanks again."

Maggie hung up the phone and began to consider how to get ahold of Heidi. *I think she is the key to getting more historical information. She seems to know Alex better than anyone else.* Lost in thought, she didn't see Adam return to the control booth.

"Find anything out from the gym?" Adam asked.

"The name of the girlfriend, but no phone number. I plan to go to her apartment."

"Guess what?" Adam said. "I discovered where this guy works, and you won't believe it."

CHAPTER 2

Adam paused, hoping to create more drama. "So I ran into the lab tech picking up the samples of urine and blood and told her about this patient and the difficulty we were having getting any information. She asked his name, and when she saw him on the monitors, she exclaimed, "Oh my gosh. That's Alex who works in the lab."

"Are you kidding me? He works here?" Maggie responded in disbelief.

"Not only that, he works in microbiology and virology."

"Yikes. Could he have caught something here in the hospital? I haven't seen any patient in the last two weeks with any illness close to this."

"All I know is that he would be at risk of getting something," said Adam. "This should make Tuttle, the CEO, pee his pants. Can you imagine the publicity from this?"

"I'm going to head to the lab now and see what I can find out from Alex's fellow employees," said Maggie. "Maybe they can give some insight into what's happened or more information on Alex. Oh, by the way, I have the name of his girlfriend, and an address but no phone number. I may try to head over to her place after work. She hasn't come to visit, has she? Her name is Heidi Campton. I guess she's a lot like our patient: a loner with very few friends."

"I haven't seen any visitors," Adam told her, "and certainly no cute girls."

After leaving the control booth and the biocontainment area, Maggie took the elevator to the third floor and the central laboratory. Arriving at the reception desk, she was greeted with, "Hi, Dr. Hamilton. Coming to check on cultures?"

"As a matter of fact, yes," said Maggie, "but I know for this patient it's too early to expect results. I really would like to talk with someone in micro. Anybody around?"

"Oh sure. Tess, the director just arrived for her shift. I'm sure she would be happy to talk with you. I'll get her up here."

Maggie heard the receptionist dial the number and tell the director that she was there. Soon, a thirty-five-ish woman flew through the swinging doors into the waiting room and extended her hand to Maggie.

"Dr. Hamilton, what can I help you with? You don't often come down to the lab. We usually talk to you by phone."

"I know that is usually what happens," replied Maggie, "but that's because I just need to know culture results. Certainly, on the patient I'm going to tell you about, we are very interested in what infection he may have contracted. But in this case, I need more personal information, and I hope you can help. You see, the patient is Alex Williamson, and I understand that he works here."

"Alex, sure, he does work here," Tess said with concern. "We wondered why he hadn't shown up. It isn't like him. He's quiet but compulsive. He's never late and always does his job—and in fact is very good. He started working here about five years ago, just out of school. So what's going on?"

"He was found semicomatose at his apartment with high fever and low blood pressure. He can't give any history. His kidneys are shutting down, and there are no family or friends that we can get any information from. Has he complained of being ill or has he looked sick recently?" Maggie asked.

"He was here about a week ago and hasn't answered any calls to his cell phone," replied Tess. "He looked fine then. I'm not aware that he has traveled anywhere. In reality, he never takes time off. He's said that he doesn't really have anywhere to go. Often, he seems somewhat sad. I guess his parents died of cancer, and he has no siblings."

"Do you know of any odd infections that have cultured out recently? I wondered if perhaps someone had tularemia or anthrax or something weird. Not just the usual MRSA or strep."

"No," said Tess, "just the boring usual infections, I believe. You would probably know about any of these as well, because they would most likely call you to see the patient."

"Well, yes and no," said Maggie. "If the patient died before I was consulted, I probably wouldn't know about it. We have our patient in the biocontainment area because this looks like a contagious disease, and we're treating it like that. After all, Deaconess spent a few million dollars to create this facility, and it has never been used. I'm grateful they had the insight to design a space like this. I can't imagine what would happen if we had been faced with one of these highly contagious infections and had no place to put the patient. Do you know of any family or friends I could call about Alex?"

"Sorry, I don't," Tess admitted. "As I said, Alex did a great job here but didn't mingle with the staff, never went out after work with the other employees, and I never saw him with anyone."

"Thanks for your help, Tess. If you think of someone or something, please call me. And I'll be interested in seeing the results of his tests, so whenever you find something out, just page me."

Maggie left the lab heading to the parking garage. She was eager to visit Heidi Campton's apartment. She found her Toyota Camry on the second level of the garage and dialed in the address on her cell phone's MapQuest.

For Maggie, a car was simply a form of transportation. She didn't really care about its looks—just that it ran and didn't give her trouble. She did get a little excited about picking out a bright red color, but otherwise, no frills.

Her GPS device suggested that it was about five miles to Heidi's apartment and estimated that she would arrive in thirty minutes. Maggie knew, however, that traffic could be bad, and it might take longer. She figured if she could get there about suppertime, she would have a better chance of finding Heidi at home.

The area where Heidi lived was a very middle-class neighborhood. There were long streets of row housing, and some of these homes had been made into apartments. Arriving at Pine, she found the address. It was a tall row house.

She went through the gate and to the front door, where she found several doorbells to ring for the inhabitants. Heidi's apartment was listed on the second floor. She pushed the button and could hear the bell ring, but no one answered the intercom connected to the doorbell.

Maggie glanced around to see if there was anyone in the

hall as she peered through the door, but it was dark, and there was no activity. Finally, giving up, she turned to go back to her car. Just as she was leaving through the gate, she saw a young girl walking to the door.

"Excuse me, but do you happen to know Heidi Campton?" Maggie called out. "I understand she lives here?"

"Oh, sure, she's on the second floor. I see her coming and going, but honestly, I never talk to her. She pretty much keeps to herself."

"Have you seen her recently?" Maggie asked.

"No, not in the last several days. Maybe's she's on vacation. Not sure."

"Is there someone who would know where she might be? I'm a physician caring for her boyfriend," Maggie said in explanation, "and he's quite ill. I thought that she could give us some insight as to where he might have caught an infection."

"Hmm … I've seen her with this guy, but they just hang out. Don't seem to associate with anyone here at the apartment. I guess he must be her boyfriend, but like I said, they stick to themselves."

"OK," Maggie replied, "but if you think of something, here's my card. Just page me at Deaconess Hospital. They can reach me at any time. Do you have a number if I need to reach you?"

"Sure, no problem. Here's my cell phone number. You can call me if you need to. I'm Kim, by the way. Kim Schneider."

"Thanks, Kim."

As Maggie left the apartment and found her way back to the parked Camry, she decided to check on her patient one more time before heading home. When she arrived at the biocontainment center, she saw that Adam had started the patient on dialysis. Alex's vital signs were stable, but he continued to have a high fever, reduced consciousness, and low blood pressure.

It appeared to her there was little more she could do for the patient for the night, so she let the nurses know she was going home but asked them to be sure to call if Alex's girlfriend, Heidi Campton, showed up. She made her way back to her car and realized she was exhausted. She had eaten very little that day.

I think I have a salad or a wrap at home—but right now, I think I could really use a glass of wine.

Maggie had bought a modest home in the Chicago suburbs. She figured she didn't need much. After all, most of her time was spent at the hospital. She had no boyfriend or husband, and a large house would just take up a lot of her time. The twenty-five-hundred-square-foot patio home fit her lifestyle perfectly. Someone else cared for the yard; she had a pool she could use, but she didn't have to maintain it; and there was good security.

She parked in the garage and headed toward the kitchen, kicking off her shoes and locating that bottle of Chardonnay. She had a leftover salad with grilled chicken that tasted surprisingly good—maybe because she was starving. She pulled out her laptop and began searching for answers to her patient's infection.

She decided to simply put in search symptoms like *fever*, *blisters*, and *renal failure*. A number of unusual diagnoses popped up, including vasculitis, Steven Johnson's syndrome, and herpes zoster—but also smallpox, chickenpox, and Ebola. *Wow,* Maggie thought. *What a variety of illnesses.*

Where would this guy who never goes anywhere, never mingles with anyone, is in excellent health from working out, contract some strange illness? she wondered. *I guess I just need to sleep on it and see what the cultures show.*

She got into her pajamas and tried reading for a while but fell asleep holding the book in her lap—only to be awakened by her phone ringing. She grabbed the phone and sleepily answered, "Dr. Hamilton. He's worse? What's going on? Pressure is lower? Still high fever? Rash seems to be worsening?"

As she became more alert, she said, "I want you to give him a gram of solumedrol." Maggie was beginning to think that Alex likely had an overwhelming infection that was leading to a total collapse of his organs, and additional cortisone in the form of solumedrol might help stabilize his condition. She couldn't think of anything else that could be done.

As in the past when she'd had patients like this, she decided to pray. "Father, guide me in how to treat this young man. Help me find the cause of his illness, and if it be your will, let him survive."

She had dealt with death and dying many times, and she always asked God for guidance. She had been humbled enough to know that you couldn't possibly cure every patient, but it gave her solace that she had sought every avenue to help her patients.

With that, she fell asleep.

CHAPTER 3

Maggie could see the sun just rising through her bedroom window as she rolled over in bed. She thought for a moment, trying to remember if she had gotten any more calls in the night but realized she hadn't. She figured that if Alex had died, they would have called her—but she was curious, so she grabbed the phone by her bedside and dialed the biocontainment center. The charge nurse who had called her during the night was still on duty and answered the phone.

"This is Dr. Hamilton," said Maggie. "I believe you called me last night, and I just wanted to find out how our patient is doing."

"The steroids seemed to do the trick," the nurse replied. "His pressure came up, and overall, he seems better. Still has a fever, but the steroids helped that as well. Still no urine output, but I didn't think you would anticipate any change there."

Maggie was relieved to hear Alex had survived, but she knew he had a long way to go if he was to ever get out of the hospital. She got up, slipped out of her pajamas, and stared at herself in the mirror. *I don't look so bad,* she thought. She was five foot six inches tall, with blonde hair and blue eyes. She cut her hair short; made it easy to care for.

She showered, found a different outfit for the day, and fixed a pot of coffee. Today, she would need more than one cup of java to help her think clearly.

After arriving at the hospital, Maggie made her way to the biocontainment center and called micro.

"Anything showing up on the cultures so far?" she asked. "I know it's early, but I thought with this guy's condition, it might show up more quickly."

"Sorry, so far nothing," answered the lab tech.

"Be sure to call if something pops up," Maggie requested. "Oh, and by the way, I want you to send samples to the Centers for Disease Control. I'm worried that this patient may have something strange that's not going to show up on the routine tests that we do. If you want, I can call them. I know some people there that I trained with."

"Sure, Doctor. It might be a good idea to give them some background on the patient."

Maggie hung up the phone and searched her cell phone contacts. She knew she could find Jamie's number—her friend from fellowship.

Ah, here it is.

She dialed, and Jamie answered on the second ring.

"Hey Jamie," she began, "it's Maggie Hamilton. I'm sending you some blood samples on a sick one here in Chicago. Who knows what he's got? He's in renal failure, covered with blisters, in shock, and has a high fever. It's early, but so far, the cultures are negative. I obviously thought that maybe he contracted some weird infection traveling outside the United States. Problem is, he hasn't gone anywhere. It turns out he works in the micro and virology lab here at the hospital. We haven't had any strange infections that I'm aware of, but you never know. Anyway, we need your help."

"Sure, Maggie. Sounds interesting. We'll run the blood through several panels. You know, the viral hemorrhagic fevers: Lassa fever, Ebola, malaria, Marburg virus, typhoid, etc. I'm sure you've checked the usual stuff: influenza or measles."

"It's in the works," Maggie replied. "We're concerned that he could have caught something in the lab."

"Understandable. I'll let you know."

Maggie reviewed the labs from the day. *Still low white count and further drop in his hemoglobin or red cells. Not surprising with the bleeding he's having. Renal function looks bad, and now his liver appears to be going to pot.*

"Got a cure yet, Maggie?" Adam Foster interrupted her thoughts.

"I only wish. This guy's a mess. I decided to call in reinforcements. My friend at the CDC is going to check out the weird stuff. It'll take a couple of days. I hope we have time to get the results back. His blood pressure dropped overnight, but steroids helped. And your part isn't that great either. No pee! But the dialysis seems to be going OK."

Adam said, "I've had the biotechs handle that dialysate that is expelled as if it's contaminated with infected material. I figure we can't be too careful."

"That's a great idea," Maggie agreed. "Have you seen any sign of the girlfriend? I thought I'd try again today to reach her. Unfortunately, I don't have any phone numbers. Just an address and no friends."

"Nope, nothing from my end."

"Wait a minute," said Maggie, "my phone is going off. The ID says it's the gym calling. Let me get this. Maybe Jake from the gym will have an answer."

"Dr. Hamilton," Maggie answered as she picked up the call.

"Hey, Doc, I thought I'd let you know we had someone call here looking for your friends. Told them that we hadn't heard from them and had been trying to reach them."

"Did you get a number?" Maggie asked hopefully.

"Sorry, Doc. They hung up as soon as I said they hadn't been in for several days. It's just curious, because no one has ever cared about them before, so I thought it was unusual."

"You're right," Maggie agreed. "It's funny, isn't it? The loners suddenly have someone who cares. Well, if they call back, try to get their number."

"Will do, Doc."

Figuring there was little else she could do today with Alex, Maggie decided to see her other patients in the hospital, and then she could try swinging by Heidi's apartment again. Maybe this time, she would be lucky and catch her at home.

As she was about to leave the hospital to go to the parking garage, her phone began to chirp.

"Adam," she asked, answering his call, "have you got something for me?"

"Yes, I do. Heidi Campton has shown up."

"Really?" Maggie asked. "Can she shed some light on our friend?"

"I'm afraid not. She was brought in by ambulance. Same story. Fever, semicomatose, low blood pressure, covered with skin lesions and bleeding. We've got a problem here. A big problem."

CHAPTER 4

Maggie grabbed the elevator and hurried to the ER. "Listen, everyone," she called out. "It is critical that you completely cover with protective gear. We have a huge issue here. This lady's boyfriend is upstairs dying from something. We haven't diagnosed his condition, and now his girlfriend shows up with what appears to be the same thing. We must treat this with the utmost caution. Anyone who has had contact with her and was exposed to any body fluids needs to go immediately to the biocontainment area to be decontaminated. You'll need to shed your clothes, and we'll get you scrubs to wear. I can't emphasize this enough. Anyone in the ambulance also needs to be instructed to get decontaminated, and the ambulance itself needs to be completely cleaned."

Two nurses who thought they might have gotten some of Heidi's serum on their clothes headed to the biocontainment area. Everyone else denied any exposure. Adam followed right behind Maggie and pulled her aside after she finished talking.

"No family again," he said. "No friends. No history.

But whatever the hell this is, it's not good. This could create panic here and probably in the city as well—and rightly so. I think we need to let John Tuttle know what's going on. Once the press finds out, we're going to have a flood of reporters."

When she arrived at Tuttle's office, Maggie asked to speak to immediately. "This is urgent!" she exclaimed.

His secretary buzzed his office, and Maggie was allowed go in.

"Dr. Hamilton, good to see you," said Tuttle. "You never stop by administration. What brings us the pleasure?"

"Actually, you may not find this so pleasurable. We have admitted two patients to your new biocontainment center. Both appear to have a very serious and contagious disease. We're still trying to sort out just what they may have, but there is a good chance both will die. They have multi-organ failure, and no organism has yet been identified. I have the CDC working on this as well, because it's just not the ordinary infection we would tend to see. I wanted to warn you about this, because I think it's likely the press will find out about these patients, and you will be inundated with calls. Also, I'm concerned that the staff may get frightened and stop coming to work."

"Oh my gosh," said Tuttle. "Well, this could be an opportunity. With this new center, we can tell the press how we were prepared for something just like this. Any clues where they got the infection?"

Maggie shook her head. "That's the problem. These types of infections tend to occur in Third World countries. But these patients don't appear to have traveled anywhere. Moreover, the man works in our hospital, and of all things, in the microbiology and virology lab. This has us concerned, because he could have contracted the illness right here if he got exposed to samples of one of these unusual infections. I've visited with the lab director, and she states they haven't had anything like this, but seem with no travel history, this could still be a possibility."

"We need to quietly go through every culture in the lab to ensure that nothing like this has been cultured there," Tuttle said urgently. "I want this done without drawing any unwarranted attention. You know how people can panic over these things."

"I agree," said Maggie, "but we also need to ensure for everyone in the lab that the infection didn't originate there. We want no one else to get exposed."

"Sure, sure, I understand," Tuttle said. "Just keep it under wraps for now."

Maggie walked out of Tuttle's office shaking her head. *Does he not realize how serious this could be for the people who work here? He's always worried more about the hospital's image.*

Her next stop was the lab director's office. She went inside and closed the door behind her.

"Tess, I need you to help me," she began. "We need to carefully go through every culture from the lab over the last thirty days. As I mentioned to you, Alex seems to have an infection like we see coming from Africa, and since he hasn't been there, where could he possibly catch anything like this? Well, the lab! The incubation period is about three weeks, so he could have been exposed in the last two to four weeks, and then the symptoms would occur."

Tess nodded. "I've been thinking about that, but like I said, we haven't seen any report from other physicians about patients with an infection anything similar, and we haven't cultured anything out. Plus, no one here has had any alarming symptoms."

"All I'm saying is, keep a look out for anything similar," Maggie advised, "either from the cultures that you are doing or from your staff. We don't want to overly alarm them, but at the same time, treat this with great vigilance."

Frank Lee turned to Susan. "You've done a great job getting information from Jason. The Party will be happy with you. This is exactly what they wanted us to do. These Americans are trying to destroy us with tariffs, but our country will prevail, and we will be the greatest nation in the world. We just can't let the economic damage inflicted by them stop us, and this could be our opportunity to change the dynamics. The United States will be attacked by a weapon that their superior military cannot combat.

"Now we have to be concerned about Alex and our own personal safety. Who knows? Maybe he caught it, but what if he's alert enough to disclose where he acquired the illness? Our plan would be destroyed quickly. He hasn't answered his cell phone, which isn't like him—and the hospital said they have a patient in the biocontainment area, but they wouldn't give me a name. It's got to be Alex. I called from a coffee shop's phone to avoid giving out our caller ID."

"I think we need to talk to the Centre," said Susan. "We've got to get advice about the next steps. Do we need to change locations?"

"Don't panic yet. Let's see what the Centre says," Frank responded.

—◄▦▦▦▦►—

Maggie retuned to the biocontainment area and found Heidi already started on continuous dialysis. Her vital signs were much like Alex's: low blood pressure, high fever, and no urine output. She was covered with skin lesions, including blisters, some of which had ruptured. The staff now was particularly astute at monitoring their two sick patients and ensuring that they wore all the protective gear. Maggie had already ordered broad-spectrum antibiotics, and the vasopressors were being instilled to bring up Heidi's blood pressure. She found Adam looking over the lab results.

"What do you make of all this, Adam?" Maggie asked. "I just talked with Tess in the lab, and she is looking through the cultures over the last thirty days. She feels certain that we haven't cultured anything like this, but she's going through all the cultures just to be sure."

"I don't know," said Adam, "but these two people are fighting for their life. I'm not sure they're going to make it. Sad, isn't it? I'm doing my best, but they aren't responding well to the antibiotics, vasopressors, or dialysis. No other family available. Is that right?"

"None that I know of," Maggie said, "and history is really sketchy. Oh, by the way, Jake from the fitness center called and said someone had called there asking about Alex. No one had ever called before, so he thought this was un-usual. I agreed with him, but the caller hung up before he could get a name."

"Interesting, isn't it?" Adam mused. "No idea where these two could have caught this infection, no family or friends, but now we have someone unknown who doesn't come to the hospital but seems to have an interest in them. I'm not sure what to make of this."

"I expedited the samples sent to Jamie at the CDC. I suspect she is going to get back with us soon. She is extremely bright and was an outstanding fellow at Johns Hopkins. We'll probably have an answer before long."

The call came into the administrative office, and Tuttle's secretary answered.

"This is Channel 10 news," said the caller. "We have received information that there may be two patients admitted to the new biocontainment unit with a contagious infection. It is our understanding that both patients are very seriously ill. Is Mr. John Tuttle available for comment?"

"One moment, please, and I'll check." The secretary buzzed his office, and Tuttle picked up her call.

"Mr. Tuttle," said the secretary, "a Channel 10 reporter is on the line. She wants to talk with you about the patients recently admitted with infections."

Damn, how did they find out so quickly? he thought. "OK," he told the secretary, "I can talk with them. Just put them through." He waited for a moment before being connected with the reporter.

"Mr. Tuttle, this is Janet Rivers from Channel 10 news. We've received a report about two patients who have been admitted with a concern about a very contagious infection. We would like any information you can give us to help inform the public."

Tuttle spoke carefully. "You are correct that we have two patients admitted to our new unit. It's quite fortunate that we were prepared to handle any patients with potentially highly contagious diseases. As you are aware, we cannot disclose any confidential information about these patients. I've been informed that we have things under control, and we're taking all the necessary precautions to protect our personnel. We haven't, as yet, identified the source or the organism, but you can rest assured that we are monitoring this situation very closely. We will let the public know if additional measures need to be taken."

"Thank you, Mr. Tuttle," said the reporter. "I will plan to check back with you in a few days, if this is OK, but we would appreciate a call if there is anything new that would be important to disclose to our citizens."

"Certainly. We want to work with Channel 10 in any way we can to keep our city healthy."

He thought to himself as he hung up, *Drat. I wonder who called the news? Probably someone in the ER or the biocontainment unit. Maggie was right.*

CHAPTER 5

Maggie got the call early in the morning from an excited Jamie Sessions.

"You're not going to believe the results of the tests," Jamie said. "They're coming back with Ebola on your first patient. We're testing the second set of samples you sent and should have the results sometime today. Are you absolutely sure Alex didn't travel outside your city?"

"From all the reports from people who know him," Maggie replied, "this guy goes nowhere, knows virtually no one, and keeps to himself. So far, we haven't found many people who can give us much information."

"We're going to be sending a team of people to Chicago to help you," Jamie said. "This is a very serious matter, and we've got to find out who he has had contact with, because those people may need to be isolated. We're doing further testing on the virus, because it seems to have some unusual features. It's not the typical Ebola. May be more lethal."

"When will you be here?" Maggie asked.

"Probably tomorrow," Jamie replied. "We're assembling the team now. Just so you know, this is going to create national news. I'd expect CNN, Fox, and MSNBC to be all over this. You know how paranoid everyone is about this virus getting into the United States."

"Yes, and they should be," Maggie said. "It's a lethal disease and very contagious. Listen, I'll take all the help you can give me. I'm going to let the CEO of the hospital know that you're coming, and I'm sure he will want to meet with your team. He's already concerned about the hospital's reputation, but is spinning the news, pointing out that the hospital made a wise decision in creating the new center. As I thought about it, I believe he's right. Still, he's worried about a possible infection originating from the laboratory. Jamie, sorry, I've to go. I'm getting a stat page."

Maggie grabbed a hospital phone and dialed the biocontainment unit. "What is it? ... He's coding? Oh my God. I'll be there in a few minutes. I'm sure this is difficult, trying to do CPR and have all the protective gear on. Does Dr. Foster know? ... Oh, so he's there helping with the code. Great. I'll be there shortly."

Maggie grabbed her physician coat and took the stairs instead of the elevator to get to the unit faster. When she arrived, panting from running the stairs, she found a full code team working on Alex. She monitored the event through the closed-circuit system and spoke to them. Adam Foster was gowned and in the room.

"Adam, how are we doing? Any success?"

"Well, we have a pulse and pressure, but overall, I'd say things aren't great."

"I understand, but he's so young," Maggie said. "I hope he can survive."

"For now, he's alive!"

Maggie decided she needed to give Tuttle an update on the patient, so she dialed administration.

"This is Dr. Hamilton. Can I speak with Mr. Tuttle?"

"Yes, he's right here," said the secretary. "I'll put you through."

"Mr. Tuttle," said Maggie when he came on the line, "you had asked me to keep you informed about the patients. The first patient, Alex Williamson, has just coded, but he was able to be resuscitated and is still alive. I must tell you, this is pretty much touch and go. He has an overall poor prognosis."

She took a deep breath and continued. "And my friend from the CDC has called back. They have identified that Alex has the Ebola virus. She is very concerned as to how he could have contracted the illness. The CDC is going to be sending a team of people to Deaconess to investigate the source. She also warned me to expect the major news networks to give this a priority headline. They will probably descend on the hospital and begin reporting regularly from here."

"Oh my gosh," said Tuttle. "Can things get any worse?"

"I'm afraid so," Maggie said ruefully. "Hospital personnel could contract the disease. Others in the community may get infected. I did send our biocontainment personnel to clean the patient's apartment. I wanted to be sure that his landlady did not get infected. As I had mentioned, we may have nursing staff refusing to come to work. There could be a city-wide or for that matter country-wide panic."

"Getting the CDC here is going to be essential. I can see that," Tuttle responded.

"I'm glad that you agree, because there is going to be tremendous pressure on our staff and the city as well."

The following day, Jamie Sessions and four other medical personnel from the CDC arrived at the hospital, including two PhD microbiologists and two certified lab technicians. They wanted to establish a command center, and Tuttle arranged a special conference room in the laboratory for their use. They went to work immediately.

"Maggie, you mentioned that Alex Williamson was a loner, and you haven't been able to get much information or history on him or his girlfriend, Heidi. Whom have you talked to?" Jamie asked.

"I went to his apartment and met with his landlady, and I called the local gym where he worked out. Plus, I visited Tess, the supervisor of the lab where he worked," Maggie explained. "All of them confirmed that he hadn't traveled anywhere, he rarely associated with people, and he had no immediate family. His parents apparently died from cancer, and he had no siblings. At Heidi's apartment, one of her neighbors described her similarly. Very little contact with people and never traveling. I guess in some respects this is good. Less chance to pass the disease on to someone else."

"Good point, but then how did Alex get this in the first place?" Jamie responded. "My associates will start with Tess in the lab and focus on the cultures over the last few months. They will also need computer access to the hospital's server to scan patients who were admitted with fever and suspected infections. I understand if they had this disease, you would think that the attending physician would have suspected something strange from the beginning, but maybe they died quickly. Oh, and one final thing: I've called the FBI."

"What?" Maggie exclaimed. "Why the FBI?"

"We need help tracking Alex's every movement. Where has he gone? Who has he seen? You know, every contact."

"Oh sure, that makes sense. Wow, what have I gotten myself into?" Maggie said with disbelief.

"I told you this was going to be a big deal. I wasn't kidding, was I?"

———————

After Jamie Sessions introduced her staff to Tess in the lab, she connected with the IT department and set up passwords and sign-ons so they could begin perusing the charts of patients admitted over the last sixty days. In particular, they would look at any cultures that could have been obtained on these patients.

As the staff began this process, Jamie went to the biocontainment unit to review Alex's records. She found him just as Maggie had suggested—in a very dire condition. After the code, he was less responsive, possibly from brain swelling. His fever continued unabated, and his pressures remained low.

Adam Foster had filled her in on Alex's current status, but Jamie wanted to get a closer look at his skin lesions, so she put on the protective gear and went into his room. The room was warm, in part because of all the clothing she had to wear and in part because Alex's skin was shedding, and the nursing staff were keeping the room temperature up, treating him much like a burn patient who had lost the outer protective exterior.

The skin lesions were horrendous and had multiplied even over a few hours. His face was flushed and swollen. He had swelling of his legs, and his abdomen protruded with fluid from ascites as his liver function continued to fall.

Returning to the control booth, she called Maggie.

"Maggie, this guy isn't going to make it," she said. "With multi-organ failure and a deadly virus that is out of control, he's likely to die. When that happens, it would be nice to get an autopsy, but I don't know if we can find a pathologist willing to do this. They may not want to take the risk."

"I can ask Pam Foster, Adam's wife, to see if she would consider it," said Maggie. "She is very talented, but I don't want to put her in harm's way."

"I understand. I can check with our superiors to see if they have suggestions. I didn't get into the girlfriend's room, but I can tell just from the monitors and her chart that she's going down the same path."

As they spoke, a sharp shrilling sound rang out. It was the cardiac alarm in Alex's room. He was coding again. The code team arrived and quickly gowned. The nurse in the room had started CPR, and Alex was receiving breathing by a ventilator, which had been instituted earlier. After forty-five minutes of aggressive resuscitation, the code was stopped. Alex Williamson had died.

CHAPTER 6

The following day, Maggie received a page from Jamie.

"Maggie, Mr. FBI has arrived," Jamie reported. "I know this hasn't been a pleasant thing to go through, but this may make things easier. He's quite the hunk!"

"Jamie, I haven't been dating anyone for so long, I don't even notice guys anymore," Maggie replied. "It's been work, work, and more work. Plus, those handsome men I dated didn't need someone to love them. They loved themselves. Right now, I feel bad about Alex. We need to focus on finding out where he got this and how to stop it."

"You're right, but I'm just saying—you're going to like what you see."

Maggie headed to the control room set up by Tuttle for the CDC team and bounded in to see Agent Matthew Johnson standing there, all six-foot-two height, chiseled body, tanned skin, and dark curly hair. Jamie was right. Extending her hand and smiling, she said, "I'm Dr. Maggie Hamilton. We're glad to have you here. We need your help."

"Agent Matthew Johnson, but most people call me Mack. I'll do my best. I don't know a thing about Ebola, but I can help tracking down any contacts of Alex. I've already assembled a team of agents, and we have started pursuing some leads."

"Wow, you work fast," Maggie exclaimed.

"The sooner we find the person who transmitted this to Alex, the better," Mack replied. "You and I are going to be working closely together. You are the bug expert; I'm the finder expert. We'll be a great team."

"I'm sure," Maggie said, smiling.

Pam Foster had agreed to do the autopsy after ensuring that the clothing would completely cover every inch of her body. She double-gloved even inside the suit. All the instruments used were to be destroyed after the exam.

After opening the abdominal cavity, she found internal organs filled with blood. The liver, lungs, heart, and intestine were swollen and full of hemorrhage. In her experience doing autopsies, she had never seen anything like this. The virus had virtually destroyed every major organ.

Pam wasn't going to save many samples to avoid contaminating anyone else. After she closed the incision, Alex's body was placed in two body bags and then cremated. No family so far had been identified to claim his body, so the ashes were kept in the morgue in case anyone eventually stepped forward.

"The Centre texted me," Frank told Susan. "We're to go to the safe house on Clements Street this afternoon. For now, we're to avoid any close contact with the hospital, but they are going to use their resources to find out more information. Apparently, they can hack into the hospital computer system and see the results."

After stopping at one of the locations of Lee's Dry Cleaning and Laundry, they let the manager know that they would not be in this morning, stating they had some errands to run. They notified their employees that they planned to return in the afternoon.

Their four dry-cleaning establishments had turned out to be quite successful. This allowed them to move into a moderately upscale suburban neighborhood. They had joined New Beginnings Church, and Frank was now on the church council. Today, however, they had more serious business to attend to.

After leaving their store, they drove to a residential area in a very nondescript area of Chicago, far from their home. They found the location they were looking for on Clements Street, even though they had gone there only rarely. Entering the safe house, they were met by Samuel, a gray-haired elderly gentleman, neatly groomed, with a very polished vocabulary. He smiled as he greeted them, and they gave a weak smile back.

"So, I see that the pregnancy is coming along," said Samuel. "How many weeks till you deliver?"

"I believe I'm at seven months, so they have told me to expect to deliver the baby in about six weeks," Susan replied.

'Much morning sickness?" Samuel asked.

"Only for the first few weeks. I feel fine now."

"This pregnancy was unfortunate, but your interactions with Mr. Turley have helped us a great deal," said Samuel. "We know that the Americans are on the verge of producing a treatment that can stop tropical diseases like Ebola from spreading. This makes our job even more urgent."

"Do you know what happened to Alex?" Frank asked. "We haven't seen him for two weeks."

"As a matter of fact, I do know. We entered the hospital computer, and he has been in the biocontainment unit. He has required dialysis, a ventilator, antibiotics, and medications to raise his blood pressure. Multiple different physicians are attending him. In the chart, they describe a concern about a Third World country infection, but it hasn't been totally identified. Today, his name was no longer on the list of patients." Samuel paused and added, "His girlfriend, Heidi, was admitted with the same symptoms, and she is basically getting the same treatment."

"So, did he die?" Susan asked.

"We believe so. That's how it would seem."

"Are we in danger of catching this?" asked Susan. "Do we know what it will do to my baby? What do we do now? Can they trace this back to us?"

"This baby was not supposed to be in the picture," Samuel said sternly. "You should have had an abortion when you first found out. Now this could slow us down. You won't be able to be nimble and maneuver easily when you're ready to have the baby and we're in the middle of delivering the virus. What if you get complications? We abort babies all the time in China. Why not here?"

"I just couldn't do it," Susan stated. "Send me home if this is such a problem!"

"We considered that, but we may need more information from Jason, and you're the key to getting it."

"So will we catch it?" she asked again.

"You haven't worked with the virus," said Samuel flatly. "That's precisely why we chose Alex. If he were to get the disease, he had virtually no friends, no family, and most importantly, no connection to you. Plus, he had worked in virology and knew how to handle viruses. Still, this virus is deadly, and that's why we chose it. Alex was helping us make it even more deadly. I trust that you have been using that disposable cell phone and had it set to not disclose the caller?"

"Yes," Susan replied. "We have been very careful with our communication with Alex."

"I would throw the cell phone away and get another disposable cell phone," Samuel advised.

"You know once the diagnosis is made, there is going to be a major panic, and every governmental agency will be tracing all of Alex's movements," Frank said.

"We understand, but you should go about your normal business," instructed Samuel. "Keep the elixir stored safely in the vault hidden in the basement location that we created for you. When the time comes, we can carry out the plan that we had originally outlined, but until then, just remain calm and continue to fit into this society. The Centre will give us the green light when to proceed. The information that Susan obtained was very helpful. This should allow us to have a major impact on their society and cause great upheaval."

The news had hit the major networks, and as John Tuttle stared out of his window overlooking the parking lot, he saw two large vans pull up with satellite dishes on their roofs. *Here it comes,* he thought. *I'm glad I contacted our public relations department early. Dr. Hamilton was right. This isn't going to be local news; this will be national news.*

He buzzed his secretary and warned her to expect calls. He then contacted the head of public relations and arranged to have the large conference room available. He wanted to be prepared.

Finally, he asked his secretary to reach Dr. Hamilton. Within minutes, the secretary buzzed his office to tell him she was on the line.

"Dr. Hamilton," said Tuttle, "we have large news trucks in our parking lot. I'm expecting a call soon. Would you be able to join me in the conference room and, if possible, bring your friend from the CDC? We need all the reinforcements we can find."

"Sure, no problem," said Maggie. "But I would suggest we huddle first to work out a game plan that would include the FBI. They're here now, and it would be best if we show we've thought of everything in trying to track down the source."

"Excellent," said Tuttle. Then, "Wait, my secretary is calling me, and I'm guessing it's the media on the line."

After taking the call, he returned to Maggie.

"I was right. It's Fox and CNN waiting to talk with me. I guess the local affiliates are also present, so I've asked my secretary to have all of them assemble in our conference room. Why don't we meet in my office first before meeting with them?"

"Good idea," Maggie responded. "I'll tell Mack and Jamie. We will need them as reinforcements."

Janet Goodwin from the publicity department arrived as the others showed up, and all they sat around the large conference table in Tuttle's office.

"Where do we start, ladies and gentlemen?" he asked.

Maggie was the first to answer. "I would suggest that we state the facts that we know. One person was admitted with what appeared to be a serious infection that was felt to be highly contagious, so we took the necessary precautions to place this person in our new biocontainment unit. After a comprehensive evaluation that included contacting the CDC, we have discovered that this individual had Ebola but has unfortunately passed away. His girlfriend appears to have a similar illness and is receiving treatments now. It will be a day or two before we can confirm whether she has the same illness."

She continued, "Since neither of them traveled outside of the United States—or, for the matter, outside of Chicago—we contacted the FBI to help in searching for everyone who may have had contact with them. We can let Jamie confirm the diagnosis, and Mack from the FBI will outline his plans to pursue any of these individuals' contacts."

"That sounds perfect," Tuttle replied. "We need to present a comprehensive approach that can reassure our staff and the public we are doing everything and taking measures to prevent further cases. Let's go meet them now."

Maggie entered the packed conference room and found all the national media present, along with local TV and radio reporters. The news had spread fast. She went to the front of the room as John Tuttle stepped up to the podium.

"Ladies and gentlemen," he began, "thank you for coming. We are here to answer as many questions as we can, but as you know, we can't disclose our patients' names. We still need to find additional family. I've asked Dr. Hamilton to address you first."

Maggie reiterated the history and the medical course of Alex Williamson and then turned the podium over to Jamie, who in turn discussed how this particular Ebola had unique features that the CDC was currently testing. In addition, she discussed how cultures and samples from the laboratory were being reviewed and tested to see if any other patients who weren't diagnosed would have entered the hospital at an earlier date. Mack then took the podium and pointed out that the FBI was going to pursue all of Alex's contacts to try to discover the source of the infection and track down who he might have exposed.

A CNN reporter asked what the public should do at this point.

Maggie answered, "When we're able to release the patient's name, we would like anyone who knows or has been associated with the patient to call the hospital. We will be setting up a hotline for any helpful tips."

As Maggie finished speaking, her cell phone buzzed, indicating an outside call. She excused herself and stepped into the hallway. Dialing the number, she was connected to a caller on a meet-me line.

"Dr. Hamilton. Can I help you?"

"My name is Ethyl Williamson. I'm Alex's aunt. I just heard the news."

CHAPTER 7

"Mrs. Williamson," said Maggie, I'm so glad you've called. We have been trying to reach one of Alex's family members. No one has had any information on family or friends."

"Alex kept to himself pretty much. After his parents died, he removed himself from the rest of the family. He left Champaign and moved to Chicago, finished his studies, and began working at the hospital—but he never contacted any of us. I think he was angry at the world over losing his parents, and he never had many friends. He was content to be by himself, but he seemed to enjoy school and exercising. I had heard that he had a girlfriend, but he never brought her back home to Champaign. We've been concerned about him, but what could we do? I just heard about his illness and that he passed away. We all feel so bad."

"Yes," Maggie replied, "this is a terrible disease, and we are worried that he may have spread it to others. We haven't been able to discern where he got it either. This is a rare disorder, which you may know is found in Africa predominately. He supposedly hasn't traveled, so he would have gotten this here in Chicago. If that is the case, we need to find the person who may have given this to him. That person could be spreading this illness to others."

"I'm sorry, I can't help you. He just never talked to us, so we don't know any of his contacts. Poor Alex. I believe that I would like to get his ashes and place them near his parents. He would have liked that, and we will have a private service for him with our family."

"We would be happy to give you his ashes," said Maggie. "If you can think of anyone we could contact, please let us know; but in the meantime, will it be all right if we release his name? We need to reach out to the public to see if there is anyone out there who will come forward."

"Yes, that's the least we can do."

Maggie went back to the conference room and found Mack. He seemed eager to talk with her.

"The team has been working on contacts," he informed her. "We're making some progress. Can we get together and talk about this? How about dinner? There's a place near the hospital. Simple food for a simple guy ... Emily's Diner. Tastes like my mom's cooking."

"Sure, I know where that it is," said Maggie. "I sometimes stop there after work and pick up things to take home. What time?"

"Let's meet at six thirty. Is that OK?"

"Perfect. See you then."

Maggie decided she needed to check on Heidi and headed back to the biocontainment center. Adam was grimacing as he looked over the lab results.

"Not looking good, Maggie," he said. "We're going down the same pathway as Alex. No urine output. Continued fever, chills, low blood pressure, and more skin lesions. Our vasopressors are nearly at a maximum. The dialysis is going OK, but this seems the least of her problems. Now we're having difficulty getting dialysis nurses to come in. They're calling in sick, as we guessed might happen."

"Same problem with nurses in the unit here," said Maggie. "We just need to reassure them that if they wear the protective gear, they will be OK."

"I know," said Adam, "but it's still going to be difficult to get them here."

"Hold on, Jamie's calling," Maggie said. "Let me get this." Turning away and talking into the phone, she said, "Hey, Jamie, what ya got?"

"As we guessed," Jamie replied. "Heidi has the same virus. Again, a modified Ebola. More virulent!"

"Anything else we can do?" Maggie asked.

"The main treatment is supportive care. Instilling gamma globulin may help her immune system. We can try this."

Maggie found her way to the parking garage and threw her white physician coat in the back seat. She knew it was only a few blocks to Emily's Diner, but she planned to head home after this quick meal with Mack. It had been a traumatic few days, with Alex's death, Heidi's poor condition, the plethora of news media, and a fear that this disease was out of control. *Who will it attack next?* she wondered.

She parked on the street and found Mack in a booth toward the back of the restaurant. She always thought that Emily's reminded her of something from the fifties. Metal tables and chairs with red plastic cushions, booths and waitresses wearing white aprons and white caps—it seemed so retro! But Mack was right. The food was always good.

He smiled as she approached him. "Hey, smarty-pants. How's the patient doing?"

"I'm not the smarty-pants, buster," Maggie retorted, "but for your information, not well. She seems to be following the same course as Alex. But I do have something to report. Alex's aunt called me. Gave me some information on him, although I'm not sure how helpful this is going to be. I guess once his parents died, he pretty much separated himself from the whole family. He refused to connect with them at all. He apparently was very smart but withdrawn. His aunt knew that he had moved to Chicago, but he wouldn't connect with any family members. She really didn't know of any of his friends. She did know that he had a girlfriend, but she had never met Heidi. So I guess I can say that I learned very little. How about you?"

"How did she know that he died?" Mack asked.

"I guess his landlady had called her. She found a number for the family and wanted to know what to do with his belongings."

"Well, the team has found his cell phone," Mack revealed. "We've been going through his contacts and calls. This guy was amazing. He had virtually no one on his contact list. He had the hospital's number, his place of work in the hospital, a few family members, the gym's number, and his girlfriend's. Not much else. We've been looking at who called him, and again, very few numbers. It is curious how someone can be so isolated."

He added, "There was one interesting thing. There seems to be a caller that does reach out to him frequently, but the number is blocked. We're going to see if we can unblock the number and track it to someone. We've found the grocery store that he goes to and the pharmacy that he occasionally frequents, but I guess this could be a good thing. With no friends or contacts, maybe he didn't expose anyone."

"Good point," Maggie agreed. "I thought that we should alert the press as to his name. His aunt has given us permission to tell the media, and we can reach out to the public and see if there is anyone out there who knows him or knows Heidi and can tell us more."

"Well, enough about this," said Mack. "Tell me more about you. Where did you grow up? Where did you go to school? How did you get so smart?"

"I'm afraid it's not that interesting," Maggie replied. "I grew up in upstate New York. My father was an engineer for DuPont but is retired now. My mother, for the most part, has been a stay-at-home mom. She did work for a while in a research lab, but when I was born, she decided to give up her career and stay home with me. Many people say I look like my mother but have my father's brains, but my mother was very bright too. I went to Rensselaer Polytechnic Institute, where my father had gone. He always wanted me to be an engineer like him, but that just wasn't for me. I was idealistic and wanted to save the world. Fortunately, I was able to get into Harvard Medical School and subsequently did my infectious-diseases fellowship at John Hopkins. That's where I met Jamie. Now there is a sharp girl. How about you?"

"I'm afraid not very exciting," Mack began. "I grew up on a farm outside of Fort Wayne, Indiana. I have two brothers, but I'm the oldest. My father has farmed all his life, but now one of my brothers has pretty much taken over the farming duties. My father helps some because he still really enjoys farming. I come from a very conservative Lutheran background. Went to Purdue University and got my criminal justice degree. For whatever reason, I always wanted to be in law enforcement, but my goal was the FBI. I'm glad that I made the cut and was able to get in. So, you're not married. Any serious relationships?"

"I've had a few boyfriends," Maggie told him. "Really never found Mr. Right. My mother is upset that I haven't gotten married. She wants grandchildren, and since I'm an only child, she's worried this will never happen."

"Funny, same with me," Mack said. "My mom asks me all the time, 'When are you ever going to give us some grandchildren?' I've told her, who wants to marry an FBI agent? Actually, I think she understands that I have spent all my efforts on getting through school and am now focusing on my career. Anyway, I've reassured her that when the right person comes along, I'll know it."

"So, what are you ordering for dinner?" Maggie asked, eager to change the subject. "You know this isn't exactly gourmet food."

"Oh, I know that, but that's what I like about this place. I'm getting ham and eggs. How about you?"

"Hmm, I going to have baked chicken and a salad, but I also need a glass of wine. I may be addicted to Chardonnay."

"Then I'm having a Bud."

When dinner was over, they headed to their cars. Mack turned to Maggie and said, "Well, that was a good time. We need to do this again. See you tomorrow, Doc."

Maggie smiled as she got into her car. *He's a nice guy,* she thought.

The Lees stopped at the dry-cleaner's and laundry on their way home from the safe house. The managers had completed all the tasks that they had assigned. After dropping Susan off, Frank headed to the church. He had a church council meeting. At the conclusion, he stayed for a few minutes in the church office, where he found the computer that he used from time to time and entered the password to get on.

He began searching for Deaconess Hospital and found a log-in for hospital staff. The Centre had shown him how to access the hospital charts. He reached Alex's medical record, but it showed that he had been discharged. The final note indicated that he had been pronounced dead. Although not in the laboratory results, the entry by a Dr. Hamilton stated that the patient was found to have Ebola, but a strain that was particularly virulent.

So he did contract the disease, Frank thought. *I knew that's what must have happened. They're going to be looking for us.*

CHAPTER 8

As she pulled into the parking garage at Deaconess Hospital, Maggie felt more energetic and enthusiastic than she had in a long while. *I can't remember the last time I was so attracted to a man on the first date*, she thought. *There is a world outside of medicine. I was beginning to think that there wasn't.*

She went directly to the biocontainment unit and met with the nursing personnel. Some had called in sick, so there were replacements from other intensive care units.

"How's our patient?" she enquired.

"About the same," the charge nurse responded. "I haven't seen her before, but the blood pressure requires medical support with vasopressors; her urine output is minimal. The dialysis seems to be going well, although she remains delirious. We did receive a call from a family member."

"Really? That's great. Who was it?"

"It was her mother. Apparently, Heidi and her mother have had a strained relationship, but one of the people in her apartment building had called the mother to let her know that Heidi was very sick."

"Do you have a number for her?" Maggie asked.

"Yes, she gave us her cell phone. The mother and father are divorced. The father, for the most part, dropped out of the picture, and the mother has remarried. I guess Heidi rarely goes home or calls. The mother knew that she had a boyfriend but had never met him, because Heidi never brought him home. Heidi grew up in Milwaukee and attended the Medical College of Wisconsin. That's where she got her master's degree in social work and has been working for a nursing home. The mother said that Heidi enjoyed working with the elderly and talked often about how happy she was with her job. It was Lake Center Nursing Home, so you may want to call them and get more information. I told the mother Heidi was very ill, and she should consider coming here right away. She plans on doing that. Incidentally, Heidi is her only child, and as you would expect, she is devastated by this news."

"Thanks for getting that information," said Maggie. "What is the mother's name?"

"Teresa Jones," the nurse replied. "That's her new married name."

"I'll call her now."

Maggie stepped into the physician charting room connected to the biocontainment unit and called Mrs. Jones. The woman answered after only a couple of rings.

"Mrs. Jones, this is Dr. Maggie Hamilton. I understand that you have talked with our head nurse in the biocontainment unit. She's told you how sick your daughter is, and she probably mentioned that she has been found to have the Ebola virus. Has she traveled outside of the United States?"

"No, I don't believe she has," Heidi's mother replied.

"The fact is, she rarely goes anywhere and talks to very few people. She had told us about her boyfriend, Alex, but other than him, she only talked about her clients in the nursing home. She seemed to really connect with them."

"Were there any missionaries she might have known who could have given her the disease?" Maggie asked.

"Not that I'm aware of. As I said, she hardly talks to us or to anyone. She has very few friends. She was a person who cared little about materialistic things and was willing to help anyone, and in that regard, has been such a delightful child. She hasn't been, however, that happy with life, because her father and I divorced, and she never forgave me for that. I would suggest that you talk with her coworkers at the nursing home. They may be able to give you more information."

"I will do that, Mrs. Jones," said Maggie. "Thank you for your help. When you arrive here, I would be happy to give you an update on Heidi's condition. In the meantime, can we disclose her name to the media? I hope that giving her name out may lead to people calling in who have had contact with her. Things are touch-and-go right now."

"Yes, feel free to alert the public. I know how serious this is."

John Tuttle stared out the window of his office. His balding head, wrinkled brow, and worn look reflected the pressure he was feeling. With nurses calling in sick, the press calling every hour, and another patient with probable Ebola, he had to find a way to calm his staff—and, for that matter, calm the city and the country.

Dr. Hamilton was a godsend. Her intelligence gave people confidence that she had things under control, but he wasn't so certain that anything actually *was* under control. As he pondered these thoughts, the buzzer on his intercom went off, and his secretary exclaimed that Dr. Hamilton was on the line. *What a coincidence!* he thought.

"Dr. Hamilton," he said as the call connected. "I was just thinking of you and how fortunate we are to have you on our medical staff at this time."

"Thank you, Mr. Tuttle," Maggie replied. "That's nice of you to say. I just wanted you to know that both Alex Williamson's family and Heidi Campton's family have given permission to release their names. I think this could be very helpful. Maybe we can further discover who they've been in contact with, track them down, and find the source of all this."

"I hope so. We've got to convince people that we have this under control. We do, don't we?" asked Tuttle.

"Not exactly," Maggie admitted. "Without a source, we have no idea who could be out there spreading this disease. That's what's frightening."

"Well, I certainly appreciate everything you're doing to try to get to the bottom of this. Let's meet the media now in the conference room, if this time is convenient for you. They're eager to hear anything."

"I'll head there now."

The room was packed with local and national media as Tuttle and Maggie entered. She found the space hot, stuffy, and close. Lights were directed toward the front to allow the cameras to project the images, but either the heat of the lights or the anxiety of the moment caused sweat to appear on her brow. The noisy chatter immediately silenced when they went to the podium.

Tuttle began, "Thank you for coming at short notice. We wanted to give you an update on our two patients and their status. I would like Dr. Hamilton to fill you in."

Maggie stepped forward and started speaking. "First, as you may know, our first patient has died from his disease despite many people's efforts. Ebola, I'm sure you're aware, is an infection that will attack every internal organ and is often fatal. His family has given us permission to release his name, and we would like you to reach out to your audience so we can identify anyone who may have had contact with him and may be infected or could become infected. His name is Alex Williamson. Mr. Williamson worked in the hospital laboratory in the microbiology and virology lab. We have been concerned that he could have contracted this disease working with the cultures in the laboratory, but so far there has been no evidence that this was the case."

She continued, "The team from the CDC has been diligently reviewing all the cultures and has found no evidence that this happened. So now we need to find out who was in contact with Mr. Williamson outside the hospital who could have infected him. His girlfriend, Heidi Campton, who appears to have the same infection, likely contracted the disease from him. She may have had it first. Although still alive, she is dangerously ill. Her family has given permission to release her name. Any information that the public could provide would be greatly appreciated and helpful."

"How much danger is this for someone who passes him on the street?" asked the first reporter.

"The disease would be spread by close contact with body fluids and wouldn't be a risk for a casual passer-by. On the other hand, we know that Heidi worked at a nursing home, and we will be contacting their residents and staff to discuss the situation."

Another reporter called out, "Is there someone out there walking around with active disease infecting others?"

"That's our biggest concern," Maggie replied. "It's why we have asked for the help of the public to identify anyone who has had close contact with these people."

"Have any of their coworkers gotten infected?" another reporter asked.

"We are not aware of any coworkers who are infected," said Maggie, "but we are cautioning them to look for any symptoms."

"How can we find the source?"

"That's why the FBI has gotten involved," Maggie explained. "They will be searching for the source to prevent any additional spread of the disease."

"Is there anything else that the public can do?"

"I would say stay vigilant, watching for anyone who could be possibly carrying the disease or would have the potential to spread it," Maggie replied.

The press seemed satisfied with the answers for now, so Tuttle and Maggie left the room and returned to his office.

"Well, this should really stir things up," John Tuttle said. "Can you imagine what the people who have had contact with them may be thinking?"

"Fortunately, they're both loners with very few friends," Maggie reminded him. "Because Heidi worked at a nursing home, we assume she has had more contact with people than Alex. The bigger question is, where did they get this in the first place?"

"Good question. I guess we'll see what response we get now."

—◼▦◼—

As she left Tuttle's office, Maggie got a text from Mack, who wanted to meet up with her. He said he had some updated news. She found him in the makeshift command center set up for the FBI.

"All right, give it to me," she said eagerly. "What ya got?"

"Well, we have been working on the cell phone," he began. "I told you that several calls were made to Alex with no caller ID. We've been able to open the phone up enough to identify that phone number. The calls were coming from a disposable cell phone that didn't have any single person attached to it. Interesting, isn't it? Who would have been repeatedly calling Alex on a disposable phone with a blocked caller ID? We think we'll be able to track the phone to the store where it was bought, and then maybe to the person who purchased it."

"That should be interesting," Maggie mused.

"More importantly," Mack continued, "where are we going for dinner tonight? I need to interrogate you more. That's what I'm good at."

Smiling, Maggie said, "I have to work a little later today, but we could meet around eight o'clock at the pub a few blocks away for a burger and beer. How's that sound?"

"Wow, you know me well," Mack said with a smile. "My kind of food. So, what's the place?"

"Patrick's Pub. Owned by an Irish guy."

"Great! See you at eight."

Maggie returned to the biocontainment unit to check on Heidi. Her condition seemed little changed. Blood pressures were up and down; fever continued unabated; and urine output was minimal. Maggie sat staring at the computer screen to review the lab results.

"Has her condition changed?" she asked the charge nurse.

"Not much," the nurse replied. "We have been pouring IVs into her because she has had substantial fluid loss from diarrhea and skin lesions. There have been times when she has developed heart arrhythmias. According to Dr. Foster, she hasn't had any issues with dialysis, but I'm concerned about her heart condition."

"I understand," said Maggie. "I'm considering giving her gamma globulin to help her immune system. I'm also going to check with Dr. Sessions to see if the CDC has access to an anti-Ebola viral treatment called Zendenivir. It's been used in some cases with possible beneficial results, but there was insufficient data to prove its effectiveness. I'm hoping I can get Heidi some to try. It doesn't appear that there is much else that I can do tonight but keep me posted if her condition changes."

Frank Lee had the nightly news on when the announcement came: "The Ebola infection in the two patients at Deaconess Hospital has led to the death of Alex Williamson. His girlfriend, Heidi Campton, is still alive but critically ill. If anyone has had contact with these individuals, they are to call Deaconess Hospital or the FBI."

As I thought would happen, Frank reflected grimly. *Now the FBI is involved, and they aren't going to stop until they track down the source. If the Centre wants us to disperse the virus, it better be soon. Since Susan found out from Jason that the government may have a preventive treatment to stop a pandemic, it's urgent to implement the plan soon. I'm glad*

I threw away the cell phone and am now using the church's computer to check on the infected patient. We need to keep ourselves as much removed as possible. We need to create pandemonium.

Maggie left the hospital and found her way to Patrick's Pub. This was the highlight of her day—to get away from the death and disease at the hospital and see Mack again. She found him in a far corner of the bar.

"Hey, big guy. How's Mr. FBI? Have you found our source yet?"

"We keep looking. We've identified the number on the disposable cell phone, and tomorrow I plan to go to a Target store where we think it was bought. Believe me, this is right up our alley: tracking people down. But enough of that. I just wanted to track you down. Tell me about your day."

"Really the same old thing," Maggie replied. "Heidi looks pretty unstable. I'm going to check with Jamie to see if I can get an experimental drug called Zendenivir. It's not clear if it helps, but we don't have a lot to lose here. I'm just glad that I have this time with you. I know that our upbringings were totally different, but it seems so easy for me to talk with you. Right now, however, I'm starved. Let's order something."

After the waitress brought menus, they both ordered hamburgers with a slew of toppings, plus French fries for Mack and a salad for Maggie. Maggie even decided tonight was Bud night. She had a beer along with Mack.

"So, where do you hope to be in five years, Maggie?" Mack asked. "I'm always trying to decide what's in my future."

"Well, I guess I never really consider that," she admitted.

"I'm always so busy with my work and the patients, I hardly know what tomorrow will bring. I guess I hope I can find the right man to meet, maybe even have a family, but at my age, I better get started soon. Time is running out."

"Fortunately for men, we can wait longer to have children," Mack noted, "but I want to get married someday and have a family as well. I'd love to have some boys to coach. After all, sports were something that I enjoyed growing up— mainly football and baseball. I liked them both, but I was never really good enough to get into the big time."

Listening to Mack, Maggie realized how easy it was to talk with him. There was no inhibition telling him anything. She realized that this had never happened before with anyone she'd dated. With other boyfriends, she always held back from exposing her inner thoughts.

Dinner passed quickly, and the two of them headed together to the parking lot. Mack walked Maggie to her car, because this wasn't the best part of town. Before he opened the door for her, he put his arm around her waist and stared into her eyes. She could see as he looked at her that he wasn't leaving until he kissed her. Their lips met in a kiss that started simple but became aggressive. He pulled her close to his body, and she could feel how muscular and toned he was. They hugged for a moment and then parted.

"It was great being with you tonight," he said, smiling. "I hope we can see each other again soon."

"I'm planning on it," she smiled back. With that, she got in her car and drove home.

CHAPTER 9

Maggie heard her cell phone chirping that she had a page. When a stat page came, it emitted a high-pitched shrill, so she knew this was something urgent. She jumped out of the shower and grabbed a towel—only to discover the page was from John Tuttle.

A stat call? she thought.

"Mr. Tuttle, what is it?" she asked. "The operator said this was urgent."

"I'm getting a flood of calls from Lakeview Nursing Home," he said tensely. "The staff, the patients, and their families are all in a panic. They're convinced that they will all be dying from Ebola. You have to calm them down. I can't do this."

"Do you have a contact number?" Maggie asked. "I can head over there now and visit with them. I'll probably have to set up a second meeting with families. I'm sure that many of the patients have no idea what's going on."

"Perfect," Tuttle declared. "Sounds great. I'll get you the phone number. Just take care of this. I'm feeling overwhelmed at the moment. I'll set up another general staff meeting, and

maybe Dr. Sessions could meet with them. Staff keeps calling in."

"That's a great idea," Maggie agreed. "An authority from
the CDC will give them more confidence that they are not at
risk if they follow the rules using protective gear."

—◄▐▐▐▐▐▐▐►—

Maggie dressed quickly, jumped in her car, and sped toward
the nursing home. She had called ahead to have all the staff
assembled by the time she arrived. Within twenty minutes,
she was pulling into the parking lot. Stepping into the facility,
she was greeted by the nursing director.

"Dr. Hamilton, I'm Sherrie Simmons. I'm the head of
nursing. I have all our staff in the conference room. Thank
you for coming at such short notice. These people are in a
panic."

"Hopefully I can calm them down," said Maggie.

As she entered the conference room, she found twenty
people all staring at her with concerned faces. Some were
LPNs, others CNAs, but there were also employees of the
dining room, laundry service, and cleaning service. Maggie
began slowly by first introducing herself.

"Thank you coming here today so we can discuss the
situation with Heidi Campton," she continued. "As you're
aware from the media reports, Ms. Campton is seriously ill
with the Ebola virus, a deadly infection. We have not identified whether she contracted the disease herself or whether she
may have gotten infected from her boyfriend. This disease is
spread by contact with bodily fluids, such as stool, blood, or
vomitus. So casually talking with someone does not lead to
catching this disease. A respiratory route such as coughing up
phlegm usually does not spread it. You could catch it using

the same bathroom if there was stool or vomitus that hadn't been cleaned up. As far as I am aware, Heidi hadn't shown any signs of illness while working here. Is that correct?"

A nurse in the front row spoke up first.

"No, she looked perfectly normal. That's what has frightened all of us. How could she look so good one moment and now have a life-threatening disease?"

"I understand your concern. Ebola is a very virulent virus and not one that we have seen here in the United States. The fortunate thing is that it doesn't appear that Heidi continued to work after she contracted the disease and therefore didn't risk giving this disease to you or your patients. Had she called in sick?"

Sherrie Simmons, the manager, chimed in. "Yes, as a matter of fact, she called in saying that she hadn't been feeling well and was going to be staying home for a few days. We never heard back from her, and we were getting worried. She was such a delightful person and so caring. We were devastated when we heard the news."

Maggie said, "We are doing all we can to get her through this, but I have to tell you that the overall prognosis is not good. I would suggest that you consider praying for her. She needs divine intervention to survive."

"We will certainly do that, Dr. Hamilton," Sherrie Simmons responded. "We so appreciate you taking the time to talk with us today."

"I would like to simply say that if any of you or your patients begin developing unusual symptoms," Maggie concluded, "please feel free to call me. I will leave my number with Ms. Simmons so I can be reached at any time."

The staff seemed to accept Maggie's advice and was calm for the moment. There was grumbling off to the side as she left, but Maggie felt that they understood the situation. She hoped none of them had contracted the disease.

From the nursing home, Maggie headed to the hospital to check on her patient. Arriving at the biocontainment unit, she found Heidi much the same. The charge nurse informed her that Heidi's mother was in the waiting room and eager to talk with her. Maggie found the woman in a corner of the waiting room sipping on black coffee.

"Mrs. Jones, I'm Dr. Hamilton," she began. "I spoke with you yesterday. Thank you so much for being here. I've just checked on Heidi, and at least for now, she seems stable. But she still requires medications to sustain her blood pressure and dialysis because of her kidney failure. We are exploring trying to get her an experimental drug that has been used to treat Ebola patients."

"Dr. Hamilton, thank you so much for all you are doing. I just can't imagine where Heidi would have gotten this disease. Her whole life was working in the nursing home and going out with this new boyfriend. She virtually does nothing else."

"That's what is perplexing to us," Maggie agreed. "This is a tropical disease and usually requires exposure in Africa or to someone who has been to Africa or other tropical countries. Your daughter and her boyfriend appear to have had no exposure to anyone who may have had this disease, but we're still looking. It was helpful that you allowed us to publicize her name so others who may know them or have had contact with them will come forward. The real concern is that the person who exposed them may be infecting others."

"I completely understand," said Heidi's mother. "What do you think are Heidi's chances?"

"To be frank, I'm afraid not very good," Maggie told her.

"Her vital signs are stable right now, but she really hasn't shown any improvement. I think they are fifty-fifty at best."

"That's terrible," her mother replied. "She doesn't have any brothers or sisters. She was my only child, and as I told the nurse, she has been bitter since I divorced her father."

"Have you contacted him about Heidi's condition?" Maggie asked.

"Yes, I called him before coming here. He will likely be flying in today from Vermont. While our divorce was bitter at the time, we've basically reconciled and realized that our relationship wasn't meant to be. Heidi was the real bright thing in our marriage. I know that he will be quite upset about her illness."

"I will be around the hospital all day," Maggie said, "so when he arrives, I would be happy to visit with him."

Frank and Susan Lee arrived at the Deaconess medical office building at eleven in the morning for Susan's routine obstetrical visit. Her physician's office was located on the third floor. With less than two months until delivery, she was to see the doctor more frequently, and Frank decided he would come along to hear about her progress. While the pregnancy was unexpected, they were anxious about having a child considering the upcoming plans.

After parking their car, they headed to the wood-paneled elevator of the seven-story beige brick building and selected the third floor, where the offices of Deaconess Ob-Gyn Specialists were located. The polished marble floors and sleek woodwork gave a clean feel to the entire space. After entering the reception area, Susan approached the receptionist.

"Mrs. Lee, it's good to see you," the receptionist said. "It appears that the baby is coming right along. The baby bump is growing. I see you have your husband with you today. Dr. Wheeler will see you momentarily. Just have a seat."

Susan found a seat and then picked up a magazine to read while waiting. All the reading material was educational for expectant mothers, so Frank was a bit bored looking for anything to keep him occupied. As he glanced at his messages, one from their handler caught his attention.

We need to meet again at the safe house tomorrow to discuss implementation of the plan. Is the elixir safe?

Frank texted back a simple answer of *Yes, tucked away.*

5 PM tomorrow, came the response.

Frank responded, *"We'll be there."*

The Lees were escorted to an exam room, and within a short time, Dr. Pamela Wheeler entered. She greeted Frank as she extended her hand.

"Great to finally meet you, Mr. Lee. I imagine you're excited about this upcoming event."

"Yes, we certainly are," said Frank. "It wasn't exactly planned, but nevertheless, we are eager to meet the new arrival."

"Well, let's just check your wife over to be sure everything is going well," said Dr. Wheeler.

With that, Susan got onto the exam table, and the doctor proceeded to palpate her abdomen. "The baby seems right in position," she said. "All your lab tests look excellent, and the sonograms show the baby is growing normally. Did you want to know the sex?"

Susan answered, "We prefer to keep this a surprise. It makes it more special."

"I understand," said Dr. Wheeler. "More women are choosing to do just that. I'll plan to see you every two weeks until delivery. Call me if anything comes up. I think that you know the protocol. Should your water break or you go into labor, call us and head to the admitting office. Usually with the first baby, labor can be long, but you never know."

With that, the Lees left and headed to their car. Frank told Susan about the text he'd received and how they would be meeting at the safe house tomorrow.

"Rather lousy timing with this pregnancy, isn't it?" Susan responded. "We need to carry out the plan, but with this baby coming about the same time, it makes things complicated."

"We'll get it done," Frank responded. "We've never failed the Centre before, so I don't expect anything less this time. You know they're our bosses, and we can't fail our country. They picked us for this job, paired us together to make us look like man and wife with common American names, and now they're counting on us to come through. They want confusion, anxiety, panic, and complete disruption of American society. Our job is to make this happen."

Maggie found Jamie in the conference room with the PhDs working on reviewing the viral cultures.

"Found anything so far?" Maggie asked.

"No, nothing out of the ordinary," replied Jamie. "A lot of the usual things: gram-negative bacteria, staphylococcus, streptococcus, but no tropical diseases. I think we have to believe that Alex caught this outside the hospital. This should give Tuttle a little consolation that the infection doesn't appear to have originated here. The FBI has to push harder to find the source."

"Mack's been working on it," Maggie assured her. "He's pursuing a phone number on Alex's cell that had no caller ID but frequently called him. Maybe this will yield something."

"Speaking of Mack," Jamie said with a smile, "how are the two of you getting along? I could see a connection there even when you first met."

"You were right," Maggie acknowledged. "He is a great guy. I have to admit I really like being with him. We've gotten together a couple of times, and he's so easy to talk to. Our backgrounds are very different, yet we seem to find a lot in common."

"Just call me the matchmaker!" gloated Jamie. "Will I get invited to the wedding?"

"Wait a minute!" Maggie protested. "There is a long way to go before that would happen."

"You might be surprised," Jamie responded.

"I wanted to ask you about this experimental treatment for Ebola called Zendenivir. Any chance we could get this for Heidi?" Maggie inquired.

"I'll try," Jamie promised. "But we'll need to get it soon if we are going to help her."

"I realize we're running out of time," Maggie agreed, "but I need something more to offer. You can probably tell I'm desperate to find a treatment that can turn the corner for her."

"I'll get back with you tomorrow once I make some calls," Jamie responded.

Mack had made his way to the control center, where he found the other agents. He sat down and got their attention to discuss the strategy in finding the source.

"Gentlemen, it is my understanding that the calls from the unidentified cell phone have been tracked to a disposable phone that was bought at a Target store."

"Yes," one of the agents responded, "and we have identified the exact store where it was purchased. It was only a few miles from the hospital."

"I'll plan to make a trip there today to see if I can discover the buyer," Mack replied. "At the same time, we need the rest of you to look further into Alex's cell phone to track his daily routine."

Tim, one of the agents, responded. "He would go to the local grocery store, occasionally the pharmacy, and mostly to the gym. At times he visited Heidi, but most of the time she visited him. He appears to be one of the most isolated people I've ever met. We also could see the phone being taken to another address, but it seemed to stop before ever reaching a building. It was almost as if the phone was left in a park. We think it's odd. Why would the phone be deposited there?"

Maybe he also worked out in the park and would leave his cell phone in a locker or by a tree. Who knows? Mack thought. *Perhaps we can go to the park and find out where he placed it.*

CHAPTER 10

The Lees made their way to the safe house and found Samuel, the handler, and three others waiting for them. The house was very simple and nondescript. It blended into all the houses on the block and didn't stand out in any way. White siding, blue shutters, a two-car garage, and a few trees and bushes for landscaping—in essence, it was the all-American house. After parking their car, they went to the front door and rang the doorbell.

Samuel met them at the door. He was a graying elderly gentleman who had kept himself in good physical shape. His debonair flair gave him a sense of dignity and power. He was dressed in a casual but elegant sweater. His perfectly groomed hair and wire-rim glasses projected a sense of intelligence, and his perfect English didn't disclose his Chinese background.

"Great to see you both," Samuel said. "What did your doctor say about the pregnancy?"

"Everything is going well," Susan responded. "It's only a few weeks before the baby will be born."

"That's why we wanted to meet," Samuel told her. "You

know my feelings about the pregnancy. This should never have happened, and when it did, abortion would have been the best course—but here we are now. We want to move up the date for the implementation, knowing that we're dealing with this pregnancy and also having the FBI trying to find you. We want to go over with you how to disperse the elixir. Alex did an amazing job of modulating the virus. He followed the directions perfectly from the plans we gave him. I realize that he thought he was finding the cure for cancer and had no idea what he was dealing with, but he was a perfect choice. Unfortunately, he was also the test case for the virus and has shown us its effectiveness."

Samuel looked at Frank and Susan and said, "We've devised a way for you to deliver the virus. My associates here will package it in a small vial encased in a sturdy container. It actually will be quite attractive and will be called "The Elixir of Love." Actually, it will be the elixir of death. It will be disguised as a small bottle of perfume that you can carry in your purse. This should lessen any suspicion that it maybe something dangerous."

He continued, "You may remember the opera *Elixir of Love* by Donizetti. A young man wants to charm a girl into falling in love with him, but he doesn't know how. He buys the elixir from a street salesman who promises the potion will cast a spell over her, and she will immediately fall in love with him. He quickly buys the potion to get the love of his life."

Samuel smiled. "In our case, the Elixir of Love will fulfill an entirely different outcome. Our country, China, hopes this will create chaos in the United States, and I think we can see already even with these two people that it has started. The Americans have tried to starve us out by placing tariffs on our exports and attempting to move the production of products back to the states. The bastards have massively increased their military, knowing that with our economy affected by our deteriorating economy, we can't do the same. Now it's our turn to put pressure on them. If successful, we can cause their financial markets to collapse, forcing them to focus on a killer virus and turn away from destroying us. And all this will come from a small tube of a lethal virus. We won't have to use bombs, rockets, or invasions."

Getting down to business, Samuel concluded, "The vial will be sturdy, and you won't be able to remove the cap, but you can remove the cover on the case. This will, in essence, arm the container. Once you compress the button on the bottom, the timer will start on the explosive. It will give you about one hour to get completely away from the building before the charge disperses the virus."

"So, what is the building?" asked Frank.

"You'll know that in due time," replied Samuel. "Susan, have you had further contact with Jason? He's the key, since he can get us schematics of the buildings that will give you options of where to plant the virus."

"I plan to call Jason again soon. He doesn't have any idea what's going on. He simply knows he's having an affair with a married woman. To be very honest, I think he may be the father of the child. I should have been more careful."

Maggie caught up with Mack as he was leaving the building. "All right, hotshot, where do you think you're going?"

"Chasing down leads. What else?"

"Are we going to make this another night together?" she asked.

"Funny you should ask," he replied. "I've planned our outing already. Tonight, we're going to a fancier place. No more bars. There's this restaurant, Stephano's. I want to take you there. I'm into Italian food. Plus, it's nice and quiet and we can talk. I'm expecting you to tell me how you're going to cure the patients, and I'm going to tell you where they got the disease."

"Well, it would be great if it works that way," she said, "but in any case, dinner sounds perfect. Should I meet you there?"

"Not this time," he told her. "I'm picking you up about seven o'clock. Then I have a surprise for you."

"What's that?" she asked.

"Sorry, it wouldn't be a surprise if I told you."

"So, how dressy?"

"I would say moderately so," he advised. "You may have a hard time believing this, but I'll have a sport coat on. I would suggest a dress that sways a great deal. It's part of the surprise."

"Now you have me wondering," she responded. "Sounds interesting. I'll text you my address. See you at seven."

Smiling, Maggie took the stairs to the biocontainment unit to check on Heidi. Still minimal urine, and her blood pressure wasn't good. The charge nurse let Maggie know that Mr. Campton was in the waiting room and wanted to talk with her. As she entered the waiting area, Maggie found him staring out the window. His ex-wife was close by.

"Mr. Campton, I'm glad you came," said Maggie. "I'm sure your ex-wife has told you that Heidi is very ill. Things are touch-and-go right now, but we are doing everything we can to support her through this illness. There are no approved treatments for Ebola, but I have asked a physician from the CDC to see if we can get an experimental treatment. We're not sure that this will be possible, but we want to try anything available, since the prognosis is bad."

"Dr. Hamilton, thank you for seeing me. We're just devastated over this and beside ourselves trying to decide what we can do. You know she's our only daughter that we had together, and she is very special to me. We just appreciate everything you're doing."

"I've asked your wife," said Maggie, "but I want to ask you as well. Are you aware of anyone who Heidi could have had contact with who may have had this illness?"

"Not really," he replied, "although I'm sure you're aware that she didn't contact us very often. She has remained very angry over our divorce, but recently she seemed to warm up to me, which appeared to be from having this boyfriend. She talked so positively about him and even implied to me that she might bring him to Vermont, so it appeared that this was starting to get serious."

"If you think of anyone besides her boyfriend who she may have connected with that was possibly ill, it would very helpful," said Maggie. "We'll keep you posted on her condition. As I've said, she is very unstable, and there is a high chance she won't survive, but we're trying our best."

As her work day came to an end, Maggie headed home to get ready for Mack. She took a long bath this time, and the warm water put her in a very relaxed mood. After drying herself, she found Huiles Precieuses oil to apply to her skin. It had been a gift from her mother, and she saved it for special occasions. It gave her skin a soft feel.

Maggie perused her clothes, trying to decide which skirt or dress to wear. *He said something that swayed. I wonder what this is all about?* She found a short black dress that flattered her figure and showed off her legs, and it did go side to side when she walked, so this appeared to be the best choice.

Admiring herself in the mirror, she thought, *I don't look so bad. It is somewhat low-cut, but Mom always said, you should show off your best parts, and I'm not flat-chested by any means.* Happy with her choice, she found matching high heels and jewelry that complemented the dress, then finished everything off with a Carolina Herrera perfume called Good Girl. She was set to go.

Promptly at seven, Mack arrived driving a new-model convertible Corvette. He came to her door and, seeing her, could only say "Wow." Then he added, "You don't look like a doctor tonight, Doc. I wouldn't worry about my illness if I was your patient and you came to treat me in the hospital."

Mack was wearing a slim-fitting burgundy sport coat and black fitted pants. His clothes showed off his exquisite physique, a result of regular exercise and sports. Rather than a shirt and tie, he wore a black low-cut sweater that gave him the appearance of a Hollywood model.

"I'm sorry, who are you?" Maggie asked. "I was waiting for Matthew Johnson, not George Clooney."

"Yeah, right," Mack laughed. "Well, you're lucky, because I *am* Matthew Johnson, your date for tonight. Are you ready to go?"

"Of course. But I have to say, I wasn't expecting a sports car. Maybe a tractor."

"Oh sure. Well, tractors *are* convertibles, but hey, I like cars. I can't afford a Ferrari, but for the price, this car will do. And it's fast! Plus, you know farmers are engineers today.

They farm with sophistication. Computerized tractors, scientific approach to farming to conserve the land and maximize the yield."

They headed to the restaurant. A valet parked the car for them, and the maître d' showed them to a quiet table. After they were seated, Mack started the conversation.

"Did you learn anything from Heidi's father today?" he asked.

"Not much," she admitted. "He seems very nice, but like Alex, Heidi has had little contact with her parents. Really no clear evidence of exposure to anyone with this disease."

"Similar thing with Alex," Mack added. "He has had very few people he has interacted with, and then there is this strange caller. I went to Target today to see if I could find out the buyer of the disposable phone. I guess they really don't keep many records of buyers. It was paid for with cash, so no credit card to track. The purchaser bought the phone a year ago, and now it appears the phone may have been disposed of. No real reason, but I'm concerned that the person got rid of the phone when Alex got sick. It seems odd. They were having many conversations with him, and when he gets deathly ill, they don't want any connection with him anymore? You wonder what might be going on. It's as though they don't want us to track the connection back to them."

"That is concerning," Maggie agreed. "Could they have given him the virus?"

"If so, for what purpose?" asked Mack.

"Well, enough about work," Maggie said, changing the subject. "I want to know more about you."

"Not much to tell," Mack replied. "Just trying to move up the ranks of the FBI. I think I got assigned this job because they didn't think there was much to it. You know, send the junior guy for an insignificant investigation."

"Who knows?" she said. "This may be a bigger thing than your superiors suspect."

"I want to know more about you," said Mack, steering the conversation back to the personal. "Let me hear about your love life."

"Actually, not very much to tell," she told him. "I've had a few boyfriends. None that ever became serious. Many I believe were threatened that I was a doctor and perhaps smarter than them. I hope I wasn't some dull chick that they thought was no fun, but I guess I do have a pretty serious personality. I deal with very sick patients, and being a doctor consumes my life."

"Well, you don't seem totally consumed to me," Mack assured her. "I enjoy talking with you."

"And I enjoy talking with you. In fact, I told my friend Jamie how I have found it so easy to tell you anything."

"Enough about this. I'm starved. How about some food?" Mack perused the menu. "I'll order antipasto appetizers, and you look over the menu for an entrée. I put in an order for a Barolo red wine. I hope you don't mind; I know you're a white wine person."

"I guess I'm a wino," Maggie replied. "I'll drink any kind of wine. Sounds great."

When the waiter came to get their order, Maggie ordered pasta with shrimp, and Mack ordered veal. He said if he couldn't have a rib-eye, then he would take the baby cow.

The dinner went quickly, and finally Maggie had to ask, "So, what's the big surprise? I haven't seen anything yet."

"That's because it is still to come. You might call it dessert. I know that you won't believe this, since I like athletics and working out, but I've been taking ballroom dance lessons, and the dance studio is right around the corner. I had taken dance lessons before coming to Chicago and I found this place to improve my moves. Tonight, I'm learning rumba. I thought it would be great to have a female partner rather than having to always dance with the instructor. I told him I was going to bring you, and he was excited to teach both of us."

"You know, I could have two left feet," Maggie warned.

"I doubt that. Besides, I'm supposed to lead, remember? Let's see if that happens."

Mack paid the bill, and they left the restaurant, walking to the "A Step Ahead" dance studio. As they entered, music was playing, and there was another couple taking dance lessons in one corner. It was apparent that they were beginners; they looked like sixth graders just learning to dance. Maggie spotted a wiry little guy heading directly for them. *Oh, great,* she thought. *I can't believe I'm really going to do this.*

"So, you must be Maggie," said the man. "Mack has told me all about you. He says he's tired of dancing with a male instructor and needs a female to dance with instead. Isn't that true, Mack?"

"You're absolutely right," Mack confessed. "It's a little embarrassing to dance with a male. Besides, if I'm ever to dance outside of this place, I need to practice with a female. So, here's Maggie."

"Let's get started," said Corry, the dance instructor. "So, rhumba is quick, quick, slow, then quick, quick, slow. Basically, you make a box. Mack knows several leads that we can see if you can follow. The first will be a simple under-arm turn. Then a cross-body lead with Cuban walks. We'll get to the Cuban motion eventually."

"Oh boy," Maggie sighed. "You expect me to do this? You're getting me out of my comfort zone."

"Maggie, you'll be great," Mack assured her.

Corry and Mack led Maggie through the basic steps, and she was surprised how easy it was to follow his lead. This led to the cross-body lead, Cuban walks, and a rock step.

"Hey, this is kind of fun!" she declared. "I have to tell you, I was scared to death when I saw Corry coming at us, Mack."

"See, I told you that you had nothing to worry about. I found this gets my mind off of every problem, and it's good exercise. OK, so it's not a football workout, but it's something you and I can do together."

They finished their hour lesson, and to Maggie, it seemed to pass so quickly. Thanking Corry, they headed to the car.

"Mack, I'm so glad you pushed me to do this tonight," said Maggie. "I have to admit, it was better to be a surprise, because I would have likely backed out if I had known in advance. Maybe the wine with dinner helped as well. I hope we can do this again."

"I'm glad that you said that," Mack replied. "Next week. Same time."

Mack opened the car door for Maggie and let her in. As they drove to her apartment, he couldn't keep from putting his hand on her leg, and it gave her goose bumps. *Am I falling in love with a farm boy?* she thought.

Maggie turned to him as they neared her home. "How about coming in for a few minutes?" she asked.

"Sure, I'd like that."

"I've got an after-dinner liqueur that I've saved just for an occasion like this," she told him.

Mack settled into her soft divan as Maggie found small

glasses for the Sobon Estate white port. She poured two small glasses and handed one to Mack, then sat down beside him.

"This is sipping booze, Mack," she said. "Rather sweet but great for dessert."

Mack took a sip and turned to her. "Actually, I thought that *you* were a much better dessert."

He pulled her close to him, and their lips met. The wine with dinner, the dancing at the studio, the hand on her leg had prepared her for this moment. She wanted to be kissed.

Mack pulled her close. He let his hands explore her body, and she provided no resistance. She hadn't felt this comfortable with a man before. She allowed his hands to unsnap her bra, and he proceeded to undress her. She reciprocated by undressing him, and before long, they had found their way to her bed.

The next thirty minutes went quickly. It was as though they had known each other forever. Maggie felt no reluctance to share her body with him. Afterward, they just lay there, staring at the ceiling.

"Mack, I've never felt like this before," Maggie confessed. "I can't believe what just happened, but everything tonight was so perfect. I hope this isn't the end of it. I want to continue to see you. I have to admit that you preoccupy my thoughts during the day, and I dream of when I will be able to see you again."

"It's the same for me, Maggie," Mack replied. "I noticed you from the very first time I met you and wanted to get to know you better. I guess we found that out tonight, didn't we? You have a beautiful body."

"I don't know if you tell a man his body is beautiful, but yours feels so powerful and perfectly shaped. You know, most of my patients are old with deteriorated frames. I don't have a chance to examine someone like you."

"Well, Doc," he said, "I hope you can examine me again. I think I need a very thorough exam frequently."

Smiling, she gave him a kick. "Yeah, right, and so do I!"

Mack got up, put on his clothes, and gave her one last kiss before leaving. "See you tomorrow?"

"Absolutely. I can't wait."

CHAPTER 11

The sun pierced her bedroom window, and Maggie slowly opened her eyes, staring at the ceiling. She had fallen asleep shortly after Mack had left, and she thought to herself, *I haven't slept that well in months. Was this a dream that I had, or was it real?*

Her daydreaming was interrupted when her phone began to ring. Sleepily, she answered, "Dr. Hamilton."

"Doctor, this is the emergency room at Deaconess. Dr. Singer would like to talk with you."

"Sure," Maggie said. "Put him on."

"Maggie," John said urgently, "we've had another patient come in who may have Ebola. His name is James Singleton. He's a tech who works here in the emergency room and cared for Alex Williamson when he was admitted. Jack's associates say he shed his protective gear at the time. He said they were too hot and took them off. No one noticed this, but that's likely how he got exposed. His wife called EMS when he started getting delirious and breaking out with blisters."

"Oh my gosh," Maggie said. "This is going to create a panic in the hospital. I'm just getting up and will get there as soon as possible. Find a place in the biocontainment unit for him."

Maggie quickly showered and got dressed, all the time considering what she could do to stop this. *We've got to find the source, and Jamie has to get me that treatment.*

Maggie got to the hospital and hurried to the biocontainment unit. Jack had been moved into the room next to Heidi. His pressures were low, and like the others, he was in renal failure. Adam Foster and Eric Strong had already been called, and the dialysis was to be started soon.

Maggie ordered cultures and started broad-spectrum antibiotics, but she was pretty confident that Jack likely had Ebola also. After ordering additional tests, she reviewed Heidi's chart. All in all, things didn't look very good for Heidi. She had persistently low blood pressure and minimal urine output.

I hope Jamie can get me Zendenivir, Maggie thought. *Heidi doesn't have much time. I'm going to contact the health department to quarantine the Singleton family. We can't let them wander around the community.*

Mack found his team of agents in the control room reserved for them.

"All right, guys," he began. "Where do we stand with contacts? I know Alex was a loner, but listen, he must have interacted with someone—like the mysterious caller on his cell phone. Any other news?"

"We've found his once-a-week trip to the grocery store

was usually at night," Jimmie, one of the agents, reported. "Security cameras identified him. The good news: he was a night owl. He went to a store that was open twenty-four hours a day and usually bought his groceries about nine at night—therefore, less exposure to others. His landlady said he would take many walks or runs through the park, but again, usually early in the morning or in the evenings. It would give less exposure to others."

"Fine," Mack said. "That helps identify the exposure of his disease to others, but it doesn't help us discover where he got the disease. I'm concerned this mysterious caller may have something to do with this whole ordeal. How can we identify the caller with the disposable phone?"

"If they disposed of the first phone and then bought another disposable phone," said Jimmie, "you would think they would have bought it at the same location, wouldn't you? Let's got back to Target and try to find everyone who bought a disposable phone around that time."

"Makes sense," Mack agreed. "I know those people, so I'll head back there today. Do we know when the first phone may have been destroyed?"

"That's the interesting point," Jimmie responded. "It was the day after Alex was admitted. The signal was turned off, and the phone was never used again."

"Really. Sounds suspicious to me," Mack mused. "Someone doesn't want to be found. Could it be that they wanted him infected? If so, why? He's not anyone who would necessarily spread it to others."

"You know he worked in virology," Jimmie replied. "Maybe it was an accident? Maybe the source doesn't want us to know they have this virus? But what were they going to do with this? Why would Alex be involved at all? Did he have some alternative motive to spread this disease? You wouldn't think that he would want to get the disease. How about we look at his home computer and see what he has posted on Facebook, Instagram, or Twitter—see if he had a reason to spread this disease. He seemed to be an angry person, and maybe he wanted to get back at the world. Maybe he had a manifesto. You know, maybe he's a domestic terrorist."

"Good idea," Mack agreed. "Jimmie, you take that over. Tim, you look into Alex's schedule at work. See when he would arrive and leave. See if you can find his movements either before or after work and where he might have gone. I'll go back to Target today and talk to the manager."

Mack found Maggie in the cafeteria having a cup of coffee. "What's the matter, gorgeous? Did you have trouble sleeping last night?"

"Not at all. I slept well after working out," she said with a wink.

"I'm a firm believer in exercise. Maybe I can be your trainer."

"What's your qualification in personal training?"

"Well, I'm new at it, but I can learn quickly and really enjoy it."

"I only work out with one person. Are you willing to only train me?"

"I can't imagine training anyone else," Mack said. "I hope this leads to more than fitness, or for that matter, dancing."

Maggie smiled. "Me too. Unfortunately, we have another case. This time, an employee of the hospital who was admitted this morning. This is going to create havoc amongst the personnel, so I need to go meet with the employees. I'm sure Tuttle is going crazy. He will have everyone on his case."

"Where did the employee work?" asked Mack.

"In the ER. He took care of Alex but didn't follow the protocol and shed his protective gear. That's what I need to emphasize to the employees. Follow the rules, and you'll be all right."

"What about his family?"

"We are going to quarantine them," Maggie replied. "I considered doing this at the nursing home, but there was no close contact with Heidi, as she was a social worker. She just talked to people and didn't have intimate contact with them. Similarly, Alex didn't have any close contact with people in the lab. We know that the incubation time can be up to three weeks, so the family will have to stay in their home for this length of time."

Mack nodded. "I'm still working on people Alex interacted with. Plus, I'm going back to Target today. Something is very strange about this disposable cell phone, and I don't have a good feeling about it. We're also looking into Alex's social media. We want to see if he had any thoughts of killing people in a mass-destruction way. Who knows, he may have wanted to get back at the world over something and accidentally caught it himself."

Frank Lee decided to stop at the church on his way to the cleaners. He wanted to access the hospital's electronic medical records and thought he could take a moment to do this before arriving at his business. After greeting the secretary, he asked if it would be all right to use the church's computer. He explained that his computer at home was on the fritz, and he had to check something before going to work. She smiled and told him to go right ahead.

He slipped into the library and, after booting up the device, entered the passwords that the Centre had instructed him to use. When his screen popped up with the monitor in the biocontainment unit, he found physicians logging on and off. *Oh great,* he thought. *Another person admitted with possible Ebola. This is really going to stir things up. Dr. Hamilton's note says she's going to quarantine the family. I need to let Samuel know. If they want us to carry this out, we're going to have to move quickly. I wonder what the target is going to be.*

Susan Lee picked up the phone and dialed Jason. She knew he would likely be at work, but she thought this might be the best time to talk to him.

"Jason, it's Susan. Can you talk?"

"Sure," he replied. "How are you feeling? Are you over the morning sickness?"

"I'm feeling fine now," she said. "I want you to know that I don't believe Frank has a clue that there is anything between us. I made sure that I had sex with him when I was seeing you, but I'm pretty confident that you're the father of the child. That night with you, when Frank was gone, was simply extraordinary, and I won't forget it."

"Wow, it was special for me too," said Jason. "You were amazing. It is still hard for me to imagine that I'm going to be a father, but I'm upset that I can't get to know my own child."

"We'll work something out," she assured him. "We can pretend with the child that you're just a very close friend. Do you have a name in mind?"

"Oh my gosh. I haven't even thought of that. Maybe

Henry if a boy. My grandfather was Henry, and we were always the best of friends."

"Then Henry it is if it's a boy." she told him. Then she added, "Oh, I have to tell you that Frank and I have to go to Washington, DC, on business soon, so we will be gone for about a week. We plan to take in the sights while we're there, and I know that you worked at the Pentagon. Do you have any contacts who can help us? Just to save me steps. I thought you could get us the layout of the buildings so I could make my way through the various places without walking so much."

"I may be able to do that," Jason said. "It's the least I can do. I still know several people in high places. I'm sure they could help me with that."

Mack found his way to the Target store and went directly to the manager's office. He showed his creds again and told the manager how critical it was to know the owner of the disposable phone.

"Well, I suppose we can look back at the sales of the phones at the time and see if we can identify a name," the manager, George Nelson, exclaimed. "No guarantee we can find anyone. They don't have to give us a name when they buy a phone, but maybe they purchased it with a credit card, and that could help."

"Perfect," Mack said.

The manager found the record of sales for the one to three days after Alex was admitted. There were twenty phones sold, and nineteen were paid with credit cards. One was purchased using cash.

Does anyone use cash to make purchases today? Mack

thought. Then he said to the manager, "Give me the names you have, and we will sort through them. Oh, one other question. Are they assigned a phone number?"

"Yes, I think so," said the manager. "I'm not sure we have a record of that, but I can check. It may be assigned by the manufacturer of the phone. I believe they are made by Samsung, and so it may be possible to find the phone numbers that way. We can look into it."

"That would be very helpful," said Mack. "In the meantime, we will go through these names and see if any are associated with our person of interest. Thank you for your help. Please get back to me as soon as you know something."

"Will do, Agent Johnson," George replied. "So, what is this all about?"

"We have a young man who has died from Ebola," Mack said. "You may have heard about this on the news. Our job is to find the source. He had been receiving many calls from a disposable phone from your store, which now has been turned off or destroyed. We would like to know why. We assume they probably bought another phone to replace the one they disposed of."

"Hmm, makes sense. I'll see what I can do."

Maggie was making rounds on her other patients when she got the stat page. Code in the biocontainment unit! Running, she took the stairs; on arriving, she found the code team in Heidi's room. They had been slow to attend to her because of the time constraints getting on the protective gear, but the charge nurse had already been dressed and began CPR as soon as Heidi's cardiac rhythm went to ventricular tachycardia. Fluids, medications, and defibrillating shocks were administered, but after forty-five minutes of aggressive CPR, the code was stopped. Heidi had become the second fatality from the disease.

Maggie thought, *How do I tell her parents? They were so hopeful she would survive. I wish we could have given her the Zendenivir. Maybe it would have helped. Maybe she would have made it.*

With a somber face, she went to the waiting room and found Heidi's parents in one corner. They both had a look of fear on their face and seeing hers, they sensed that the outcome was not good.

"I'm sorry, Mr. Campton and Mrs. Jones," Maggie began. "Heidi had a cardiac arrest. We tried to resuscitate her for an extended period without any success. This disease is just horrible. It attacks about every organ in your body. We had hoped to have tried an experimental treatment, but it hasn't arrived. With no response from the resuscitation and no return of a normal heart rhythm, we have stopped the code. I'm afraid your daughter has passed away."

Teresa Jones began to weep, and Maggie found Kleenex to give her. Mr. Campton thanked Maggie for all she had done. They together agreed to an autopsy. Leaving the waiting room, Maggie called the chaplain to come meet with the family and then paged Pam Foster.

"Pam, we have another death from the Ebola," she said. "I expect your findings will be similar, but would you be willing to do an autopsy on Heidi Campton? We just want to be sure we're dealing with the same disease."

Pam replied, "The autopsy went fine with the last patient, so I guess I can do this one as well. It's not easy having to wear all the gear, and I don't want to take any risk of exposing others, but I should be able to give you an idea if the findings are the same as the last victim."

"Thank you, Pam. Having two young and healthy people die is weighing on me. We have to find the source and stop this."

Maggie hung up the phone and called her friend Jamie.

"Jamie, our second patient has just died. I was so hopeful that we could try the Zendenivir. Any idea if we will get it soon?"

Jamie told her, "It's supposed to come tomorrow, but you know there is no guarantee that this treatment will work. It's brand new and not thoroughly tested."

"Look, do we have anything to lose?" Maggie asked. "Most of the time, these patients die."

"Good point," Jamie agreed. "I'll get it to you tomorrow as soon as it arrives. I understand a third patient is here. The sooner we give him the drug, the better chance of a response."

Leaving the biocontainment unit, Maggie felt very depressed. She walked slowly to the elevator but decided to take the stairs instead. On entering the stairwell, she felt a tear trickle down her cheek, and she couldn't stop herself. She cried in one corner of the landing.

I've been a total failure, she thought. *Two young healthy people. Their whole lives ahead of them. How could they have caught this?* Composing herself, she hesitated and then walked down the stairs, exiting on the third floor.

Mack had just gotten off of the elevator. On seeing her, he said, "Did you see a ghost? You look terrible."

Maggie couldn't control herself and began to cry again. "I'm sorry, it's just that Heidi Campton just died. I feel like I should have done something more. But what?"

"Look, Maggie," said Mack, "you've put your heart and

soul into treating these two patients. It's not you. It's this disease. We obviously don't have any great treatments."

"I know, but I just feel so helpless. I'm young, and some people may say a more experienced doctor could have saved them. I hope this experimental treatment will help the third patient. I don't know what else to do."

Mack replied, "Everyone knows that you are the star physician in the hospital. If you can't solve the problem, no one can. Do you want to take a walk outside just to get some fresh air and try to calm down?"

"Yes, I think that would be a good idea. Mack, you're just the greatest guy. Even though you have a macho personality, you always seem to sense my emotional state. How in the world did you think of that? I've never had any other man be so sensitive to my emotions."

"You know, I'm not sure," he said. "Maybe it's something to do with the training at the FBI. They teach us to be very observant of people we interrogate. You can tell a great deal from people's facial expressions, their responses, and their general posturing. I guess maybe that could be it, but I think I may have picked up this ability from my mother. She has an amazing instinct to know what's going on with someone, simply by talking and observing them."

"All I know is, this makes me love you," she told him. "I never knew Mr. Macho could be so kind and gentle."

Jason dialed a number in Washington, DC, and found a friend of his who worked at the State Department. He figured this would be the best person to provide schematics of buildings.

"Hey Jack," he began, "this is Jason. I haven't talked to

you in ages, but I have a favor to ask. I have a good friend who is going to be in DC, and she is very pregnant. She and her husband are there on business, but they want to take in the sights. Since it is hard for her to get around, she wanted to try and get a layout of the buildings so she could keep her walking to a minimum. Any chance you could help?"

"I can probably help you with this," said Jack. "I know one of the facility managers who is a young guy whose wife is pregnant also. He'll understand. He should have access to the floor plans of the buildings. Any idea which buildings they want to visit?"

"I'm not exactly sure, but I think the Smithsonian, the National Gallery of Art, the White House, and maybe the Holocaust Museum. That would probably be a good start."

"The White House might be the only one I'd have trouble getting, but I'm guessing he will be willing to share those plans with me if he knows the situation. I assume they would be taking the visitor's tour."

"I would think so," said Jason. "That's great if you can get these. I know that she will appreciate this a lot."

"She must be a special friend if you're going out of your way to do this for her," said Jack.

"She is. We have a very close relationship. She's amazing."

"I'm guessing she is. Sure, I'll do all I can."

Maggie's cell phone buzzed, and she recognized Jamie's number.

"Maggie, the Zendenivir has arrived," Jamie told her when she answered. "Let's get this to your patient as soon as we can. Do you have the family quarantine still?"

"Yes," Maggie responded, "It's his wife and two children.

We're delivering food and supplies to them as needed. The police have provided guards at their house to prevent them from leaving. They'll be happy to hear that we have the treatment."

"Listen," Jamie reminded her, "there are no guarantees with this. It's new and hasn't been used extensively, but it gives us some hope."

"Anything is better than nothing," said Maggie.

Maggie went straight to the biocontainment unit, where Jamie was waiting with the treatment. It came packaged in a cool container and was surrounded by spongy material to prevent breakage of the vial. The instructions said to infuse slowly over one hour intravenously. They were to watch for any signs of allergic reaction, such as a fall in blood pressure, rash, or difficulty breathing.

Well, how can we determine a drop in his blood pressure when he is on medication to keep it up? thought Maggie. *He's on a ventilator, so we're controlling his breathing. I suppose these things could worsen with the infusion, but at least we have them under control with the treatment.*

The IV was started, and the medication was infused slowly into James Singleton's vein. Maggie watched from the control booth, constantly observing the vital signs and the patient. Fortunately, there appeared to be no adverse effect as the Zendenivir entered his body. After an hour, all the medication had been delivered, and Maggie sighed with relief.

"So far, so good," she said to Jamie. "Now let's hope we see some results."

"In other patients who have received this medication, it usually takes about seventy-two hours before there is appreciable change in their condition. Let's keep our fingers crossed."

"I'm doing more than that," said Maggie. "I'm praying to God that we have a response. I can't take more deaths from this disease."

CHAPTER 12

Maggie glanced out the seventh-floor window of Deaconess Hospital. The news trucks were lined up and down the parking lot, with towers projecting to send information back to their home offices. *I'm sure they're bombarding Tuttle's office right now, since they've likely heard Heidi Campton has died. And with a hospital employee admitted positive with the disease, he's probably feeling even more pressure.*

Even though she didn't always see eye to eye with Tuttle, she decided it might be time to pay him another visit. She found him in his office pacing back and forth, exasperated, not knowing what he was going to say.

"Dr. Hamilton, nursing personnel are calling in sick. What can I say to reassure the community—or for that matter, the nation—that we have this under control?" he asked with frustrated anger. "I need help here. The reporters outside our hospital want answers too! Do you blame them? The word is out about the young girl dying, and now another hospital employee has been admitted with the disease."

"Well," Maggie began, "we can say that the employee

has received an experimental treatment and that we will see if he shows any improvement in the next three days. We can let them know that his family has been quarantined and we are watching them closely for any signs of the disease, and we have the FBI following up on leads as to Alex's potential contacts. I believe they're making some progress. How does that sound?"

"Much better than anything I could say," Tuttle said with relief. "You are a life-saver, Dr. Hamilton."

"Well, I'd like to think so, but we just lost two young people. I'm not feeling all that great about that."

"Look," said Tuttle, "you're doing everything you can do, and now giving this medication to our employee shows that we are accessing every therapy that is known to help cure the patient."

"Let's hope it works," Maggie said. "We need a success here."

"I have the media assembled in the conference room. Can you go with me now?" Tuttle asked.

"Sure. I've finished making rounds, and this would be a good time."

They made their way to the conference room and found the space to be even more packed with reporters than before. Now there were international media representatives in addition to American reporters. A podium had been set up as before, and Tuttle was the first to speak.

"Thank you, ladies and gentlemen, for assembling here on short notice. We would like to give you an update on the status of the disease and the patients affected. I've asked Dr.

Hamilton to be here again, and she can apprise you where we stand with the patients we have been caring for."

Maggie approached the podium and scanned the room. She felt uneasy as she looked at the faces staring at her. They held on to every word or statement she made. The report was being broadcast live to all the major TV networks, and she didn't want to present anything that might give false hope. Yet at the same time, she wanted to show that progress was being made. She started slowly, reviewing statements from the last press conference.

"As you are aware, Alex Williamson, our first patient with the Ebola virus, passed away, and we confirmed by autopsy that he had all the hallmarks of this terrible disease. His girlfriend, Heidi Campton, was next admitted with identical symptoms and signs of the disease, and she too has succumbed. The autopsy on her is pending, but we feel confident that she has had the same affliction. Finally, a nurse technician has been admitted, also displaying the same findings. We have taken the precaution of quarantining his family until we can be assured that they have not acquired the disease and that they are safe to be out in the community. Finally, we were able to secure an experimental therapy and have given this medication to our latest patient. We hope to see improvement in the next few days. There is no assurance that the treatment will work, but as you know, supportive care alone has not prevented the disease from killing the first two patients admitted. Can I answer any questions?"

"Do we have any idea where the first patient may have gotten this disease? That's the biggest concern that most of the public would like to know," a reporter from Fox News asked.

"I understand that concern, and we feel the same way. That's why we have the FBI onboard, and they are diligently looking for the source. Also, your audiences could help us. We have set up a hotline where they can call if they know of any exposure to any of these individuals, but particularly to our first case, Alex Williamson. He appears to be the initial source of these infections, but we have not been able to identify where he may have contracted the disease."

"Could he have gotten the disease from the hospital lab?" a reporter asked.

"We were initially concerned about this, but the team from the CDC has thoroughly investigated this possibility and found no evidence that the disease was spread from the lab."

"Can we expect an update on this most recent patient's progress soon to see if the therapy is helping?" called out another reporter.

"Yes, I hope to be able to report back to all of you within twenty-four to thirty-six hours and let you know if we are seeing a response. I will say that the CDC feels that this particular Ebola virus appears to be even more virulent than what they have seen previously, but we have no reason to doubt that the new treatment may provide a benefit for our patient."

The conference concluded, and Maggie sighed with relief as she left the room. Turning to Tuttle, she rolled her eyes. "I hope this treatment helps. Let's pray we don't see others showing up in the emergency room tonight or tomorrow with Ebola."

Susan Lee got into her car and found her way to Jason's apartment. It wasn't far from her home and close to the bar where they had met. Jason was, for the Chinese, the perfect target: lonely, smart, and with connections to bioweapons. He had the information on how the country would handle a bioweapons attack and what counterattacks they might possess. She just hadn't planned on this pregnancy getting in the way.

When she rang the doorbell, Jason opened the door and smiled broadly, scanning her body. "Well, things are growing down south, it seems. Are you feeling OK?"

"Actually," she said, "I feel great. Even better now that I'm seeing you. How about a kiss?"

She loved it as he grabbed her around the waist, pulled her close, and began passionately kissing her. She didn't feel particularly sexy, but still, Jason was very attracted to her. He let his hands feel her now-enlarged breasts, and he kissed her even more. He pulled her to his couch and proceeded to let his hands explore her more intimately.

"Listen, Jason," she interrupted, "I would love to have you seduce me again right now. You're an animal in bed, but the doctor tells me I have to lay off of this for the next few weeks until the baby is born. Any news on the schematics of the buildings? My back kills me walking any distance."

"You're in luck," Jason told her. "My friend has just sent me some attachments on an email that gives the floor plans of about every government building in DC. This should help you a lot."

"You're just the best," she purred. And with that, she proceeded to passionately kiss him as her hands explored his body. "Look, maybe we can't have sex right now, but that doesn't mean I can't satisfy you and me at the same time."

After an hour of lovemaking, Susan explained that she needed to get home. "Frank will be there soon and will wonder where I am, so I need to leave."

She got into her car and drove back to her house, where Frank was waiting.

"Any luck?" Frank asked as she came in the door.

"Sure. Did you doubt me? I have him under my control. He has emailed all the plans of the government buildings. Now the Centre has to tell us which one is the target and when we will make the drop."

"I know that they'll be happy with you," Frank said. "You always come through for them."

"We women know how to get things out of men," she said with a wink.

Mack took all the charges for new disposable phones to his team at the control center at Deaconess Hospital.

"All right, gentlemen, here are the records on the disposable phones purchased within three days on either side of when the phone was destroyed that was used to call Alex. The majority were paid for with a credit card, so we have a name with these. There was only one that were purchased with cash. Who uses cash anymore to buy anything? It's beyond me. Nevertheless, we have no name on that purchase. Once we identify the phone numbers and names of the people who bought their phones with credit cards, then I believe we can get the numbers for the phone bought with cash and begin calling this person. Hopefully, we'll find the mysterious caller, who seems to be elusive. Let's go to work."

After leaving the news conference, Maggie took the stairs and not the elevator to avoid any questions that might be asked of her. She went directly to the biocontainment area where the charge nurse gave an update.

"Blood pressure is doing a little better," she said. "Less vasopressors needed. He hasn't made much urine, but I don't think Dr. Foster was expecting any change there. His fever also has improved and now is mostly around 99 degrees. He still has altered consciousness, but I suspect that's simply from being so sick. He doesn't show any signs of a stroke and is moving all his extremities. I guess from my perspective, he's better."

"I agree with you," said Maggie. "He does seem better. Certainly not out of the woods but at least showing improvement."

Just as Maggie finished talking with the nurse, she got a call on her cell phone. The caller ID showed that it was Pam Foster.

"Pam, what ya got? Were you able to complete the autopsy on Heidi?"

"Yes, and as before, massive organ hemorrhage. This is like something I have never seen before. This virus attacks every vital organ. I don't see how anyone can survive this."

"Well, I will say that the third patient seems better," Maggie told her. "I've been checking him over now, and his vitals are improved. His temperature is coming down, and he appears to be stabilizing, so let's keep our fingers crossed. Thanks for all your help with the autopsy. I know this wasn't easy, and it puts you at risk as well."

"Believe me, I covered every inch of my body and made sure that I got no needle sticks or contamination. I certainly wouldn't want this disease."

As Maggie closed her cell phone, Mack came into the biocontainment unit. Maggie turned to the charge nurse and said, "Watch what you say here. Everything will be used against you. We've got the cops here."

"Correction," said Mack, "FBI, and I'm not here to interrogate the nurse. I'm here to check up on the TV star. I saw your interview with the media. Good job. I'm guessing they'll want me next."

"See how cocky this guy is?" Maggie said, smiling at the nurse. "Mr. Macho wants to try to upstage me. They do want to hear from you, and so do I. I want you by my side the next time this happens. Having the Jolly Green Giant like a tree standing by me will distract them and divert questions to you."

"Maybe we need to plot what we're going to say," Mack suggested. "I know a bar close by. I hear they have wine and appetizers."

"I know that you think I'm a wino, but I only drink occasionally. You know, like daily," Maggie answered, laughing.

"Well, I view it as truth serum. I can get the truth out of you."

Maggie leaned forward and whispered in his ear, "And maybe more than that. Tell me where and I'll be there at five o'clock."

Frank and Susan drove to the safe house. Samuel had texted that he needed to talk with them. They had printed off the schematics of the buildings and had them in hand as they entered the room. Samuel greeted them with "Zhao Lee and Huan Jiao, it's great to see you. Sorry, we shouldn't use your real names. Sometimes I slip back to Chinese. I realize that we need to keep this Frank and Susan. Let's see what you brought us."

"Samuel," said Susan, "I believe we have what you have wanted. Jason came through for us. We've printed out the schematics, and you should be able to design the route that we will need to take. Has the Centre decided on the target?"

"If they have, they haven't told us yet," Samuel said, "but we expect soon. You could have a problem traveling by air to Washington, DC, with the pregnancy. Either you're going to have to try to hide how advanced you are in the pregnancy or drive to the destination. If you drive, it will be a long distance, but this may assure no issues."

"Good point," Frank responded. "I think driving may be the best option, but we'll need enough advance notice so that we have time to get there."

"The Americans, as I've said before, appear to be on the verge of being able to stop an outbreak of Ebola," Susan interjected. "Jason was confiding in me that this treatment would be available soon, so besides this pregnancy, if we hope to be successful, we have to carry out the plan now."

"I'm sure that they understand that," Samuel answered. "We will have an escape plan also, just in case things get complicated."

"That's good," said Frank. "You never know. We've been fortunate so far. We've kept ourselves under the radar. But this is a tricky operation, and with the FBI involved, they're looking for us."

CHAPTER 13

"OK, gentlemen, we need to start calling," Mack began as he assembled his team. "Here are the phone numbers we were able to get from the cell phone manufacturer. As I told you, some of these phones were bought with a credit card and one with cash. The previous phone of the mystery caller was bought with cash and then destroyed. We assume that he or she bought another phone at the same location with cash again, but we don't know for sure. We found out that twenty phones were sold within three days of the other phone being destroyed. Nineteen were purchased with a credit card and one with cash. I'll call the number for the one with cash, and I'll have John call the others. Let's call from a hospital phone, not letting the owner of the phone know that it's the FBI calling."

John dialed the first number, and a Hispanic woman answered. He tried talking with her, but she spoke very little English.

"Hey, Jack, can you help me?" John called out. "You speak Spanish, don't you? I need help. Only Spanish speaking on this first call."

"Sure."

As Jack proceeded to talk with the caller in Spanish, it became apparent he was getting nowhere.

"No luck here," he said as he hung up. "She doesn't know Alex at all. I suspect she's an illegal. Once she found out that I was FBI, she quickly hung up. I'm working on the other numbers now. So far, no one seems to know him. Some had heard about the case on the news, so they were willing to help but said they never met Alex. They wondered why they were being called. I explained the situation that Alex had gotten many calls from a disposable phone like theirs, and then they seemed to understand."

Mack said, "I'm going to try the number for the phone bought with cash. This should be interesting."

Dialing the number, he heard it ring multiple times. There was no answer and no voicemail. *Interesting? Oh, I promised to meet Maggie.*

"Sorry, guys," he said. "I've got to go. Important business. The doctor is calling."

"Sure, right. We understand. Only official business," John chuckled.

Frank heard his cell phone ring. The caller ID suggested that it was an extension of Deaconess Hospital.

Who from Deaconess would be calling us? he thought. *I hope this isn't a bad sign. Do I destroy this phone too? I may need to give Samuel a call and get his advice.*

Maggie went to the biocontainment unit, hoping that the treatment James Singleton was given would be showing promise. She could see from the charge nurse's expression that things were looking up.

"Well, what's the verdict? Any improvement?" Maggie inquired.

"Yes, he seems better. Less dependent on the vasopressors, so his blood pressure is improved. Not much urine output, but his skin may be clearing up. Fewer blisters, less bleeding, and the diarrhea is improved."

"We never saw that in the other two patients, so I'm going to celebrate it," said Maggie. "I know that we're not out of the woods, but let's hope the improvement continues. The family is still quarantined, and we need to wait for at least another week to be sure that none of them contracted the disease, but thank goodness so far they haven't."

Mack met Maggie at a bar two miles from the hospital. It was a casual place, but with outstanding wine and food. He had ordered a few appetizers, but his favorite was the calamari, and he was munching on it before Maggie walked in.

"Hi, gorgeous. I've got your wine decanting now. The sommelier said it needs to breathe. I had no idea that this juice was alive. I don't see any air going in or out! Mack said sarcastically."

"You've got to be a wine snob to appreciate this," Maggie replied. "But I will say, if the wine is an older bottle, it's best to allow it to be exposed to the air. You know, it's been cooped up in a bottle for a long time. So, if it's allowed to be opened for a period of time, it will taste better."

"Really?" Mack asked. "I think I'll breathe with it. *In, out, in out.*" He mimicked breathing for the wine.

"If you don't stop that, I may think you've had a respiratory arrest and have to perform CPR," she joked.

"I can only hope. Maybe I can fake it and get that kind of attention."

"Listen, I can tell the difference between fake and real, so don't test me, Mr. Big Shot. Let's get down to business. What about these cell phones? Any luck?"

"Well, we did track down an illegal most likely," Mack began. "She only spoke Spanish, and once she understood it was the FBI, she quickly hung up. I called the phone bought with cash. No answer or voicemail. The guys are still calling the other numbers, but I told them I had a very important appointment that required my immediate attention." He smiled at her and then continued. "I'm checking on tracking the phones to see if this could help us. I'm still curious about this cash-bought phone. They really don't want us to talk to them or for that matter find them. And the question is, why?"

"I wouldn't know," replied Maggie. "But I would keep at it. We're starting to get calls from the gym. Those folks are nervous. Maybe rightly so. He was sweating a lot there. So was the girlfriend. While I don't think sweat alone would transfer the disease, I can understand their concern."

"Samuel, it's Frank. We got a call from Deaconess. It showed up on the caller ID on our cell phone. Should we be concerned?"

"Frank, everything is a concern," Samuel snapped. "If these keep coming, we will need to destroy this phone. I wonder how they got your number. Maybe it was a fluke. In any case, if it happens again, we are going to have to make a change. Also, we have looked over the schematics that you got from Jason. We're going to need more information."

"Like what?" asked Frank.

"We need to know what times we will have access to these buildings. We also need to have an idea of the security and camera locations. Any chance Susan can get this information from Jason?"

"Susan can get him to do anything," Frank replied. "The only question is whether he will have access to this information. He may not, but we can try. I'm trying to think of a reason we would need this from his perspective. I don't think that the times will be a problem, but the security may cause him to be suspicious."

"Perhaps you could say that Susan will be using a wheelchair part of the time, and she wants to know if she will need to go through metal detectors. Something like this may work. We could send one of our operatives into the buildings, and they could chart the locations of the cameras."

"Yes, that might work," Frank agreed. "I'll have her get with him tonight. He's always eager to see her."

Mack and Maggie finished their wine and appetizers and headed to their cars. "How about stopping by my house?" Maggie said.

"Sure, love to. I'll follow you home."

Within ten minutes, they were pulling into Maggie's driveway. After unlocking the door, she turned and gave Mack a passionate kiss.

"Now that's a good way to be greeted at your house," he remarked.

"Listen, big guy. I did that for my sake, not yours. I've wanted that all day."

"So have I. You're making it difficult, however, to concentrate on this investigation. I can't get you out of my mind."

Leading him to her couch, she got on his lap and proceeded to kiss him more. He explored her body like the first night they were together, but then stopped.

"Listen," he said. "I want more, but we need to focus on this case. I sense this is a much bigger thing than either you, me, or the FBI thought it might be. What if there is some form of plot? You know, a terrorist plot. What if there is something bigger coming? I just sense there's more to the story than we've uncovered. There was no reason for these two young people to get this disease unless they were either intentionally infected or were part of something bigger. We're checking Alex's social networks to see if he had any reason to be taking destructive action. Who knows? He may have wanted to expose a large population to the disease but accidentally infected himself."

"If that were the case, where did he get the virus?" Maggie inquired. "Where did he keep it? How did he manipulate it to alter the virulence? These would be important questions."

"You're right," Mack agreed. "I'm just saying, something isn't adding up, and there may be a much larger issue out there than we see now. I'm going to talk with my team about tracking all the phones that we have identified to see if we can see any pattern as to where they go. That might give us a clue to an underlying plot. And we will see if Alex's social media explains anything."

"All right," Maggie said. "I'll give you the night off." Then she put her hands into his pants and said, "One final physical exam to be sure that you're healthy—and I see that you are!"

"Jason, I have to see you tonight," Susan said urgently. "Are you available? Frank's out for the evening."

"I'm available to you anytime. Sure, come on over."

Hmm, I wonder what she wants, Jason thought. *Maybe the pregnancy is getting to her and Frank isn't supporting her. She sounded upset for some reason. This lady remains mysterious to me. I can't quite figure her out. Always upset with her husband but never willing to leave him.*

Thirty minutes later, Susan pulled into his driveway and made her way to the door. He had opened the garage so she could enter his house from the garage rather than the front door and not be seen.

"Even pregnant, you look sexy," he said. He pulled her close to him, and she reciprocated with a kiss. Susan was five feet six inches tall. Her dark short hair and curves made her appearance very sexy. When he had first met her in the bar, she wore a tight-fitting dress with a plunging neckline that accented her full figure. He couldn't resist watching her. Now, even with her pregnancy, he still found her attractive and sexy.

"That pregnant abdomen doesn't prevent me from loving you," he said as he explored her body. "It may get in the way for now, but within a few weeks, it won't any longer. What about leaving Frank when the baby is born? We could have a fantastic life together."

"Jason, I would love to," Susan replied. "You're just a spectacular person. Good looking, sexy, fun to be with, and now the father of my child. But it could be a problem. Frank won't let me out of this marriage very easily, but let's see. Anything is possible. In the meantime, I've got to think about our upcoming trip. Frank is getting me a wheelchair to get around. Am I going to have to go through metal detectors? If so, should I avoid some of the buildings or locations in those buildings? Can you find out for me?"

"I would think that this is possible. You know security has gotten much tighter everywhere in the United States since 911. I suspect they have security checkpoints throughout. My friend should be able to help. I'll call him tomorrow."

Susan gave him one last hug and kiss before leaving through the garage door and getting into her car. As she was leaving, Jason paused and thought, *I really don't know much about Susan. I don't even know where she lives. We met in a bar, ended up at my house, and had a fantastic night together. She said she was lonely at the time and her relationship with her husband was on the rocks. But now, she tells me that it's going to be difficult to leave him. Which is it? I think I should follow her home just to see where she lives.*

As soon as Susan was a short distance away from his house, Jason got into his BMW and followed her from a distance. Surprisingly, she didn't live far away. As she pulled into her driveway, he made sure that he stopped a significant distance away so she would not recognize him.

At least now I know where she lives. She says he wants nothing to do with her, yet he won't let her leave him. Something doesn't add up.

CHAPTER 14

Mack was energized as he arrived at the FBI control center.

"Gentlemen," he began, "today we are going to begin tracking all the cell phones' paths. I know you've called all of them, and this may lead to nothing, but I want to know if we can find any connection between Alex, Heidi, and this Ebola virus. The agency has given us the tools to begin this tracking process. Let's see if it gives us any clues as to whether they had an association with our two young people who died."

"So, Mack, we have retrieved Heidi's cell phone and have begun looking through her contacts and calls," Tim piped up. "She is a female Alex. We see that she would call him frequently, call the nursing home, and occasionally talk with her mother. The total number of people in her phonebook was five. We don't see that she called any of those who Alex called, so they didn't seem to have any mutual friends. There were a couple of girls in her apartment, so we reached out to them. They told us that Heidi would occasionally ask them to check on her cat or make sure that her apartment was locked, but they didn't socialize with her. When we called, they expressed concern about contracting the virus, but we reassured them that without close interaction, there shouldn't be much to worry about. They seemed satisfied for the moment, but we also gave them Dr. Hamilton's contact information if they needed additional information."

"Did anyone say that they knew Alex when you talked with them?" Mack asked.

"The girls in the apartment would see him come around, but again, they did not socialize with either one of them. The others we called who had the disposable phones only knew of Alex through the media's reports on the Ebola outbreak. They denied any association with Alex or Heidi."

"Very strange. I guess the only individual we don't know much about is that person with the phone bought with cash. They never answered their phone. For now, let's just track them and their movements and see where they go. If there is an alternative plot, we don't want to give them any idea that we suspect them so they will get rid of this phone. It allows us to surveil them without alerting them. This may be nothing, but you never know."

Life seemed so much better to Maggie as she entered the hospital. Suddenly, everything was more enjoyable. She just hoped that this relationship with Mack would not be a passing thing. She always planned out her day so she could meet up with him, and when she did, it made her smile. Heading to the biocontainment unit, she was hopeful that her patient would be better.

"How's Jack today?" she enquired of the charge nurse.

"Steady progress. We have his medications down to a

minimum, and his blood pressure is holding. He may be starting to have some urine output, even though the lab values don't show improvement in the kidney function. Dr. Foster didn't seem concerned about this. Many of his skin lesions are starting to dry up, and his liver enzymes are coming down. All in all, I would say we are going in the right direction."

"I couldn't agree with you more. I stopped many of the antibiotics. I'm just keeping the remaining ones going that might treat the skin lesions if they're infected," Maggie said, smiling to herself. *Finally, some positive news. I'm going to fill in Tuttle. He'll be happy to hear this.* Leaving the unit, she headed to administration.

"Mr. Tuttle, Dr. Hamilton is here. She needs to talk with you," the secretary said, calling through the intercom.

"Send her in. In fact, send her in anytime no matter what I'm doing and cancel everything else."

Maggie entered his office, this time with a smile on her face.

Tuttle said, "I hope this smile means you have some good news for me."

"I do," she replied. "James Singleton seems to be turning the corner. He may make it. Nothing is for certain, but the experimental treatment we gave him has made a significant difference. His vitals are better, his skin lesions are improving, and Dr. Foster is confident that he will recover his kidney function. So we have much to grateful for."

"We have to address the media," Tuttle said eagerly. "We need to give them a positive report, so let me have my secretary round them all up."

Within thirty minutes, the conference room was filled with national and international media outlets eagerly awaiting some news on the Ebola outbreak.

"Ladies and gentlemen, we called you together at a moment's notice because we have some positive news about our third patient infected, so I'll turn the podium over to Dr. Hamilton."

Maggie stood up to move toward the podium—but at her side was Mack. He had promised he would be there to support her and answer any questions regarding the investigation.

As Maggie began, she felt more uplifted knowing that she had something positive to report.

"Unfortunately, as you are aware, our two young patients passed away from the Ebola infection, despite our best efforts. The autopsies on both confirmed that they had all the hallmarks of this disease: a disease which is devastating. Our third patient, an employee of our hospital, has been fortunate in that he has received an experimental treatment provided by the CDC."

Maggie could see Jamie Sessions smiling in the back of the room as she continued to address the crowd. "This patient appears to be turning the corner. His vitals are improved. His skin lesions are beginning to resolve, and he appears to be starting to recover kidney function. We are so pleased to give you this update, but you need to realize that he still has a long way to go, and we are still not sure he will survive. Time will tell, but the improvement has been dramatic, considering how lethal this disease can be."

A reporter in the back interrupted Maggie with a question. "So, do we still have no clue where they may have contracted this disease?"

"I'm going to let Agent Johnson address that question," said Maggie.

Mack came to the podium and perused the crowd. "We have been looking at all the contacts of Alex Williamson and Heidi Campton," he said, "and have tracked their movements as much as possible. The good news is that their interactions with the public have been minimal, which means they would have exposed virtually no one. The question that remains is, where did Alex get this in the first place? The answer to that question is still unknown, and we understand that this leaves everyone very uneasy."

He continued, "If they haven't traveled to Africa or a Third World country and have interacted with so few people, how could they have gotten this disease? We would like to know that as well. We hope that with your broadcasts, we will have someone step forward and tell us how this happened. We're working on a few other angles that I can't discuss at this time, but any information that the public can give us would certainly be helpful. We have had calls identifying these two young people from their pictures, but they haven't had any explanation for the exposure to the virus. We need the public's help regarding that."

"Do you think that there is any foul play or intent with regard to this infection?" the same reporter asked.

"That is a very good question," Mack acknowledged. "We haven't found anything that would suggest that. We've looked at Alex's social media and his contacts, and we don't find any reason that Alex would have tried to expose others to this disease. We're still working on his personal computer to see if there is anything there to give us clues as to how he got infected."

The media seemed content with that answer for the

moment, but several reporters were grumbling about having no answer as to the source.

As Maggie left the conference room, Tuttle stopped her momentarily.

"Good job again, Dr Hamilton," he said. "You know how to deal with these people. I want you to know that we are getting more calls on the hotline that was set up. Several are from people who have been going regularly to the gym where Alex and Heidi worked out. Others are coming from family members of the people who live at the nursing home. What should I tell them?"

"Perhaps we can have an open forum where we invite them to the hospital to hear about their risks and options," Maggie suggested. "I want to check with Jamie on something that could be of significance for them."

"What's that?" Tuttle asked.

"Well, there's work being done on a vaccine for Ebola. People at the CDC will know about this, and Jamie could help us get our hands on some. I suspect that it is in limited supply, but for selected people, such as those at the gym or nursing home, this could be an option that would give them a degree of protection. With this virus, which appears to be more virulent, it may be less effective, but we don't know for sure."

"Certainly this is worth looking into," Tuttle agreed. "I'll talk to our public relations office to set up the place and time, but you'll need to give them your schedule to be there. Will tomorrow or the next day work?"

"Should be OK, but I need to be sure that I've had time

to talk with Jamie. We want to find out if we can get the vaccine."

"I understand. Call me later and let me know."

Maggie found Jamie in the cafeteria having a light lunch. She was off in one corner, which Maggie thought was good. *Away from the employees where we can talk without being heard*, she thought.

"Jamie, I'm glad I caught up with you. What did you think of the news conference?"

"Went well, Maggie. I feel good that the Zendenivir is helping."

"So am I. I've been getting so depressed over these deaths and having a sense of helplessness."

"Does the relationship with the Big Guy help?" Jamie asked mischievously.

Blushing, Maggie answered, "Well, it certainly does. We're getting along well. You were right. He's a hunk. And I'm a bit snowed by him. I just hope he feels the same about me. I don't want to be hurt by another bad relationship. But this time it seems different. I can talk to him so easily. It's as though I've known him forever, and he makes me laugh. It has distracted me from all this death and disease."

"I've always thought a guy that makes you laugh is the best," Jamie said. "Nothing can be better. How about the intimate stuff?"

"I can't talk to you about the specifics. I'd be embarrassed. But let's just say he knows how to push the right buttons. It feels great."

"You don't have to tell me more," Jamie assured her. "I

get it. I can see it in your eyes, and quite frankly, in his as well."

Maggie felt it was time to change the subject. "Well, I actually came to talk with you about the Ebola. I've read that there may be a vaccine in the works. Is there any chance we can get any of this?"

"You're right," said Jamie. "A vaccine *is* being developed and is undergoing human trials. I hadn't mentioned it because it's new and may not be available. Still being tested. I can check into getting it, but the patients who take it will need to give informed consent that they are taking a vaccine not yet fully approved. I'm guessing they would consent if they're really nervous about catching the disease."

"I'm sure they will," Maggie agreed. "When will you know?"

"I'll call this afternoon or tonight. I know the chief medical director of the project. He's a friend from training. I'll bet if I twist his arm, I can get the vaccine if it's available."

Three Centre agents arrived at the Lees' home in the evening after dinner. They were sullen-faced and all business. Knocking on the door, they stated that they needed to check on the product in the basement.

"Sure, no problem," Frank said as he led them down the stairs.

After the agents found the safe, they entered the code and carefully removed a tray with several vials of liquid in test tubes. Wearing gloves, masks, and face guards, they cautiously placed the trays on the table. They then removed from their briefcase multiple metal cases with the inscribed name *Elixir of Love*.

Smiling, one of them said, "Here is your new perfume."

"It's just a killer," the other two said, laughing.

Cautiously, they placed the test tubes in metal containers that would prevent accidental breakage. The containers had a base that was about one-half inch below where the tubes rested, and the base contained a charge that could detonate when a button on the bottom of the case was compressed. It was set on a timer, and as Frank and Susan had been instructed, the timer would allow one hour before detonation. The final step was to cover the case with a special cap that prevented accidental detonation or compression of the button to start the timer. Once the agents felt comfortable that they had gotten all the vials properly encased, they moved the cases back to the vault.

"We have enough vials that you should be able to place several in different locations," one of the agents instructed Frank, "if the Centre thinks this is necessary. We don't need to tell you that you have to treat these with the greatest caution. You've seen what it has done to Alex and his girlfriend."

Frank responded with a serious look. "No, we understand completely.

Mack stared at the plots of the pathways that the owners of the disposable cell phones were taking. *It seems like they all go to pretty ordinary places. Grocery stores, schools, pharmacies, dentists, and sometimes restaurants. Our mysterious owner who bought with cash also never goes to Alex's or Heidi's apartment. It's odd that the person goes to multiple dry-cleaning establishments, and they are all the same company. Maybe he or she works for them or owns them. He did go to the hospital medical office building on a couple of*

occasions. He or she must be seeing a physician there. I guess for now we just keep tracking this group and see if anything shows up.

He called out to the other agents, "Hey guys, what do you have on Alex's computer? Anything that can help us?"

"There are some interesting things," said Tim. "He seems to search the internet frequently for topics on cancer. We were told that both of his parents died of cancer. But probably more interesting is that he has been searching websites to manipulate viruses. As you know, he did work in virology, so perhaps this would be related to his work, but I wouldn't think that he would be modifying viruses. Why would he want to do this working in a hospital laboratory? He doesn't seem to have any intention of harming anyone; at least his Facebook and social media don't indicate any reason to create havoc. And there was no manifesto or evidence of anger against society. So, it isn't clear why he would be trying to explore this aspect of viruses." He paused, then asked, "Do you remember that the doctor from the CDC said that the Ebola virus was more virulent? Maybe modified."

"I do remember she mentioned that. Interesting!" Mack said. "Do you think he could have been working for someone or with someone to do that? The big question is why? I'll ask Maggie about it. Maybe she'd have an idea."

Mack left the control center and set out to find Maggie. He texted her, and she said she was on the seventh floor of the hospital. He told her he needed to talk. Smiling, he found her reviewing a patient's chart in the physician's charting area.

"Hey, gorgeous, are you saving the world here?"

"Not really, just trying to cure a few infectious diseases. What's up?" she asked.

"We've come across something that I need your help with. In looking at Alex's computer, he spends time looking at sites that deal with cancer and cancer treatments, but he also looks for ways to modify viruses. Would he use this in his job at Deaconess?"

"I wouldn't think so," Maggie responded thoughtfully. "This seems odd. You might try to change a virus to make a vaccine by reducing its virility."

"Well, don't do that to me!" Mack quickly answered.

"No chance. You have more than you need." She smiled, then continued, "All joking aside, changing a virus could be for the better or for the worse. It could make the virus harmless, or it could make the virus more lethal. Viruses can sometimes change by themselves into more dangerous infections, but if you were intentionally doing this, it could be part of a bioweapon."

"Now you're talking my language," said Mack. "In the FBI, there's always been a concern that our enemies would develop bioweapons and use them in warfare. Infections like smallpox and anthrax are already thought to be part of their weaponry. It's easier than developing a new bomb and certainly easier to bring into this country. The real question is, if Alex was doing this, what would be his motive?"

"What if he didn't know he was developing a weapon?" Maggie asked. "What if he thought he was doing something that was beneficial to mankind? He might have been misled to change the virus with the idea it was going to do some good."

"Hmm, maybe this has something to do with his searches on cancer cures," Mack mused. "His parents apparently both died of cancer."

"There it is!" exclaimed Maggie. "He could have been told that modifying the virus would allow the virus to attack a cancer and destroy it. But all along, he was developing a lethal virus to kill."

"Wow," said Mack. "If this is true, we are dealing with something much bigger than an isolated infection with a lethal virus. The agency sent me here thinking this was a minor problem to deal with. This may be much more serious. I'm going back to talk with my agents. We need to think through this. I don't want to create panic, but we need to cover every possibility, and this is certainly a new twist. I hope it doesn't occupy so much of my time that I can't see you."

"You can multitask. I do it all the time." Maggie smiled. "I'll make sure you don't forget me. Have you looked at his apartment to see if he had any kind of laboratory equipment to change a virus? You know, a table with a microscope, culture media, pipettes, things he could use to manipulate the germ?"

"No one mentioned that, but I'll send the boys back to check it out."

"I'll go back to the lab and talk to the director to make sure he wasn't using the equipment on the side to carry out the same thing," Maggie said. "I'm guessing this is unlikely, but who knows."

CHAPTER 15

Mack returned to the control center and rounded up all the agents.

"All right, guys," he began, "we're taking a new turn in this investigation. We still want to find the contacts of Alex and Heidi. We need to be sure the disease isn't spreading, and if necessary, quarantine people suspected of having the disease. But now, Maggie has proposed another alternative. What if Alex was modifying a virus thinking he was going to help mankind but in actuality was developing a bioweapon that was very virulent? It's possible that he was accidentally infected, and the people he was working with are trying to keep as far removed from us as they can. I believe we need to look closer at those disposable cell phones. I've always come back to the phone bought with cash. It was the only phone where the individual who owned the phone never answered. Where were the places you said they traveled?"

Jack replied, "This was the phone we tracked to multiple dry-cleaning establishments and on a few occasions to the hospital medical office building. Nothing seemed out of the ordinary, other than that their trips to the dry-cleaners were frequent and included several different ones."

"Have you looked up the name of the dry-cleaners?"

"Yes, they were all Lee's Dry-Cleaners. All of them were the same name, so we thought that they must be owned by the same people."

"I think we need to pay a visit to one of these cleaning establishments, but I don't want to raise any suspicion. Who needs some dry-cleaning done?"

"Are you kidding? All of us!" Tim joked. "Our wives normally take care of this, and here we are in Chicago."

"Fine," said Mack. "Hand something over. I'm going to spruce you up. I'll be your wife for now."

Each day, James Singleton was showing progress. He had started to make more urine, and his lab values continued to improve. The pulmonologist was doing a trial to get him off of the ventilator, and his family had been taken out of quarantine. Maggie was thrilled that finally there seemed a chance that one of these patients would survive.

She reported daily to Tuttle, who fed the positive news to the media through the public relations department. The lingering question asked daily by the reporters, though, was, "Where did he get it?" There was no answer, which left everyone uneasy—including Maggie. She made her way to the lab, as she had promised Mack that she would talk with the lab director.

"Tess, I need to visit with you about Alex Williamson and his work here in the lab," Maggie began. "We have some concern that Alex may have been working on modifying a virus, and that virus could have been the Ebola virus. We don't know if this was really happening—but since we haven't, as of yet, found any connection to a source of the Ebola. we want to look at his lab space. He could have been trying to modify this virus right here, and maybe in the process, he accidentally got infected."

She added, "We don't have any evidence of this, so please don't say anything to anyone. But we have found on his computer that he was investigating how to make changes to a virus, and this could have been applied to Ebola."

"Wow, that's a wild idea," Tess exclaimed. "We can look at his workstation, but I don't remember seeing anything there that would indicate that he had a side project doing something like this. Let's go look."

As they walked to Alex's station, they avoided causing any consternation amongst the other employees. Alex's area was toward the back of the laboratory space and was removed from many of the other lab technicians.

"Here we are," Tess said. "Maggie, you can go through his desk and paperwork and see if you find anything."

They found a few notes that Alex had made regarding the cultures he had set up the few days before he left work. There were pipettes, test tubes, and culture media. Everything was neatly arranged, but after a thorough review, they weren't able to find any indication that Alex was working on a virus modification.

"Not much here," Tess sighed. "I just can't believe that Alex would be intentionally working to develop a dangerous viral change for a nefarious purpose. It would seem so out of character for him. He was a quiet and somewhat sad person, but he never seemed like a person with a vindictive personality. I suppose you never know what's in a person's mind, but I would be shocked if this were the case with Alex. He always seemed so kind and concerned about people."

"I agree with you, Tess. This seems out of character for Alex. I didn't know him, but I sense he was the type of person you've described. Kind, aloof, sad, but bright, with no desire to hurt anyone. Nevertheless, I felt it was necessary to be sure that he wasn't doing something so unexpected. You just never know about people. He may have had another side that was not apparent. I do feel better after looking at his lab station. We're looking into his apartment as well, and I hope we find nothing there."

Mack and two additional agents showed up at Alex's apartment. They rang Gretchen Summers's doorbell, and when she arrived at the door, Mack flashed his credentials.

"Ms. Summers, we need to take another look at Alex Williamson's apartment," he said. "Have you rented it out?"

"No," she replied. "No one wants to be in the apartment for fear of catching this disease. Sure, I would be happy to let you in."

She led them to the apartment and opened the door. There was a distinct odor of lingering cleaning materials, with a bleach and alcohol smell, likely from the disinfection that had occurred after Alex was diagnosed. The landlady left the FBI agents to go through the apartment on their own.

Mack and the agents began combing through all of Alex's private things, using gloves and masks to avoid any personal contamination. They found no evidence of a microbiology lab—no microscope, culture media, tubes, or any lab paraphernalia. There didn't appear to be any evidence that a lab had been set up.

"Not much here," Mack exclaimed. "It looks like a dead end again. Let's go back and rethink this. Where do we go next?"

Tim piped up, "Let's look at the cell phone owners once more. Let's get the dry-cleaning done like you suggested."

"Good idea, Tim," Mack responded. "I'll take the clothes in."

After returning to the hospital, Mack called Maggie.

"Hey, gorgeous, what's the word on the laboratory? Any clues? You've become my Sherlock Holmes."

"Not quite, Mr. FBI," Maggie responded. "No, nothing interesting. His workstation was pretty much unremarkable. He had it very neatly arranged, going along with what everyone has said about Alex. He was supposedly very obsessive, compulsive, quiet, hard-working, somewhat shy, and sad. But nothing to indicate he had side projects like we discussed. How about you? Find anything at the apartment?"

"Same thing. No laboratory equipment. No set-up for experiments. Even if he were doing something like this, where would he have gotten the virus in the first place? It's not like you can order this on Amazon. Or can you?"

"Don't be silly," Maggie chided him. "Of course not. That's why, if he were doing this, it would seem he would have to be working with someone else. Someone who would have access to the virus. But you just don't carry this around in your back pocket."

"That's what makes me concerned," Mack agreed. "Access to a deadly virus like this has to come from a major source—a country or some radical faction that may have plans to create havoc and harm. It doesn't seem like a young kid who works in the lab and never travels anywhere could get his hands on anything so deadly."

"I agree. There has got to be more to the story, and we're not finding the missing link."

"Tomorrow, I'm taking some clothes to the dry cleaners," Mack remarked.

"I was going to mention that it's about time."

"Yeah, right, not really. We want to find the mysterious caller on the disposable cell phone who we believe bought another one and won't answer our calls. He or she seems to run between multiple dry-cleaning establishments that are all likely owned by the same person or persons. They are all Lee's Dry-Cleaners. So, if it is the Lees, we want to meet them. I'm not going to show any creds. I don't want them to get suspicious if they could be someone who was involved with Alex."

"Good idea. Should I send some of my clothes?"

"Sure. Here, let me help you take them off."

"Not here. Are you crazy? But later—now that's OK."

"Deal. Where are we going to go eat tonight? I'll plan on that dessert afterward," Mack smiled.

"Hmm," Maggie mused. "Let's see. We've gone to a diner, a pub, and fine dining. How about dinner at my house? I make a mean lasagna."

"Do you mean you can cook?" Mack said with mock surprise.

"Don't be so surprised. I'm not too bad at cooking. You'll see. Six thirty OK?"

"Perfect. See you then."

Mack found his way to the nearest Lee's Dry-Cleaners. With a stack of clothes that he had collected from the agents, he pushed through the door and was eagerly greeted by a petite young lady who appeared to be college-age.

"Well, you must not have been to the cleaners in a while, by the appearance of all those clothes!" Sally Higgins said with a smile.

"You're right," he said sheepishly. "I let them build up. Been too busy at work. When do you think you can get these done?"

"Are you in a hurry?" Sally asked politely.

"No, not really. Just that if it takes a long time, I'll run out of clothes, and that could be a problem."

Laughing, Sally responded, "We won't let you streak around town. They should be done in three days."

"Wow, that's great," Mack exclaimed. Then he added, "By the way, you're one of the most pleasant people I've dealt with in a long time. I'd like to tell your boss what a great job you're doing. Who do I contact?"

"The Lees own these dry-cleaners," she replied. "They're great people to work for, and I would really appreciate the compliment. I can get you an email address. They don't usually give out their phone number. You know how angry people can get over their clothes. But I will tell you, I'm not sure they're still in town. They were planning a trip. I believe it's a vacation, but they didn't mention for sure where they're going. I don't believe they've left yet, but if not, it's soon. Poor Mrs. Lee; she is very pregnant. I don't know why they would plan to go anywhere in her condition."

"Email will work fine," said Mack. "I can send them a note specifically about you."

Sally was smiling broadly as Mack left the store.

Heading back to the hospital, Mack was thinking that he should try to get more information on the Lees.

I could access background information, he thought, *where they came from, where they went to school, their parents, etc.* He thought that this could be helpful. He would get his agents on this right away.

—◀▬▬▶—

Frank felt a buzz on his cell phone indicating a message. Glancing down, he saw that Samuel wanted him to call. He pressed to redial back to Samuel's phone.

"Samuel, Frank here. From the brevity of the message, I sense this is urgent."

"Frank, the Centre is getting concerned," said Samuel. "Things are too quiet out there. The reports from the media keep asking the question of how Alex and Heidi got infected, but the hospital isn't releasing any information on how they're pursuing finding the source, other than they keep mentioning that the FBI is working on this. It concerns us that they haven't indicated what they're doing, and they could be trying to track you."

"But how? We have been very careful to avoid contact with anything with Alex after he got infected. We immediately disposed of the cell phone, and we've accessed the hospital computer through the church's computer using the credentials you provided. I can't imagine how they could connect us."

"I know that you've been very careful," Samuel agreed. "It's just that things are a little too quiet, which suggests to us they have something going on. We should have the final plans soon, and we can implement them. The trip by car to Washington, DC, is going to be long. Can Susan handle this?"

"She's feeling great," Frank assured him. "We have checked into hospitals along the way just in case we would have to stop. If that happens, I'll deliver the package and go back and pick her up. We have set up a tentative schedule for visiting the sites in DC but will finalize those plans once we know the final site."

"It sounds like you have things under control," said Samuel. "This pregnancy has thrown a curve into everything. I had thought maybe she should have aborted the child."

"We considered that as well," said Frank, "but Jason would have gotten upset. He doesn't believe in abortion and is excited about the child coming. We thought that he would stop giving information if that were to happen."

"I see," Samuel replied. "That makes sense. I believe you're going to be starting your trip in the next two to three days. Are you all packed and ready to go at any time?"

"Yes, we have gotten everything together and tried to think of every contingency. What if the FBI starts coming after us?"

"We will have a backup plan. Don't worry. We always have a backup plan. You can't be too careful."

Mack made his way back to the control center and turned to his agents to begin a background check on the Lees.

"All right, guys, we're going to search for information on our people of interest. Tim, I'm going to have you contact the home office. See what you can find out on these people. They seem as ordinary as anyone. The young lady at the cleaners said they were either on vacation or going soon. She mentioned that Mrs. Lee is very pregnant, which probably explains the trips to the Deaconess medical office building. But I wonder why they would decide to take a vacation with Mrs. Lee at the end of her pregnancy? I would assume they won't be able to fly. Maybe they have family where they're going for a visit, and the baby would be delivered there, but it seems odd. I would think most women would want to be delivered by the obstetrician who has followed them through their pregnancy."

John piped in, "My wife would never let anyone but her obstetrician deliver the baby. That isn't usually the case, but my wife wouldn't accept any other option."

"That's what I'm saying," Mack remarked. "It would appear to be risky for the mother and not something she would agree to—but as I said, maybe there is a plan for her to deliver where they're going. We'll see."

Maggie finished up her rounds early so she could get home to prepare dinner. She didn't often cook for herself. She liked to cook, but it wasn't fun making dinner for one person. Now she had a reason, and she was excited to put effort into this for Mack.

Since she didn't have all the ingredients, she stopped at the grocery store on her way home and picked up fresh garlic, basil, and romaine lettuce. She also bought some lasagna noodles, tomato sauce, and Parmesan cheese. She tried to remember all the things her mother had taught her, but it all seemed to be a blur. *I've got to call Mom,* Maggie thought. *She'll know what I need.*

She dialed her mother, who answered on the third ring.

"Mom, I need help," said Maggie. "You always know

how to prepare these things. I'm having a friend over for dinner tonight, and I want to make your lasagna. It has always been my favorite. Can you help me?"

"You never call me for recipes," her mother said suspiciously. "This must be a special friend. Is it a man?"

Maggie quietly said, blushing, "Yes, just someone I've met at work. You'd like him. So different from me, but it has been so easy to talk with him. He's very handsome. You've probably heard in the news about the Ebola patients at our hospital. Well, he's an FBI agent in charge of trying to find the source where our patient might have contracted the disease. It's really been quite a mystery, and Mack—his real name is Matthew—has been working with me on the case."

"It sounds like working not only on the *case* but on *you* as well," her mother observed. "I've never heard you sound so excited about someone. I sense this may be something more than solving a mystery?"

"It's too early to say, but I'll admit to you, I really like this guy. I hope that he feels the same about me. Now what about those ingredients?"

"You will need to buy onion, Italian sausage, and mozzarella cheese," her mother instructed. "Pepperoni slices will add extra flavor. Oh, and an Italian wine to set the stage. Maybe a Sangiovese. Don't forget garlic bread, but don't use too much garlic."

"Yes, Mom, I've got it," said Maggie. "Thanks for the advice."

Hanging up, she headed to the store and was able to get all the ingredients, including the wine her mother suggested. *Now,* she thought, *I need to get home. I want to get this dinner prepared and have time to take a hot bath.*

—◄━━━►—

Frank Lee printed off a MapQuest page that plotted their trip from Chicago to Washington, DC. *Hmm*, he thought for a moment. *It appears that we will need to travel through Toledo, Cleveland, Pittsburgh, Baltimore, and eventually to DC. That's good. If Susan has trouble, these are large cities where we could stop for help. The Centre wants us to leave soon, and they're concerned that the FBI maybe getting closer to us. I hope that the escape plan will work.*

As Frank mulled over the travel plans, Susan arrived home from the cleaners.

"Well, Frank, you seem to be lost in thought. What's going on?" she asked.

"Just planning our trip," Frank replied. "Take a look at the map. We will be going through major cities. I think this is good for you, just in case there is a problem with the baby. This whole pregnancy thing has been unfortunate, but look, we can make this work. We always do."

Susan told him, "I have been having a few false contractions from time to time, but the doctor said that this is to be expected."

"The Centre wants us to pack and start the trip," Frank said. "How about tomorrow? Can you be ready?"

"Sure," Susan replied, "no problem. We'll have the floor plans that the Centre got from Jason, and honestly, I think the sooner we leave, the better."

"Tomorrow it is," Frank said decisively. "We'll take our time. I believe we should drive this in two to three days. I don't want to stress you too much."

"Look, I can handle it," Susan responded, "but I will admit my back begins hurting and my feet start swelling the longer I'm sitting. So you're probably right."

Maggie arrived home and spread all her groceries out over her kitchen island. *Now I'll get the sauce started, boil the lasagna noodles, and get the spices combined,* she told herself. *While this is slow-cooking, I think I can take that bath I've been thinking about.*

She filled the tub exceptionally full of warm water so she could fully submerge deep into the bath and just relax. *Wow, this feels great,* she thought. *I could lay in this tub for hours, but I can't ruin the food, so unfortunately this must end soon.*

She got out, dried herself off, and found a causal jumpsuit that clung to her body. Staring in the mirror, she thought, *not bad. Beats the white physician coat I wear every day. I think that this could appeal to a guy.*

She got the table set, putting out both wine glasses and water glasses, and put on dinner music to set the mood. She chose Michael Bublé. She had always liked his voice—a modern-day Frank Sinatra with romantic lyrics. She dimmed the lights and set up candles on the table.

Thirty minutes later, her doorbell rang, and she felt her heart speed up for a moment. *I'm acting like a schoolgirl,* she thought. *Why am I so jumpy tonight? He just seems to do this to me.*

She opened the door and felt at ease as soon as she looked at him.

"Mack, how about this," she said. "You've gotten me to cook. You know I rarely make anything for myself."

"Wow, it smells great in here," he said. "I love Italian food. All those spices just fill up your nasal passage. I can't wait to try it. But honestly, you're the best thing in this room. You look fantastic as always. Red is your color. I swear you look more attractive every time I see you."

"You know how to make a girl feel good," she said as she

threw her arms around his neck and gave him a passionate kiss.

"Now that's the right way to start off an evening," Mack exclaimed as he let his hands feel her waist, her back, and her breasts.

"All right, enough of this," she said. "I can't let this food get cold. We need to sit down and eat."

Mack ate voraciously, as if this was his last meal. "Did you put illicit drugs in this food? I can't get enough of it. I think it's addicting. Cocaine maybe?"

"True confessions," Susan replied, "these recipes are my mother's. She has always been a great cook, and lasagna has been my favorite meal of hers."

"How does a doctor who is a workaholic find time or have the ability to make such a great meal?" Mack asked.

"Well, I do enjoy cooking, but being a doctor doesn't leave me much time."

"I think I need to meet your mother," Mack joked, "except I may gain about thirty pounds if I keep this up."

"I suspect you would exercise and work it out and burn off all these carbs. Plus, we can't eat like this every day."

"I know a way to burn off the calories," he said with a smile. Rising from his chair beside her, he pulled her close to him and resumed caressing her as he had before dinner. Before long, they were in bed together.

Staring into Maggie's eyes, he said, "Dinner was great, but this is the part I was waiting for. I can't resist you. All I do is think about you all day. You've cast a spell over me."

Maggie thought to herself, *love-making has become easier, more relaxed, and more comfortable. I'm mad about this guy.*

CHAPTER 16

Mack sat staring at the documents his agents had procured from FBI headquarters. *There are about a million Lees in the database. This must be the most common Chinese name ever. And Frank and Susan have to be the most common first names for Lee. This is going to take some time. If I limit this to Chicago, it helps, but there are still hundreds or even thousands.*

Frank had gotten word from the Centre. It was time to leave, so on arriving home, he told Susan the news.

"We're to leave tomorrow. It's going to be a long drive to Washington, DC. You've seen the route, and I've plotted stops along the way that include those hospitals. This is just in case you have issues with the pregnancy. This damn pregnancy was very inconvenient for the assignment we have. Can you think of anything additional we need?"

"Not really," said Susan. "I'll take along the names of physicians that I've seen, in case they need to be called. I feel pretty good right now, but you never know. I'm hoping Jason isn't going to be a problem. He doesn't know much about this trip, and if he starts calling or wanting to get together, it might be a problem—or if he calls his friends in DC to watch out for me, that could be an issue."

"Good point," said Frank. "Do you need to see him again?"

"Maybe. It might be wise to be sure he doesn't interfere. I'll call him and see if I can talk with him tonight."

"While you're at his house, I'll prepare the elixir," Frank said. "We're to take several vials, just in case we need more. They've given us a sturdy case to transport the product. We certainly can't risk breakage of the vials on the way. That would be disastrous."

"No kidding," Susan agreed. "Hit from behind by a car with the virus in our trunk. Yikes! You know, this could be our most dangerous mission for the military and our country. Our leaders want this to succeed. They know this is a way to get back at the American president for his sanctions and restrictions. It's allowed the Americans to advance their military while suppressing ours. Now it's our time to collapse their economy and get even."

Susan picked up the phone and called Jason. He answered quickly and, with the caller ID, knew it was her.

"Susan, I haven't been able to stop thinking about you," he said. "I've been worried that maybe the pregnancy wasn't going well. Are you all right?"

"I'm fine, Jason, but I miss you. Frank is going to be out tonight. It will be a chance for us to be together before we leave on this trip. Can I come over?"

"Of course you can," he replied. "I can't wait to see you. Are you coming now?"

"I'll be there in fifteen minutes."

Susan backed her Hyundai SUV out of the garage and drove the short distance to Jason's house. He was eagerly waiting for her as she entered through the garage.

"I'm really glad you called. I have trouble keeping you out of my mind. I'm worried about you traveling. Do you think you'll be OK? It's a long trip. I hope that the floor plans I got for you helped. I know that you wanted to know more about my work but my friends at the Pentagon can't share much with you. Plus I suspect it would be boring to you anyway."

"I'll be all right," she assured him. "I feel fine, and everything with the pregnancy is going well. And the floor plans were great. I told Frank I downloaded them from the internet, and he was fine with that.Your work has always been interesting to me. When I get back maybe we can talk more about that"

Jason persisted. "I'm just worried that something could happen to you or the baby. I'm so excited about becoming a father."

"I'm excited too," she said. "This will be a whole new experience for me—and for you. Jason, you have been such a wonderful friend and lover. Maybe we can find a way to work this out so we can be together. But in the meantime, while I'm gone, I would simply lie low. If something serious comes up, I'll call you. You can count on that. Will you do that?"

"I'll try. And I expect a call if something happens. Right?" he asked.

"Yes, of course."

With that, she threw her arms around him and gave him a passionate kiss. He was totally in her control, and she knew it, but she was beginning to like his kindness and concern. She had never experienced this back home or, for that matter, with Frank, her surrogate husband. It was all business when it came to the Centre and their country. It was all about following orders, carrying out the plan, and allegiance to the state. Here, she found a warmth and caring from someone she hardly knew existed except for the sexual escapades, and he was really passionate in bed.

It had started out as business, but now she was beginning to feel an attachment. She knew it could only lead to disappointment for him, and she had to put these thoughts of feelings and love out of her mind. Maybe the pregnancy was making her more sensitive. Who knows?

The FBI agent assigned to find the Lees eventually was able to tie them to the dry cleaners. But any search of their past connections seemed to lead to a dead end. He couldn't find any marriage agreement between them. It wasn't clear where they had lived before moving to Chicago. It was as though they had come out of nowhere. His thoughts were interrupted when Mack came into the room.

"All right, Tim, what's the answer? Who are these Lees?"

"That's a really good question," Tim replied. "Do you know how many Lees are in Chicago? Literally hundreds. But I have tied our Lees to the dry-cleaning establishments. Even so, everything seems to stop there. I can't seem to move back from that point. I can't find any marriage license, where they moved from, relatives. Really nothing."

"How strange," Mack said. "Do you have their dates of birth?"

"Yes, I think so. Frank Lee was born in 1981. Susan

appears to be younger. She was born in 1985. At least those are the dates on their driver's licenses. I haven't been able to determine when they were married or even if they were married.

"They started their dry-cleaning business five years ago and expanded it rapidly. That's when they incorporated. They used about $100,000 to establish the business and didn't take out any loans. They have been able to generate enough money from their companies to avoid bank loans. They purchased a small home and again were able to put down cash without borrowing. So, they must have come to Chicago with money in their pockets. Probably sold a house somewhere else and used the equity that had built up to buy this house without borrowing. I think they are quite entrepreneurial.

"I have no idea where they moved from, and I'm checking the birthdates to see if I can discover where they were born. Even that seems difficult. There are so many Lees, you have to tie these Lees to that birthdate, and there are several Lees with the same birthdate."

When Tim finished his report, Mack said, "This is getting more interesting all the time. Their employees said they were leaving on a trip, even though Mrs. Lee is very pregnant. The employees don't know where they're going but expect them to be gone about two weeks. I wonder how we can find out their travel plans. Probably not that easy. I guess we can track the phone and see where they go that way. I do have their email address, but it's doubtful that will be helpful. Keep me posted, Tim. Good job."

Mack left the control booth. His whole demeanor was different these days. He had never been so content. Work was now a second interest, where it had always been his first. He wanted to give Maggie an update on the Lees, but maybe it was just an excuse to see her. He found her in the biocontainment unit.

"Well, Miss Infectious Diseases. Are you stamping out pestilence?" he asked.

"Trying," she replied. "Are you a pestilence that I should stamp out?"

"Hardly, but I do need tender loving care. I'm here to help in more ways than one. How's your patient?"

"Better, thank God. It is so rewarding to see him improve. We have him off of dialysis and the ventilator. He's very weak, but we're on the road to recovery. His family is out of quarantine, but we can't let them visit him. That's the rules here in the biocontainment area. He's eating but still predominately on liquids. I think we should be able to advance his diet tomorrow."

"You've done a great job," said Mack. "I know that his family and the hospital are very appreciative. But let me say that I appreciate you more than anyone else." He smiled as he looked into her eyes.

Maggie smiled back, lost in thought about last night. "And you probably know that I feel the same about you. If you don't, I've failed, and I don't like to fail. So you better watch out, buster."

"You haven't failed," he assured her. "Remember, I'm FBI. I can get into your inner self. I know what's inside."

"I would say that is literally true. You do know me from the inside out, and I'm happy that you do. I haven't felt this way about anyone else."

Their conversation was interrupted when Adam Foster arrived and, smiling, told them that the dialysis had been stopped. "How about that? Kidneys are better. I've done my job."

"All right, Mr. Nephron," joked Maggie. "I've done my part as well. His temp is down, and it looks like he'll recover. Don't take all the credit."

Mack chimed in. "If I were you, Adam, I would take her advice if you value your life. She can take you apart. She is very feisty. I know from experience."

"Oh, come on, guys," Maggie protested. "I'm five foot six and weigh one hundred thirty pounds. I don't think you have a lot to worry about. Besides, this has been a group effort. All of us have contributed to his recovery."

"You're right, Maggie," said Adam. "I just want you to know that it's great working with you. You're so smart and yet not haughty. That makes it easy."

Susan returned home to find Frank in the bedroom, packing clothes.

"Well, how did it go?" he asked.

"Fine," Susan replied. "Jason is concerned about me. Worried that I may have problems with the pregnancy on this trip. He's eager to become a father. He actually is a very nice guy."

"You're not starting to like him, are you?" Frank asked.

"No, this is all business. You know, all for our country. But still, I can't help but appreciate how caring and tender he is. I've been thinking how great it is living here. We don't have the freedoms in China that we experience here. And Jason is such a great person. His excitement over this new baby maybe has influenced me. I'm getting excited too just thinking that I'm bringing a new life into the world."

"You know this can't to lead to anything," Frank snapped. "After this, we may be heading home."

"What about the baby?"

"What about the baby? I don't know. This was not a planned event. Maybe Jason will get to raise the child after all. It's going to be really about what happens to us. We may need to escape."

"I know," Susan responded with a sad, downtrodden face.

"You need to start packing. We're leaving in the morning."

"I will. I'll start getting my things together."

Tim stared at the computer. *I can't find a maiden name for Susan Lee, mainly because I can't find when they were married. There are Susan Lees in the database, and there is one with her birthdate, but that person lives in Canada. This is so weird. The Frank Lee I've found with his birthdate has died. Killed in a motorcycle accident in Utah. This is getting stranger all the time. Who are these people?*

The frantic call came through to Maggie. "Dr. Hamilton, it's Jake. You know, Jake Johnson from the gym. We've got people going crazy over here. They heard about Alex and Heidi. Now they're scared to death that they're going to be next. What do I tell them?"

"They should calm down," she said reassuringly. "This requires more intimate contact, usually with body fluids or blood."

"Exactly. Sweat. That's what we do here. Sweat, sweat, sweat. Well, at least some people do," said Jake.

"Usually sweat wouldn't be so much of a problem,"

Maggie said, "but if Alex had injured himself and spilled blood, that could be a concern. There may be a solution for these people. There is an experimental vaccine that is being developed. My friend from the CDC is trying to get us some, and people like your members could participate in a trial. Do you think they would do this?"

"In a heartbeat!" he exclaimed. "They'll do anything. They're panicking."

"Let me get with the people from the CDC and see what I can do. It will be best for me to come to the gym and you assemble your members so we can talk to them about the risks. Will that work?"

"Wow, that would be fabulous. Just let me know, and I'll make it happen."

Hanging up, Maggie called Jamie and told her about the call. Jamie had already been looking into the vaccine for the nursing home people.

"Maggie, I think I can swing it and get people enrolled in the trial of the vaccine. You know that they will need to able to understand the consent and agree to participate. Do you think all the nursing home residents can do that?"

"I'm not sure," Maggie replied, "but we can pay them a visit and find out. I'm betting that many of them will qualify and agree to participate. Like I said before, they may be low risk, because Heidi mainly just talked to them. There wasn't a great deal of physical contact. The gym may be a different story. When Alex and Heidi worked out, it was all business, and they would sweat a great deal—maybe even bleed if they nicked up a hand or knee. I'm planning on talking with them also. Can you come along?"

"Sure," Jamie agreed. "Just let me know when."

Frank Lee began putting their bags in the trunk of the car. He placed the rack of elixir toward the front of the trunk and put the bags toward the back. *You can't be too careful,* he thought. *If we get hit from behind, the bags may act as a cushion.*

Looking at the map, he concluded that driving to Cleveland the first night was going to be too hard on Susan. *Stopping in Toledo may be better. She's going to be miserable on this trip. It's just too bad this pregnancy had to get in the way.*

John Tuttle got Maggie on the line. "Dr. Hamilton," he began, "we are still getting the same question over and over. Where did these people catch the virus? This uncertainly has created a great deal of alarm throughout the country. It's even shaken the financial markets. The Dow is down about six hundred points today. You know anything can create turbulence in the markets, which triggers computer selling by the big institutions."

"Well," said Maggie, "I don't know much about that, but unfortunately, we don't have much to report. Mack has this one family he's keeping an eye on, but so far, nothing terribly suspicious. They haven't traveled outside the United States as far as we can tell. They have a strange past, and the agents are having difficulty piecing it all together, but we'll see. It's probably nothing."

"When you find out something, please tell me," Tuttle said. "The media can drive a person crazy."

Frank got Susan situated in the front seat. He had brought along a pillow that she could use for the lumbar area of her back and another she could lay her feet on so they could be elevated to reduce the swelling.

"That was kind of you to think of bringing the pillows," Susan said. "They do help with my aches and pains. I'm ready for this pregnancy thing to be over. I feel swollen and bloated."

"I can imagine," Frank replied. "We won't drive very far the first day. I want to just take our time and make it as easy on you as possible. Let's just hope we don't get into trouble along the way."

"I'll be fine, Frank," Susan assured him. "I've been through a lot tougher things back in China. I come from a very poor family. We struggled to get everything we had, and I felt fortunate to be chosen for this job. They've promised me that my family would be taken care of if anything were to happen to me."

"Same with me, Susan. Or should I say, Huan. We can speak our Chinese names out here on the road."

"Sometimes I like hearing our real names again," Susan admitted. "But it does make me homesick. I miss my family from time to time. I wonder what they would think of me being pregnant. I'm guessing they would be happy for me even under these circumstances."

"I have to say, there is a beauty in women when they're pregnant. There is a certain glow about your face."

Susan smiled. "Those first few weeks with the morning sickness were rough, but now I feel relatively good, apart from the back pain that I get from time to time. Oh, and the kicks that I get from the baby. I don't mind them at all. It tells me he or she is alive and well. I was glad I elected to not know the sex of the baby. It's kind of fun having it be a surprise."

"I get the sense that you're beginning to like the idea of being a mother."

"I suppose all those hormones begin to work on you," Susan replied. "Yes, it is exciting to think that I'm having a baby. But I know that this can't lead to much. I'm not sure what will happen to the baby. What if we have to escape?"

"I guess we'll deal with that if it happens."

The nursing home director, Sherrie Simmons, eagerly greeted Maggie and Jamie at the door. "We're so glad that you have agreed to come and talk with our residents and their families," she said. "As you can imagine, they are all very nervous about what's happened. I've tried to reassure them that their risk is low, but it's going to come better from you."

As they entered the dining area, they found a motley group of people, with some in wheelchairs, others on walkers, and still others just sitting in chairs. Several appeared to be confused and disconnected mentally, but for the most part, the rest seemed to have all their faculties.

"Well, ladies and gentlemen, I'm Dr. Hamilton, and this is Dr. Sessions. We would like to give you an update about the virus, Ebola, and allow you to ask us any questions."

Maggie proceeded to tell the story of Alex and Heidi and how they became critically ill and ultimately died. She related to the attendees that the third patient was doing much better with the experimental treatment. She went on to explain the trial with the novel vaccine and let them know that this was going to be available to them. However, because it was experimental, they would have to agree to take an experimental medication.

The majority nodded approval that they would be able

to get the vaccine, so Maggie asked Jamie to go over the protocol with the residents and their families. Jamie carefully reviewed the benefits and potential side effects of the vaccine and then let them know that a research coordinator would visit with them individually to gauge their interest and, if they were still willing, have them sign the consent to proceed. Most seemed eager to participate. There were a few questions by the families, but for the most part, it appeared that they were ready to sign the consent at any time.

As Maggie and Jamie were leaving, they thanked Sherrie Simmons.

"Ladies, or I guess I should say doctors, we are so happy that you came today," Sherrie replied. "You don't know how much this has helped to calm the people who live here and their families. They may be old, but many are still very active and have a good understanding of the circumstances."

"I'm glad we could help," Maggie exclaimed.

As they were leaving, she turned to Jamie. "All right, girl, it's on to the gym. Now this should be a completely different crowd."

Frank drove slowly on their trip, intentionally avoiding speeding and any bumps or jerking. He wanted to make this as comfortable for Susan as possible. Even though they weren't husband and wife, they still had a great affection and respect for each other. He had planned ahead for a hotel, and he had reservations for a Hampton Inn.

They had been traveling for about four hours, and Frank concluded that this was enough driving for the day. Susan was tired. They had stopped for a light lunch but intentionally parked the car outside the Wendy's where they could keep an eye on the vehicle to ensure no one attempted to get into it. Now using their app on their phone, they were able to drive directly to the hotel.

Frank left Susan in the car as he checked in. He gave the clerk his name and proceeded to pay for the room with cash.

Frank went back to the car and helped Susan get out. He escorted her to the room and let her in to lie down. He then returned to the lobby to park the car and take their luggage to the room. Again, he attempted to place the car in a position that could easily be observed from their room. He knew it was critical not to have anyone break into the car or find the elixir.

"Boy, Frank, this bed feels wonderful," said Susan. "I was ready to stop. My back was killing me, and I think we drove far enough for today. The baby seemed to know that we were on a road trip and was having a heyday kicking me."

"I'm glad we could stop now," Frank agreed. "I could tell you were getting tired. With a good night's rest, we can get started tomorrow early after breakfast."

John turned to Tim in the control room. "Well, our mystery couple appears to be on the move. I'm tracking the cell phone, and they have been traveling down Interstate 90 going east. They've been driving for four to five hours, and they appear to have stopped for the night in Toledo. There could be several places they're going. We'll just have to see. Any luck with their background, Tim?"

"Not really. They have had no traffic tickets or crimes. They moved here rather mysteriously with cash to buy everything, and it's been difficult to find a past. They just came out of nowhere."

CHAPTER 17

Maggie and Jamie found their way to Rick's Gym and Fitness, where Jake was eagerly waiting for them.

"I've got everyone here," he told them. "I've set up chairs, and I believe they will be able to hear you there. No basketball going on."

"This will be fine," Maggie assured him. "It looks like there are about two hundred people. So, you're right, they're very concerned."

Maggie started by introducing herself and then going over Alex and Heidi's course. Some in the audience nodded their heads when they heard their names, having recognized them from the gym. She introduced Jamie, who reviewed the protocol for the vaccine, and then they opened it up for questions.

"So, if I agree to take the vaccine, will I get any side effects?" a lady in the back of the group asked.

"This is still an experimental treatment," Jamie explained, "but in the preliminary studies, we have only seen problems with a sore arm after getting the injection. Some have had a mild fever for one to two days, but most remain asymptomatic. Still, it is experimental, so there could be side effects that haven't been identified. This is purely voluntary to receive the vaccine—but as you probably know, we don't have anything else to protect you, and the treatments have been mostly supportive. We have used an experimental medication for the third patient with the disease, and he is recovering."

"Will this cost us anything to receive the vaccine?" a gentleman in the front row asked.

"No, the treatment is free—and actually, you will be compensated to participate. Generally, you would receive fifty dollars for each visit to the research site, and all the testing associated with the vaccine would be provided free. We do expect you to report any and all unusual symptoms you might have. We even want you to report accidents. You see, if for some reason the medication changed your vision or your balance, it could have contributed to the accident. Basically, we need to know everything. The physician you will be seeing will make a determination as to whether he or she believes the vaccine was responsible or not."

There were a few more minor questions, but in general, the people attending were appreciative that there was something they could receive that might prevent the illness. This led to a concern by a younger member as to their chances of getting the virus.

Maggie stood up to answer this question. "I believe that for the most part, your risk of getting this Ebola will be very low. The disease is transmitted by bodily fluids, predominately blood. It isn't spread through coughing, for example. On the other hand, if Alex or Heidi happened to scratch themselves on the equipment and left fresh blood on the handles, there could be a chance that it could be transmitted to whoever used it next. So, there is a risk, but as I said, I believe that the risk should be low. The blood would have to get into your system."

The explanations by Jamie and the comments by Maggie seemed to quell some of the anxiety of the crowd attending, but many remained concerned. About seventy percent indicated an interest in participating in the trial on the vaccine, so Jamie gave them information as to where they could go to review the informed consent and sign up if they qualified.

Leaving the gym, Maggie and Jamie looked at each other and sighed with relief.

"Well, I'm glad that's over," Maggie exclaimed. "I understand their concern. Who would have thought they would be exposed to Ebola in a gym in Chicago? Really, this is just crazy, if you ask me."

"I agree with you, Maggie. It's very unnerving to think that someone in United States who hasn't traveled anywhere outside of the states could show up with this disease. I wonder how in the hell he got exposed?"

"Mack's working on it. So far, no clear answers, but I have confidence that he will come up with something."

"Or maybe it's that he can do no wrong?" Jamie teased.

"Well, there could be a little of that," Maggie admitted, "but I believe he's on the right track, and before long, we're going to be getting some answers."

The sun pierced through the window of the hotel room through a crack in the curtain and directly into Susan's eyes. Groaning, she rolled over and asked Frank, "Why did we have to leave the curtain open?"

"I had to keep an eye on the car," he told her. "We can't be too careful. I got up several times last night to peek out and look at it. No traffic around it or anything to suggest any unscrupulous activity. It's time, however, to get up and shower, pack our bags, have breakfast, and get on the road."

"Wow, this bed was fantastic last night," Susan said. "Can't I just lay here, and you go ahead?"

"Yeah, sure, no problem, I'll just pick you up on the way home," Frank said sarcastically. "Are you kidding?"

"Yes, of course," she replied. "I know that we have to get going. Next stop Cleveland?"

"You got it, sister. It shouldn't be too bad today."

Maggie returned to the hospital and found James Singleton sitting in a reclining chair. *Now this is a change!* she thought. *What an improvement.*

Turning to the charge nurse, she said, "Wow, James looks great today. Sitting up and eating. We have made great progress. This is so encouraging. I'm sure his family is thrilled, but so am I."

"Yes, they've been up to see him," the nurse replied, "and they are so appreciative of all that you've done."

"And you and the staff as well," Maggie added. "This is a team effort. It's great to have a positive outcome when things had been so dire with Alex and Heidi."

"I agree. Mr. Tuttle came down here today to see the patient through the monitors and talk with him. He wanted to report this positive news to the media."

"I don't blame him," Maggie said. "He has been harangued by them. He needs a break. I wish we could give them a clear answer where this started in the first place. That question has been very elusive."

Mack found John in the control center. "All right, John," he said. "Where are they now?"

"They stopped in Toledo, Ohio, and appeared to spend the night," John reported. "Now they're on the road again down Interstate 90. They appear to be going toward Cleveland. What an interesting couple. Very mysterious, if you ask me. They have a legitimate business that appears to be quite successful but a background that is hard to discover. Going on a crazy trip at a time when it would seem they should be hunkered down at home waiting for delivery of a baby. The only one of the bunch we discovered that has a disposable phone bought with cash. Strange. Plus, their home and business were bought with cash. No way to trace any of this without loans or credit cards. And now we can't find any past on these people. Something isn't right."

"I agree," Mack nodded. "Keep on them. We may be on to something."

As Mack left the control room, he thought it would be a good time to meet up with Maggie and update her about the Lees. If nothing else, it gave him an excuse to see her. He found her in the biocontainment area with the charge nurse.

"How's our patient?" he asked.

"Fantastic, actually. Take a look through the monitor. See, he's sitting up and eating. It just makes me feel great."

"You should. What an accomplishment with a disease like this. At least there haven't been any new cases. That would really spook people."

"You're telling me. So, any news from your side?"

"Not really. Those two young people who died had the most boring life possible. They knew no one, went nowhere, did nothing, except perhaps apart from exercising—and still they catch a disease found only in a tropical environment. This is just a weird story. Our mystery couple is equally strange. Traveling east by car, reportedly on vacation, and the lady is very pregnant. We don't have a final destination, but they're traveling on Interstate 90. They've made one stop in Toledo, but they appear to be on the road again. None of the other cell phone owners seem to be of interest."

"I have an interest," Maggie said. "Not in them, but in you. When can we get together again?"

"Are you trying to distract me from my work?" Mack asked, grinning.

"Absolutely. Isn't that what I'm supposed to do?"

"Now that I think about it, you're right," he laughed. "We could take that other dance lesson we talked about."

"That sounds like fun. Tonight?"

"Why not? Let me check with the instructor."

Mack pulled out his cell phone and found Corry's number in the contacts. Corry answered on the second ring.

"Corry, Mack here. Maggie says she is ready for round two. Can you work us in for a dance lesson tonight?"

"For you, no problem," Corry replied. "What's it going to be? Bachata? This is an easy one—and a sexy dance."

"Perfect, I'll take it. Seven o'clock?"

Turning to Maggie, he said, "We're all set, but we start at my place. Where I'm staying, they have a kitchen, and I'll cook."

"You cook?" she asked.

"Don't be so surprised. See you then."

Susan and Frank packed their bags. They had a light break-fast, and then Frank loaded the car with the luggage. He left to refuel the car while Susan waited for him in the lobby, reading *USA Today*.

No New Cases of Ebola in Chicago, the headline read. *Still no answer how this started in the first place.* Smiling, Susan set the paper down.

A lady sitting on the couch beside her turned and re-marked, "Strange, isn't it? I couldn't help but notice you reading that headline about the Ebola. Why do you think this showed up in Chicago?"

"No idea," said Susan. "Maybe it was just a fluke."

"Odd, though. It has certainly made everyone nervous."

And that is exactly what we hoped would happen, Susan thought.

"Sorry," she said, "I have to leave. My husband is here to pick me up."

"Good luck with the delivery," the lady responded. "It looks like it could be any time."

"Thank you. We're excited. Our first."

Frank found his way to Interstate 90 east and eased onto the turnpike.

"Well, so far so good, eh, Huan?" he remarked.

"I like having you call me that, Zhao. It makes me think of home. How long will we be driving today?"

"That depends on how you feel," Frank replied. "We can drive a relatively short distance to Cleveland or farther, if you feel OK. I'm in no hurry, even though Samuel is nervous. He wants us to get there and deploy the elixir."

"I'm with you," said Susan. "We'll just mosey down the highway. After all, we're on vacation, right?"

—◄▉▉▉▉►—

Mack stopped at the grocery store on his way to the long-stay hotel where he had been living. He found salmon, broccoli, a salad in a bag that was easy to prepare, and a bottle of Chardonnay. *This should do,* he thought. *They have a grill outside the hotel that guests can use. I'll cook the salmon on the grill.*

He arrived home and set out the food on the counter. He carefully applied the seasonings to the salmon that the butcher had recommended. He didn't want to start the grill until Maggie arrived, so he washed the broccoli and set it aside. Thinking he had time, he jumped in the shower and slipped on casual clothes. Thirty minutes later, his doorbell rang, and Maggie was there in skinny jeans and a white blouse.

"You never cease to amaze me," he said. "Cool outfit. I like it. Now let's see if you like my cooking. There is wine in the fridge if you want to pour yourself a glass. I'll get the grill going and start the vegetable and salad."

"Yes sir, Mr. Chef."

"Well, don't get too excited. The people in the grocery store helped me a lot. We'll see how this turns out."

Mack proceeded to light the grill and cook the salmon on a moderate temperature setting. While it was cooking, he quickly started the broccoli and made the salad. The bag of Asian salad came with a dressing and sesame seed crackers to top it off. As he finished the salad, he checked on the salmon and concluded he had cooked it to the right temperature. Not too much, just pink in the center.

"All right, gorgeous, dinner is about ready," he announced as he brought in the salmon from the outdoor grill. "Let's toast with a sip of wine before dinner." He clinked his glass against hers and then, setting down the wine glass, he folded her into his arms and gave her a kiss.

"Sorry, no more hanky-panky," he said, stopping suddenly. "My food might get cold."

Scowling, Maggie sat down at the table. "Party pooper. Let's eat."

Taking her first few bites of the salmon, she was amazed at how great it tasted. "Wow," she exclaimed, "you can cook!"

"Well, as I said. I had a lot of help from the clerk at the seafood counter who got me the salmon," Mack demurred. "He said, 'Be sure not to overcook the fish. You've got to leave it medium,' so that's what I tried to do."

"Well, you did great. Now how about that dessert we always have?" she said, smiling.

"Sorry, on to the next thing," Mack announced. "Dance class, remember?"

"Oh, shoot. Maybe later?"

"Guaranteed."

Frank drove only at the speed limit on the highway. He didn't want to raise any suspicions or create any undue stress for Susan. They had driven most of the day and it was getting toward evening. With the pregnancy, she had to make several bathroom stops, and she asked Frank to take the next exit so she could use the restroom.

"Susan, there is an exit in about a mile. Is that OK?"

"Sure, Frank. I can make it that far."

Frank pulled off the highway and saw a McDonald's. He parked next to it, and while Susan was in the restroom, Frank bought them both Cokes to drink. She found the restrooms busy because there was a lot of traffic on the highway, but a stall became available. As she finished urinating, she glanced in the toilet. The water was red.

"Oh my God," she exclaimed. "I'm bleeding. This can't be."

She finished and hurried out to find Frank. Seeing her coming, he could tell something was wrong.

"Susan, what is it? You're frazzled."

"No, Frank, I'm bleeding. This isn't good. We're going to have to find a hospital. I need to be checked out."

"Cleveland is only another twenty-five miles," Frank told her. "It won't take us long to get there. Can you make it?"

"I think so," she said. "I'm only having a few light contractions. Nothing that seems severe."

"I was afraid this might happen," Frank said. "Let's get going."

When Mack and Maggie walked into the dance studio, Corry hurried toward them with a big smile on his face.

"So, I didn't scare you away with the first dance lesson?" he said to Maggie.

"I was surprised how much I liked it," she told him. "I never thought of myself as being able to dance. Plus, it was fun. So, what's it going to be tonight?"

"Ahh, I'm glad you asked," Corry replied. "Another Latin dance. Very sexy. Bachata. You're going to like it. It's not too hard, but you can do a lot with it."

"Lay it on me," Susan said. "I'll give it my best effort."

"Let's start with this," Corry began. "Simply go in a horizontal line with step, step, tap. Then reverse directions and go step, step, tap. Try this first. You can get Cuban motion going by bending your leg that has the weight on it and then shifting and bending your opposite leg. Give it a shot."

Mack and Maggie began going back and forth, following Corry's instructions, and before long they had the basic moves figured out. They even started moving their hips by bending their legs as he'd described.

"Well, this is kind of fun," Mack said. "I think I could do this in my sleep."

"Don't fall asleep yet," Corry advised. "We need to move on. Next, let's try an underarm turn. Mack, as you move to your right, lift your arm, giving Maggie the signal that it's time for the turn. She'll get the message."

Doing as he said, Mack lifted his arm, and sure enough, Maggie followed along, doing the underarm turn.

"Hey this really works!" Mack exclaimed.

"I told you."

"Do you have suggestions of things I can do to make her follow other commands I give her?" he asked.

"Only in dance," Corry said, laughing. "I'm staying out of the rest of it."

The three of them worked on some additional moves, but after an hour, Mack and Maggie decided they'd had enough.

"This is the maximum amount of moves I can handle for the night," Maggie stated. "I'll be lucky if I can remember these."

Mack drove them back to his home, where Maggie had left her car. He invited her in, and they quickly found the couch to sit and talk.

"Mack, you are so much fun to be with," Maggie marveled. "I would have never thought that I would be taking dance lessons, especially with an FBI agent."

"I know it seems a bit crazy, but I find it lets me wind down. I'm not great at it, but I don't plan to be on *Dancing with the Stars*."

"You probably could if you wanted to. I think you could do about anything."

"Maybe you really don't know me that well," Mack replied. "I may be a jack of all trades but a master of none."

"I don't think so. You've mastered me, and no one else has done that."

With that, he pulled her close, and their lips met. Lovemaking had become easier each time, and they both enjoyed the moment—but everything was interrupted when Mack's cell phone let out a chirp indicating a message.

"Gosh, I never get paged at night," he said. "It's a message from John. He's been tracking our mysterious couple. He wants me to call him. Sorry, babe, work is calling."

"I know all about that. Remember, I'm a physician."

He grabbed his phone, dialed the number, and quickly asked, "What is it, John? ... So, our couple have stopped in Cleveland. They're at the MacDonald Women's Hospital? Mrs. Lee must be having issues. Keep an eye on them. There is still something fishy here."

Hanging up, he asked, "Maggie, do you think it strange that a very pregnant lady and her husband decide to take a vacation at the eleventh hour of her pregnancy? It seems so to me."

"I'm surprised that her obstetrician would let her," said Maggie. "I would have thought that she would have been told that she couldn't travel."

"Even their employees thought the same thing," Mack

noted. "Why a vacation now? There is something screwy here. We haven't found any connection with Alex or Heidi, but they have an odd past as well, so we're going to follow them closely. They may be the contact we've been looking for."

CHAPTER 18

Frank stopped at the emergency room of the MacDonald Women's Hospital, and Susan was taken into a room immediately because of her bleeding. She was given a hospital gown and undressed. Frank stayed with her until the doctor arrived.

"So, Mrs. Lee, I'm Dr. Stanley Smith. I see you are from Chicago, but you were traveling when the bleeding started. And how far along are you?"

"My due date is in three weeks," Susan told him.

"Well, it seems a bit risky to be out on the road, being this advanced in your pregnancy. Are you doing something important?" the doctor asked.

"Yes," Susan replied. "I have an elderly mother whom I must see. She has become very ill, and I feel I need to be with her."

The doctor frowned. "With your bleeding, we need to put you on bed rest, at least for the night, until we can determine if things have settled down. There are potentially many factors that could be causing this bleeding, but it may stop, and you could be all right. Other causes are more serious.

I'm going to arrange for a bed for the night, and then we can decide in the morning what we'll need to do. It's possible that you may need to deliver here."

"Oh, doctor, I don't know if I can do that," said Susan. "You see, it is very important that we make it to my mother. She's on her deathbed."

"We'll do all we can, but I can't promise you that. I'll have the nurse find you a room, and we'll monitor the baby's heartbeat overnight."

After the doctor left the room, Susan looked at Frank. "What are we going to do?" she asked.

"Spend the night, like he said," Frank replied. "Let's see how things are in the morning. I'll find a room in a nearby hotel but call me if something comes up. I'll let the Centre know what's going on."

Frank found the Choice Hotel near the hospital and checked in as before, using cash. He again found a parking space for the car so he could check on it from time to time. Frank unpacked his bag and laid out a Glock 19. He had put the gun in his suitcase just in case they ran into some trouble. He shed his clothes, took a shower, and then called Samuel.

"Samuel, we have an issue here. Susan is in the hospital with bleeding. The physician warned us that she may need to deliver here if the bleeding continues or if she goes into advanced labor. We were fearful something like this might happen. What should we do?"

"This isn't good—I agree with you," Samuel replied. "I think we may have to get proactive and release some of the virus where you are, just in case you never reach Washington, DC. I would consider finding the ventilation system of the hotel or a nearby building. We know this will create total panic. Washington, DC, the heart of the federal government, would be best, but believe me—this would make a big impact even if cases of Ebola occurred right there. Search for a spot and let me know. But when you release the vial, you need to be on your way. Don't stay around to see the results. Although the virus is best transmitted with bodily fluids, if it lands on devices or furniture, it can last for several hours and be transmitted that way."

"Believe me, when we release it, you'll see us running out of town. We're not going to wait and see what happens. I'll check back with you in the morning."

Samuel added, "Oh, and by the way, after you release the Ebola, throw away the phone. We can't be too careful. You'll probably have to get another one, but it would be best to get rid of it so no one can trace you."

"I understand."

Frank slept better that night than he had the night before. He now knew that there was a back-up plan. After eating breakfast, he decided to walk around the hotel, where he found the fitness center—and the vents from the heating and air-conditioning system. It seemed ideal to him. No one was using the equipment at the time, so he could explore the best place to deploy the virus.

The vent covers were easily removed, and because this area required more ventilation with people exercising, it appeared to have more flow of air. The virus would be aerosolized better and hopefully land on the equipment. Breathing it might not spread the virus but contact with it would. Since people exercised with earphones, they would not likely hear the soft sound of the explosive.

This is perfect, Frank decided. *Time to go see Susan.*

After finding the car, he drove the short distance to the

hospital and found his way to her room. "Hey, Susan. How are you feeling?"

"Fine," she told him. "No contractions overnight. It seems to me that the bleeding has stopped. The doctor is supposed to be in soon. Why don't you wait, and you can hear what he has to say?"

"Sure, no problem. Oh, and by the way, Samuel gave us some new orders. He feels we need to deliver one of our presents here. I found a spot at the hotel, so as we're leaving, I think we can deploy the gift."

"Really!" she exclaimed. "That should be interesting."

"He still wants us to try to get to DC, but he's concerned that with your condition, that might not happen. He's convinced that it could have almost the same effect here, and he might be right."

At that moment, Dr. Jones entered the room, accompanied by the charge nurse. "How are you feeling, Mrs. Lee?" he asked.

"Actually, I think pretty well. I'm ready to go anytime."

"I'm not sure that's a good idea," the doctor replied. "We have just watched you for a few hours, and this could all get worse quickly."

"But doctor, like I said, I need to get to my mother. This is very important."

The doctor simply replied, "Let's see how you're doing tomorrow and then make that decision."

"I just don't think that's a good idea," Susan protested. "I understand your concern, but I believe I will be fine."

"We'll check on you later and see if anything has changed." And with that, the doctor and nurse left the room.

Susan turned to Frank. "Now what Frank?"

"We can't stay. With no symptoms, I suggest that I go back to the hotel and pack our bags. I'll get us checked out and, on leaving, I'll plant the package. You gather your things. I saw a back exit where we can take the stairs—so when I get back, be ready to leave. You'll have to move quickly as we leave; we won't have much time."

Frank smiled at the nurses as he left the obstetrics floor to return to the hotel. He stopped the car in the parking lot in a remote location so he could carefully remove one of the vials from the tray. He wrapped it in clothes that he had lying in the trunk and carefully took it to his room. After packing, he took all their luggage to the car.

"The hotel was perfect for the night," Frank told the receptionist. "I just have to get a couple more things, and then I'll be leaving."

"Where is your wife?" she enquired.

"Oh, I have to pick her up at the hospital. She had some bleeding, but everything is fine now, so we can be on our way."

"That's good to hear. I'm glad that everything worked out. Thank you for staying with us."

Frank took the elevator to his room and carefully carried the vial of elixir hidden in his hand with the clothes. The fitness center was located on the second floor, and he first checked to be sure there was no one in the room. He slipped in quietly and removed the vent cover near the entrance. Once the vial was planted, he set the charge, returned the vent cover, and hurried to the exit. He quickly got into his car and went to the hospital.

Finding a location near the back of the hospital, he discovered an entrance that appeared to be used for maintenance people and housekeeping, so he parked his car nearby. He assessed that he could exit the hospital from this location, then he walked to the front of the hospital and to the main entrance. He smiled at the security guard and found the elevator to Susan's floor, slipping quietly into her room.

As he had told her, she was completely dressed and ready to go. He cautiously peered out of the room, and when there were no nurses around, he signaled her to follow him. They found their way to the stairwell and began descending to the first floor. The exit Frank had identified was toward the back of the hospital and away from the entrance. They stepped through the door, and the car was waiting where Frank had left it.

"Susan, jump in. We need to get going. We don't have a lot of time."

As they left, Frank tossed the cell phone in a garbage can just outside the exit. On their way out of town, they found another Target store and purchased a new phone.

Mack smiled as he entered the hospital. *Who would have guessed that this job would be this much fun? Maggie is great. I've never met a girl like her before.*

He found John and was curious to know if there was anything new with the mystery couple. "Have they moved?"

"No, they seem to be stuck at the hospital. In fact, there has been no movement at all on the phone. I suppose he must be with her at the bedside. I wonder if we should call and see if we can find out any information?"

"Maybe I could call, indicating that I'm her obstetrician, and see if she delivered."

"Sure, Mack. Good idea. Here's the number."

Mack dialed the number and reached the hospital operator. "Could I have the maternity floor where Susan Lee would be located?" he asked. "I'm her obstetrician from Chicago."

"Certainly, doctor. Let me connect you to the floor."

"Third floor maternity," the unit clerk answered.

"My name is Dr. Mack Johnson. I understand my patient, Susan Lee, was admitted with complications from her pregnancy. Could I speak with her nurse?"

"No problem—with one exception. Mrs. Lee left the hospital AMA this morning. When the nursing staff went to check on her, she was not in her room, and she appears to have left the hospital."

"Really," Mack replied. "I told her that I felt it was too dangerous to travel, but she insisted. Do you have any idea where she might be going? She never advised me."

"Let me have you talk to our charge nurse. She may know."

After a few moments, a female voice came on the line announcing herself. "This is Shirley Templeton. I'm the daytime charge nurse. Can I help you?"

"Ms. Templeton, my name is Dr. Mack Johnson. I'm Susan Lee's obstetrician. I understand that she has left the hospital."

"Yes," Ms. Templeton replied. "Our physician had wanted her to remain at least one more day for observation. She kept insisting that she had an elderly mother who was dying, and she had to get to her soon before she passed away. She left on her own. We didn't dismiss her."

"Do you know where the mother lived?"

"No. She never gave us any information about that. She implied that she was going east, but she didn't give the name of a city."

"I had discouraged her from traveling, but she wouldn't listen to me," Mack said. "She never mentioned to me that she had a sick relative."

"All I know is that her bleeding had stopped, and she left before the doctor could talk to her further."

"Thanks for your help. Let's hope that the baby and mother will have no further complications."

Hanging up the phone, Mack shook his head in disbelief. *This whole story gets stranger by the minute. Something very fishy is going on.*

"Hey John," he called out. "She checked herself out of the hospital against the advice of her doctor. Actually, she never told him she was leaving. She just left. And the phone is not moving—I'm guessing they dumped it as they left the hospital. Can we get someone to go to the hospital and find it before the battery dies?"

"Sure, Mack," John replied. "We have agents in Cleveland as you know. They can probably use the signal to help find it as long as the battery stays charged."

"Perfect."

Tom Simpson had finished his insurance work and was packing his bags in preparation for leaving the Choice Hotel and returning to his home in Hollywood, Florida. He stopped for a moment and thought to himself, *I don't have to be in a big hurry to leave today. My work is done here in the city, and now it's just a matter of getting home for the weekend. I've got time to get in a quick workout.*

He put on his gym clothes and found the fitness center on the second floor. He used his room key to enter and decided to run on the treadmill. Walking into the room, he didn't notice a weight that had been left on the floor. His foot caught in the handle, and he fell forward, hitting the mat hard.

Damn, he thought. *How did I miss seeing that weight? I guess it's because it was black and blended with the black floor. What's this?* He glanced at his hand. *Blood, shit,* he thought. *I'll just hold some pressure on it and hopefully the bleeding will stop.*

He had been gaining weight from so many trips on the road. Now he was trying to trim down by restarting running again. Donning headphones, he started to run while watching the morning news. Within a short time, he was perspiring heavily and gripping the handles of the treadmill tightly. Glancing down, he saw some blood on the handle. *I'll just clean this off when I'm done,* he thought.

Halfway through his workout, a young lady entered the center and joined him running on another treadmill close by his. He could tell she had been exercising regularly by her very slim physique.

"Looks like you've been doing this much longer than me," he said as he removed his headphones. "You don't even get short of breath running at a much faster speed."

"I've always enjoyed running," she said. "It lets me burn off energy and forget my problems. I have a big meeting today for some investors, and I thought this could help reduce my stress level. But I've got a runny nose. I must be catching something." She wiped her nose. "How about you?"

"I'm done here. I couldn't get back to Florida last night, but I'm leaving today. Sorry about the blood. I cut my hand when I tripped on that weight. I'll get it cleaned up before I leave. I get a whole four days off, and I'm eager to see my kids. Are you finished after today?"

"Yeah, after this presentation, I head home to Philly. Just have two dogs that will be waiting for me. But they're always eager to see me. I'm Sally Schneider, by the way."

"Tom Simpson. Well, I'm done here. Good luck with the presentation and have safe travels."

"Same to you."

CHAPTER 19

Mack made the call to the Cleveland FBI office and identified himself

"This is Agent Matthew Johnson. I'm currently on assignment in Chicago, and we have two people of interest that we have been tracking. We've been following a disposable cell phone, and it appears that they may have dumped the phone somewhere near MacDonald Women's Hospital. Our suspect was hospitalized there overnight but left against medical advice. We're not sure of their final destination, but we thought finding the cell phone could help us identify some of their contacts."

"Sure, no problem, Agent Johnson," Agent Andrew Schmidt replied. "I'll get someone over there right now."

"If they ask who you're following," Mack advised, "I would simply imply someone who was recently hospitalized and leave it at that. We hope the battery will last long enough that you will be able to find the phone. I'll send you the number so you can track the signal."

"Will do. I'll get back with you."

Mack wandered into the hospital cafeteria to find Maggie. She was in one of the corners having a bagel and coffee.

"Maggie, I've got to give you an update on the Lees," Mack said urgently. "Mrs. Lee was hospitalized at a maternity hospital in Cleveland for bleeding, but she left the hospital on her own. I was told that her attending physician wanted to keep her for another day, but she was adamant that she had to see her dying mother. She left the hospital without telling anyone. I think this gets crazier all the time. What do you think?"

"You're right," Maggie agreed. "This is very strange. She should never be traveling this late in her pregnancy, and then to just leave the hospital doesn't make sense. You mentioned that their employees thought they were going on vacation, but now Mrs. Lee says that she must see her dying mother. Things aren't adding up."

"It appears they threw away the cell phone as they were leaving, so I have agents in Cleveland on their way to find it. If the battery holds out, we should be able to locate it. From there, we can try to analyze who they've been calling."

"That's going to be interesting!" Maggie exclaimed.

"I think so too. How's your patient?"

"He's great. He may be able to go home soon. His strength is improving each day, and his kidney function has almost returned to normal."

"You should feel good about that," Mack told her.

"I do. And we've started vaccinating the people from the

nursing home and the gym. That's giving them some reassurance that they are protected from the disease. In reality, I don't believe that the nursing home people are at very high risk, since the contact was very social. The gym could be another story if bodily fluids from our patients got in contact with people working out at the gym. That could be a problem."

"I'm sure they're happy that you and Jamie met with them and offered the vaccine as an option," Mack said. Then he added, "Hold on a minute—I'm getting a call. Yes, Andrew? ... That was fast. You must have raced down to hospital. So, it was in a garbage can? I'm glad you acted so quickly. The garbage could have been dumped and the phone lost. Can you get it up to us? ... Sure, sending a courier with the phone will be perfect. That way we can start analyzing the contents immediately."

He hung up and turned back to Maggie. "Found the phone. Now we can do some real FBI business. This should be interesting. We should have it here in the next four hours."

"I hope you will tell this doctor what you find."

"You know I can't keep many secrets from you. After all, you're my sidekick in this investigation. I need you, and you need me to solve the puzzle of how this got started in the first place."

"You're right," said Maggie. "My job in diagnosing an illness isn't so dissimilar to you solving a case, is it?"

"So, as I see it, we complement each other. In fact, we complement each other in more ways than one."

Mack got the call from John. The phone had arrived, and they had already started working on it. They first had to crack the code for the password to get on the phone, but they had programs from the FBI that helped solve that problem. Then they began to look at the calls that had been made. Many were to a number with no caller ID. There were also several phone calls made to a person named Jason Turley.

The agents had already found Jason's address and began exploring his background. He was an analyst for a local brokerage firm. Single, no past criminal record. He had lived in Chicago for only one year. Originally, he came from Indianapolis, where he studied economics at Indiana University. He had been employed at the Pentagon for three years doing work for the Department of Defense. The real question was, what was his relationship with the Lees? And what did he do for the DOD?

He didn't have any ownership in the Lee's businesses. He didn't appear to be related. Although he lived close, they didn't seem to have any texts from him. The relationship between them had been going on for at least eight months.

"What do you make of this, John?" Mack asked.

"I don't know. It's hard to make a connection. They're not related. No business interests. Not from the same cities or backgrounds, although that's hard to know since we aren't sure where the Lees came from. We don't want to spook him, but maybe we should text him? We could act like we're one of them?"

"Clever. Sure, give it a try. That call should be interesting!"

Mack found Maggie in the usual place: the biocontainment center. As he walked in, her cell phone was ringing.

"Now it's my turn for a call, since it seems you're the one

always getting the messages," Maggie responded. "This time I've got a message from Jamie. ... Hey, Jamie. What's up? ... Are you kidding? Where in Florida? Hollywood? How would the virus get there? Any information on the patient? ... Let me tell Mack about this. So, you want me to join you?"

Maggie was flushed and rattled as she hung up the phone.

"There may be another case of Ebola in Hollywood, Florida, Mack. They probably wouldn't have considered this initially, but the physicians have been following the news from here, and when the patient was brought into the emergency room with similar findings, they became concerned and called us right away. How in the world would someone in Hollywood, Florida, contract the disease? It is nowhere near Chicago."

"Good question. Now you need to put on your investigative hat and think this through."

"Jamie wants me to meet her there. She says I know everything about these cases and feels I can help the physicians deal with this. I'm supposed to leave tonight."

"You need to go." he said. "You understand this infection, and it could help with our investigation here. I'm going to work on the phone and the contacts of the Lees. We'll see if we come up with something significant."

Maggie finished her bagel and coffee, made her final rounds at the hospital, and then headed home to pack. She let John Tuttle know of what had transpired, and she began mulling over in her mind what to pack and wondering how long she might be in Florida. Jamie hadn't given her many details.

When she arrived home, she threw clothes in a medium-size suitcase, thinking she might be there for a week. She took a quick shower and changed into a suit, thinking it would give her a more dignified appearance. She tossed her bag in the car. She had plenty of time to make it to the airport, so she stopped by Mack's hotel on her way. He had just gotten home.

"I couldn't leave without saying goodbye," she said. "I'm not sure how long I'll be gone, but I'll miss seeing you. Don't get a big head over this, but you're in my thoughts all the time. Do you know that you're a distraction?"

"Well, I'm glad that I'm a distraction for you," Mack said. "No one else I'd rather distract."

With that, he pulled her close and kissed her. "You smell great," he said. "Is that the same perfume you had on the first date?"

"As a matter of fact, yes. Marc Jacobs—one of my favorites."

"Don't let other guys smell that. They'll be chasing after you."

"If they do, it will be to my advantage, because it may make you jealous."

"It absolutely would," Mack agreed. "Just don't let them. I may need to take them out."

"There wouldn't be a need for that," Maggie responded. "You know that I'm yours."

"Let's just keep it that way. Call me when you get there."

Maggie left his hotel and went to her car. For a moment, she felt the moisture build up in her eyes and a tear trickle down her cheek. *Am I really that controlled by this guy?* she wondered. *Yes, I really am. I feel like turning around and going*

to bed with him. Isn't that awful? Too bad I can't. I'll just have to dream about it.

Maggie got to the airport in plenty of time to catch a bite of supper at the Chick-fil-A. It was one of her favorite fast foods. She always got the grilled chicken sandwich, thinking it would be healthier than any of the fried chicken. Waiting for her flight, she debated whether to text Mack. She tried to resist but couldn't.

Hey Mack. Do you miss me yet?

Within moments, the text returned. *You've been gone too long. It's time to come home.*

She texted back, *Silly, I haven't gotten out of town. I'm waiting for the plane. But I'll be thinking of you the entire flight. Anything new with the cell phone?*

His reply came after a moment. *This is very interesting. They seem to have a friend, Jason Turley, but we can't find any relationship between them. No family connection. No business connection. But there have been many calls between them. We're considering calling him on their phone.*

She texted back, *Let me know what turns up, and I'll let you know what I find in Florida. It's a long way for the virus to have traveled without something in between.*

Putting her phone away, she began thinking more about the patient in Florida with Ebola. *This could create major national panic if we begin to see sporadic cases in different cities. And then try to connect the dots as to how these cases have a common thread.*

As her mind wandered, she got a text from Jamie. *Maggie, we've just gotten notice that there may be another case in Philadelphia. This young woman has all the hallmarks of the other cases. I may need to have you cancel your flight and go there instead. I can't be two places at once.*

Texting her back, Maggie wrote, *Oh my gosh. I was just thinking what would happen if there were erratic isolated outbreaks in different cities. This could create a nationwide meltdown.*

Jamie replied, *Exactly. We need to get on this as soon as possible. Mack needs to find us the source.*

Maggie texted, *He's pursuing the Lees. They may have some connection to all this. I'll cancel this flight and rebook to Philly. Hopefully there's a flight I can get on tonight.*

With that, Maggie went to the desk at the gate to talk with the attendant.

"Excuse me," she began, "but I'm supposed to be on this flight to Florida, but something has come up and I need to switch the flight to Philadelphia. Is that something you can do for me?"

"Sorry," said the attendant, "but you will need to go back to the ticket counter and make those changes."

"Is there a flight tonight?" Maggie asked.

"Let me check." Staring at her computer monitor, the attendant finally looked up and said, "Yes, there is one leaving in an hour and a half. Did you check any bags?"

"Yes," Maggie replied. "I had a medium-sized bag that I checked."

"I can have the bag pulled, and I will let the ticket counter know that you're coming, but I would go there right away," the attendant said. "It shows that there are three seats left, so I would expect that you can get on the flight."

Maggie gave a sigh of relief and thanked the attendant for her help. She hurried past security and made it to the American Airlines ticket counter. She was able to get the flight switched, so she turned around and went through the security checkpoint again, this time finding the gate for the new flight. Once she was settled, she decided to call Mack.

"Hey, Mack. I know you must think I'm a pest, but something has come up. There may be another Ebola case, but this time in Philadelphia. I just wanted you to know that I've had a change of plans and now will be leaving for Philly."

"Babe, you're never a pest," he replied. "I'm glad that you called. I would have worried about you if you hadn't arrived in Florida."

"This is really disturbing. Can you imagine if we start getting cases all over the United States with no connection between them?"

"You're right. In fact, I'm surprised that we haven't heard from the TV networks already. By the way, we're trying to decide what to text our new friend from the Lees' phone. We're not sure if it should come from Frank or Susan. I'll let you know what happens."

Maggie closed her phone and glanced up at the TV in the waiting area for the passengers. *Oh my gosh*, she thought, *Mack was right. The CNN reporter in Florida is talking about the case.*

"This is Justin Anderson broadcasting from the entrance to Memorial Hospital in Hollywood, Florida," came the voice from the TV. "We have just learned that a patient has been admitted to the hospital yesterday, and there is concern that the patient may have Ebola. As you recall, there have been three cases of Ebola discovered in Chicago, where the source of these infections has never been determined. It appears we may have this new case outside of Chicago. It's our understanding that the infected individual has not traveled outside the United States. We have asked the hospital administration to comment on this individual, but we have been told that they are waiting on confirmation of the disease and assistance from the CDC. They have representatives here who are involved in the investigation, and we have been promised a report tomorrow."

Maggie wondered when they would find out about the case in Philadelphia. Her thoughts were interrupted when the gate attendant announced that boarding was starting. She quickly texted Mack to tell him about the CNN report and told him to turn on the TV, explaining that she was just boarding her flight. She ended the text with "Love ya."

Mack got the text and quickly turned on the TV to CNN.

"Hey, guys, check this out. A possible new case of Ebola in Florida, and Maggie tells me there may be another in Philly. How are we going to connect the Lees to these cases? They aren't anywhere near Florida or Pennsylvania.

"Good question, Mack. Let's just reach out to our new friend Jason. I think maybe we should text him from Frank. What do you think?" John asked.

"Frank is good as any. How about asking him to check on the house while they're away?"

"Sounds pretty benign. Sure, I'll send the text."

Jason saw his cell phone chirp, indicating a new message. *Hmm, a text from Susan. Wait a minute. It says it's from Frank. I didn't think he even knew I existed. What would he want? I hope he's not coming after me. What? He wants me to check on their house while they're out of town. Strange. What does he know about me? Did Susan tell him? What do*

I do with this? I think I'll just text him back saying I don't know who this is.

"Check this out, Mack," said John. "He texted back stating he doesn't know who this is. How strange. He has had multiple calls made to his number from this cell phone, and now he says he doesn't have any clue who's calling him? What do you make of this?"

"I'm not sure. Do you think we chose the wrong person? Maybe he only talks to her?"

"Wouldn't her husband know about him as well?"

"Maybe or maybe not," Mack mused. "Perhaps they're having their own personal relationship. If that's the case, he may be shocked that Frank texted him."

"You may be right. He's probably peeing his pants right now if he thinks the husband found out."

"How about texting him back and telling him it was Susan?" Mack suggested. "We can say that she just wanted to give him a hard time."

"OK, let me try that."

Within minutes, the text came through to Jason. Chills ran down his spine when he heard the chirp. Then he read: *Sorry Jason, I just wanted to see what you would do. I had a free moment and wanted to reach out to you.*

Jason sighed with relief when he saw that the text had

come from Susan. *Thank God,* he thought. He quickly texted back saying, *You're crazy. I about had a heart attack.*

"I think this answers your question, Mack," John said. "They're having an affair. I don't think we should push this too much for now but wait until tomorrow and maybe text him again. Send him a final message."

"I just did, and it said, *Have a good night. I miss you.*"

The return text answered with, *I miss you too. I can't wait until you return, and we can see each other again.*

CHAPTER 20

Maggie reached her hotel room near Philadelphia General Hospital. Jamie had arranged the room and texted her the address. After arriving, she realized how exhausted she was. She took a hot bath, slipped into her pajamas, and found the contacts of the people she was to reach out to at the hospital.

She thought she should give the infectious disease physician a call so they could touch base before she met him in the morning. She called Andrew Perkins, the head of infectious diseases at the hospital.

"Dr. Perkins," she said, "this is Dr. Margaret Hamilton, but most people call me Maggie. I believe that Jamie Sessions called to let you know I was coming to go over your case with you and see if I can provide any assistance. Can you give me some background on the patient?"

"Dr. Hamilton, we so appreciate you taking the time to come here and give us a hand. The patient is twenty-eight years old. She travels for work but hasn't traveled outside the United States. She is Caucasian and single. Her name is Sally Schneider, and she works for a wealth-management company.

She is very physically fit and, according to her friends, is never ill, so when she developed a high fever, nausea, vomiting, and diarrhea, this was quite out of the ordinary for her. They called EMS, who found her delirious and not responding normally.

"When she arrived at the emergency room, she was found to have multiple blisters on her body, a high temperature, and low blood pressure. She was in kidney failure. All in all, she appeared to have all the symptoms you had described on the CNN report, which made us concerned that she may have the same infection.

"The tests are still pending, but we believe this may be the case. Her parents are coming, but her girlfriends have confirmed that she hasn't had any contact that they are aware of with anyone from a Third World country. Still, with all her travels in the states, they couldn't be certain."

Maggie said, "I'll get into the hospital early in the morning. Where should I meet you?"

"You should come to the intensive care unit. We don't have a specific isolation area, but we have cordoned off the back section of the ICU for her, and everyone is using full protective gear. We did interrogate her friends, and it appears that they did not have any close contact with her. She doesn't have a close boyfriend or anyone else who might have been exposed."

"I'll meet you there at eight a.m.," Maggie said. "Thank you for the information, and we can talk further tomorrow."

Frank turned to Susan as they approached Baltimore. "How are you feeling? Any contractions?"

"No, actually, I'm feeling great. No more bleeding. I would have loved to have seen the look on Dr. Smith's face when he found that we just walked out. He probably wondered who in the world he was dealing with."

Frank smiled. "Well, he probably thinks we are totally unreasonable people, but he doesn't know us at all or why we left so unexpectedly. Thank goodness you recovered. I did text Samuel to let him know that we are back on the road toward the target."

At that moment, the Sirius XM radio Fox News channel announced that there was a suspected new case of Ebola in Hollywood, Florida. The Fox reporter who described the situation had an element of desperation in his voice.

"It looks like we are getting around," Frank smiled as he turned to Susan. "The virus was dispersed in the fitness center, so someone who used the area was going to be at risk of contracting the disease. We now can see that aerosolizing the virus and letting it contact surfaces allows us to spread the disease. Samuel is going to be happy to hear this. And from the reporter's tone of voice, I think we're getting the desired results. He seems to be very anxious. We should stop here for the night. I want to go slow and not push you too hard."

The next day, Maggie found the fourth floor of Philadelphia General Hospital, and Dr. Perkins was there waiting for her. He had a cup of black coffee that he had picked up from the cafeteria for her, anticipating she might need caffeine after her travels.

"Andrew," he said in introduction as he extended his hand. "Here's some coffee for you, but there's sweetener and creamer in the lounge if you like."

"Black is fine. Nice to meet you, Andrew. I'm Maggie. Sounds like your case is similar to ours in Chicago. Can you tell me anymore since I spoke with you?"

"Not much," Andrew replied. "This girl is quite athletic. Runs all the time and is very fit. Apparently, she travels a great deal for her work, but not outside the country. Her girlfriends tell us she is all work. No time for boyfriends. Her family is from Georgia, and they are on their way. She has an older brother and sister. We've had to start dialysis, apparently like your patients. She's on pressers and we did start broad-spectrum antibiotics, but from her clinical condition, she seems to follow the pattern that you described in your patients. Did you want to gown up and see her?"

"Sure, that probably is the best thing."

Andrew led Maggie to the dressing area, and the charge nurse helped her get into all the protective gown, gloves, and headgear. Maggie was taken into Sally's room, where Sally was intubated on a ventilator. A CRRT machine was providing continuous dialysis and IV fluids, and medications were dripping into a central venous catheter. Sally was sedated and not responsive. There was a foley catheter that led from under her bedsheets, but very little urine was in the collection bag.

Maggie was given a disposable stethoscope to examine the patient. She proceeded to pull back the covers on Sally, exposing a massive number of blisters; some had ruptured, and some were still distended with fluid that appeared to be filled with blood. When she pressed on Sally's right upper abdomen, the patient groaned as if in pain.

Sally had swelling of her lower extremities, but it was not confined to her legs. Her face appeared to be bloated and puffy from the excess fluid. The dialysis machine was removing fluid each hour, which would likely help correct this fluid imbalance.

After completing her exam, Maggie was escorted to a different area to remove the protective gear and rejoined Dr. Perkins. "Well," she began, "this certainly looks like the

Ebola patients we've taken care of. This disease simply causes a massive shutdown of internal organs, and the blisters she has are so typical of our patients as well. I would suggest we try to get the experimental treatment that was successful with our third patient, and the sooner the better. This disease will destroy all her organs. I'll call Dr. Jamie Sessions with the CDC, who helped us get the treatment for our patient."

"We would really appreciate that," said Andrew. "We are doing everything we can think of, but I fear that without something like that treatment, we have no hope she'll survive."

"Do we have any information on her contacts or travels?" Maggie asked.

"She has girlfriends, and I thought we could contact her office and find out where she's traveled. Do you think that would help?"

"Yes, especially her recent travels. This may give us a clue on her exposure plus who she might have exposed."

"Let's call her boss now and see if he has that information," Andrew suggested. He dialed Grandview Wealth Management and reached the receptionist, explaining that he was Dr. Perkins caring for Sally Schneider.

"Oh, Doctor, we are so upset that Sally is this sick," the receptionist said. "Jack, her boss, I know will want to talk with you. Let me put you through to him."

When the intercom buzzed, Aaron Davis picked up the phone. "Aaron Davis, can I help you?"

"Mr. Davis, my name is Dr. Andrew Perkins, and I'm here with Dr Margaret Hamilton. We're here seeing one of your employees, Sally Schneider. We can't really disclose much of her medical problems because of the privacy act, but can you tell us about her recent travels working for your company?"

"We have been worried sick about her. We just pray she

will make it through this. She is not only a beautiful girl; she's extremely bright and has been one of our best employees ever. Let me check our calendar and see if I can give you some idea where she's been."

Andrew and Maggie heard him clicking through the pages on his computer, and eventually he returned to the phone.

"Here we are. She was in Connecticut on Monday for two days; then traveled to New York City for two days; and finally, Cleveland for two days before flying home."

"Did she report to you any symptoms of being ill?" Andrew asked.

"No, not at all. You probably know that she's a health nut and has a perfect diet, plus she exercises all the time. She never takes time off for any illness."

"Do you think she would have met with anyone from a Third World country?" Andrew asked.

"Not that I'm aware of. All our clients are Americans. We don't deal with investors outside of the United States."

"Could you fax us her schedule so can peruse it further?" Maggie asked. "We may get a clue where she might have gotten this disease. From your recollection, was she ever in Chicago?"

"No, hasn't been in Chicago for months. I'll send the fax right over. And please tell Sally how much we're thinking of her."

"We'll certainly do that," Maggie said, knowing that Sally was in no condition to hear anything.

After hanging up, Maggie turned to Andrew. "That schedule is going to be very important for us to look at. See if we can identify any contacts that could have exposed her to Ebola. In the meantime, I'll call my friend Jamie, and we'll try to get Zendenivir. It worked well for our other patient."

"We're so grateful that you've made the trip here," Andrew said. "Let us know if there is anything else we can do."

Maggie left the hospital and headed for her hotel, mulling over in her mind where this young girl could have contracted the disease. When she got back to her hotel room, she reached out to Jamie.

"Hey, Jamie, it's Maggie. I've seen the patient here, and she has all the hallmarks of the disease. Very sick like the others. I was wondering if you would be able to get Zendenivir for her. This will likely be her only chance of survival."

"I should be able to. I'll call tonight and get working on it."

"How's your patient?" Maggie asked.

"He's a man in his fifties. He does a lot of traveling. He's self-employed and sells insurance. His wife says that he will be on the road for several days at a time. She wasn't sure where he had traveled recently and was going to check with his secretary. His symptoms and exam are like your patient, and he is also very sick. I'm sure they both will have the disease. Have you seen the media camped out here? They are lined up in full force."

"I suspect they haven't heard about this case yet, but I'm sure it won't be long. I'm planning on heading home tomorrow, unless you think I should stay."

"You wanna get back to your honey?" Jamie chided her.

"Well, there may be something to that, but I also need to get back to my patients. The physicians here seem very capable of caring for this girl."

The news media were set up in the parking lot outside Hollywood Memorial Hospital. A makeshift stage had been erected, and the hospital administrator and public relations director, along with Jamie Sessions, were standing waiting to take questions.

The first came from a CNN reporter. "Mr. Campbell, can you tell us the status of your patient? Does he have Ebola?"

"We are not able to disclose the patient's name, and we don't have final confirmation on his disease, but we have a physician from the CDC who I believe can answer this question the best."

Jamie stepped forward. "My name is Dr. Jamie Sessions. I just arrived last night, but I have had a chance to examine the patient, and it does appear that he has all the hallmarks of the disease. We should have confirmation within forty-eight hours if this is the case. We're exploring where the patient has been over the last seven to ten days to see if we can pinpoint where he might have contracted the disease. His secretary is going to get us his itinerary so we can try to establish a point of contact."

A Fox News reporter was next to ask a question. "We have just been told that there may be another case in Philadelphia. Is this true?"

"I have sent a good friend and colleague to investigate that case, and you are correct, it does appear that this young lady may also have the disease."

"So do we have an explanation as to how we have five people, three in Chicago, one in Philadelphia, and one in Florida contracting this disease?" another reporter called out.

"I'm afraid we don't have a good answer," Jamie said. "We do have the FBI working on the contacts from our first three cases, and these last two cases have just surfaced, so we haven't had time to really look into their travels or contacts thoroughly, but we are intending to do that."

"Do you think that someone is intentionally infecting these people?" came a final question.

"We have no evidence of that," Jamie replied, "but we are certainly keeping all options open."

The media disbursed, but there was great unease amongst the reporters. They were mumbling and talking amongst themselves about how frightening this was, with no known source of the infections. The following day, the anxiety was reflected in the stock market. A CNBC reporter commented about the stock futures as Jamie listened in her hotel room.

"We are seeing a lot of red occurring this morning," a downtrodden business reporter stated. "It appears that the reports of Ebola in Chicago, Philadelphia, and Florida are causing a great deal of worry among investors. The impact that could take place on the financial markets could be substantial, and at the opening today, we expect markets will be down about eight hundred points. I suspect it's the uncertainty of the source that is creating this anxiety."

Jamie thought to herself, *those investors aren't alone. I'm worried too. How can we have multiple cases and no clear connecting thread between them?*

Maggie got her bags packed and called an Uber to get to the airport. She checked one more time with Dr. Perkins to see how the young girl was doing, and he informed her that she appeared to be holding her own. Jamie had texted that the

Zendenivir had been approved; it would most likely arrive the next day. Like Jamie, Maggie was mulling it all over in her mind, trying to find a link between the new patients with the disease and her patients in Chicago. There just didn't seem to be any relationship that was apparent.

When she arrived at the airport, she checked her bag and made her way to the gate. As she was walking, she saw parts of the interview that Jamie had given the night before. The business reporter then gave a bleak outlook for the stock market, blaming the falling numbers on the Ebola cases that now had occurred in three different cities.

Like Jamie, Maggie was feeling a great deal of uncertainty wondering where any new cases might pop up. These all seemed to be very random. After reaching the gate, she decided to give Mack a call before boarding. He answered after only two rings.

"Hey, Mack, how are things back home?" she asked. "I'm through here and coming back early. This young girl looks like all the others, and I'm sure this will be Ebola as well. Jamie has Zendenivir on the way for her. Have you found anything?"

"Well, it seems that Mrs. Lee has been having any affair with a man named Jason Turley," Mack replied. "We found his number in their cell phone and texted him as if we were Frank. I think he about had a heart attack and responded that he didn't know us, but on retexting posing as Susan Lee, he opened up, and it seems apparent that there is a sexual connection between them."

He continued, "Susan Lee was in the hospital in Cleveland overnight, but we discovered that she left against medical advice. She just left the hospital without telling anyone. She had told the doctor that she had to get to her dying mother. This seems odd, because their employee said they were taking a vacation. We're still not sure where they're going now; we can't track them, since they ditched the phone. We may pay our new friend Jason a visit and see if we can find anything more out, but we don't want the Lees to catch on that we're following if they are planning a devious plot."

"Wow, it appears you've learned a lot. Can you think of any connection between these two new people who are infected? They both are travelers for their job, so we are trying to get the locations they've been to recently. If we trace their paths, we may find where they are interlinked. I'm trying to get the schedule for the man in Florida. It's surprising, but his wife seems to have no clue where he has been recently. The young girl is single, very career-oriented, and her boss got us her schedule. She has been to Connecticut, New York, and then Cleveland before flying home. Once we get the schedule of the man, we'll compare them."

"See, you're becoming an investigator like me," Mack responded. "Since this young lady was in Cleveland and the Lees were there at the same time, I'm guessing there is a good chance we're going to find they interacted, likely at the same hotel. We should know soon."

He added, "The home office is starting to get more interested in all this, by the way, as they see random cases popping up. The president is worried about fear leading to panic and a major crisis. The big boss wants me reporting to him directly. I think they sent the junior guy anticipating that this was going to be nothing, but now this case is high up on the radar."

"I have all the confidence in the world that you can solve the mystery," Maggie assured him. "But in addition to the confidence I have in you, I can't wait to get home and see you. Sorry, I have to run; they're boarding the plane now."

"Love you, Maggie. Travel safely."

CHAPTER 21

Frank and Susan checked into a Courtyard Marriott in Baltimore. Frank felt Susan needed to rest up before they made the final leg of their trip to Washington, DC. Susan was glad to have stopped. She was starting to swell in her ankles and was exhausted.

"Thanks, Frank, for stopping," she said. "I really appreciate how thoughtful you've been, thinking of my condition. I'm sorry that I got myself into this mess. I know this is creating a problem for everyone. Hopefully we can carry out the mission and disappear."

"That's probably what's going to happen," Frank agreed. "You'll need to rest up tonight, but the next few days are going to be busy."

When Maggie arrived back in Chicago, she went immediately to her home to drop off her suitcase and then went to the hospital. James Singleton was improving daily. He was still kept in isolation, but he was allowed to walk the halls in the biocontainment area with help from the staff. Maggie was going to have to make a decision as to when he could come out of isolation.

The media appeared to have less interest now in the patients in Chicago and were more focused on Philadelphia and Florida. That was just fine with her, and certainly with Tuttle as well, although she was convinced, he did like having the limelight. Right now, she was eager to find Mack. Although she'd only been gone for two days, she already missed seeing him. She found him in the control room with the other agents.

"Mack how are you and the other agents doing?" she asked. "Any new clues? There is increasing pressure now nationally to find the source. With these new cases, everyone is getting nervous. Have you called Mrs. Lee's lover?"

"Not yet, but today may be the day. Our only concern is if he is involved in a plot, could he tip them off and they would get away or do something more destructive? Nevertheless, we think we need to speak with him. Anything new from your standpoint?"

"The secretary of the patient in Philadelphia got us information on her travels," Maggie told him. "Jamie is calling now to tell me about the Florida patient. Let me take this. Hey, Jamie, any news? … OK, so our patient in Florida had gone to Atlanta, Charlotte, Cleveland, and then home. Wait, so they were both in Cleveland? We need to find out where they stayed while they were there. As soon as you find out, call me back."

Closing her cell phone, she turned to Mack. "So, they crossed paths in Cleveland. Now the question will be, where in Cleveland?"

"How about the Choice Hotel, across the street from the hospital?" said Mack. "That's where we tracked the Lee's cell phone. Let's call the hotel now and see if they were there."

Mack picked up his phone and searched for the phone number of the hotel. He dialed the number and got the receptionist.

"Excuse me," he began. "My name is Matthew Johnson, an FBI agent, and I'm inquiring whether a Sally Schneider and a Tom Simpson stayed at your hotel recently?"

"I will need to check with my manager if I can give this information out. We may be restricted from doing that."

Her phone was placed on hold, and Mack could hear music and an advertisement for the hotel for what seemed like an eternity. Eventually, a male voice came on the line.

"Mr. Johnson, I'm the manager of the hotel. We're a little reluctant to release this information. Could you tell me why you need to know this?"

"First off, I can give you the bureau's phone number so you can check with them to assure you that I am an FBI agent. I can't describe too many details, but both these individuals may have Ebola, which they contracted a short time after leaving your hotel. The real concern is whether they may have acquired this disease *at* your hotel."

"How could they have gotten that disease in our hotel?" the manager asked.

"That's what we would like to know. Does your receptionist remember them at all?"

"Just a moment, and I'll put her on."

After a click, the young girl was back on the line. "I'm not one hundred percent sure," she said. "We have many people coming and going from our hotel, but I would have been working in the morning when they would have checked out."

"I believe the older gentleman was in his fifties, travels a lot, a little on the heavy side, according to my colleagues," Mack told her.

"I think I know that person. He uses our hotel frequently.

He's always very pleasant and never complains. He has told me that the traveling all the time doesn't help his waistline. I think he may have been in the fitness center before leaving."

"And the girl reportedly is very fit. Works out all the time. She's twenty-eight years old. I believe she's quite attractive."

"Oh sure, she also has been here before. She checked out I believe the same day. Are they all right?"

"Not really," Mack replied. "They're actually fighting for their life, and we're trying to track down where they may have contracted their disease. Could I speak to your manager again?"

"Sure."

After a short pause, the manager was back on the line. "So, what do you think?" he asked.

"We need to send some personnel to your hotel to do an inspection and see if we can find the source. Are you OK with this?"

"We will cooperate in any way," the manager assured him.

After getting off the phone, Mack contacted the home office of the FBI and spoke with the director. "Mr. Jamison, this is Matthew Johnson. You asked me to keep you posted on the status of our investigation. I've just gotten off the phone with the manager of a hotel in Cleveland. Our two latest people that appear to be infected with the virus both stayed at this hotel. In addition, the people we have been tracking here in Chicago may have also stayed at the hotel. We're checking on that and we believe they left the same day. So, we're getting concerned that there may be a connection between all these individuals. In particular, the Lees, who we have been watching. They have been traveling east, but we don't know their final destination. We're getting more concerned that they may be intentionally infecting people. Regarding the hotel, I would like to send a team there and have medical people skilled in analyzing the situation see if the virus was released somewhere in the hotel."

"Listen, Johnson, you let me know what you need," the director replied. "The country is on the verge of a collapse over this. I've checked with the CIA to see if we could detect any chatter from terrorists, but there hasn't been any specific data to suggest any terrorist group is involved—but that doesn't mean it isn't happening. What do you need from me?"

"I think a team from the CDC who can culture and look for the virus in the hotel. I'm not sure it can be detected now, but we need to see if we can find anything. We have been working with Dr. Jamie Sessions, and I believe she would be a good choice. In addition, Dr. Margaret Hamilton, an infectious diseases specialist here, should be a part of this evaluation as well. She has been on top of this problem and has been involved intimately with the cases in Chicago and Philadelphia. I believe she should come with us to give her opinion."

"Absolutely," the director agreed. "I will assemble people here to get all the necessary protective gear. In the meantime, the hotel needs to shut down and be evacuated until we can clear the building and ensure no one will catch the disease."

"Thank you, Mr. Jamison," Mack replied.

"Just call me Herb."

"Maggie, we need to go to the Choice Hotel," Mack told her. "Repack those bags and see if Jamie can meet us there. I'll call the manager back and let him know that the hotel must be closed for now."

"Yes, boss, I'll get right on it," she said, smiling, as she saluted him. "I'll call Jamie. She'll be interested in hearing about this."

Maggie immediately dialed Jamie and told her about the conversation with the hotel manager. "Jamie, you need to meet us at the hotel. We'll have protective gear, and with the hotel shut down, we'll be able to examine it carefully and see if we can discover anything. Do you think it's possible to detect the virus anywhere in the hotel?"

Jamie thought about it for a moment. "Normally, the disease is spread by body fluids, but there have been reports of aerosolized droplets attaching to solid surfaces that may spread the disease. Especially if the virus has been modified to make it more transmissible."

Maggie replied, "We can't take any chances when we're there, and we'll need to try to find an obvious place that could be the source of the infection for our latest patients."

"I'll get packed and catch up with you there tomorrow."

While Susan was showering, Frank made a call to Samuel on the new cell phone to get an update on directives. This was their last stop before going to DC and the final destination. Both were anxious as they anticipated their most difficult assignment. They knew the FBI was likely closing in and time was running out.

"Samuel, it's Frank. We're in Baltimore and getting close to the target. Do you have any additional information that you can give us as to our next steps? You haven't provided the target yet, and I wondered if this would be the time."

"Here's what you are to do," Samuel told him. "You should check into the Capital Hilton. Rest up and visit with the concierge about tourist sites in Washington, DC, that you could visit, explaining that your wife is pregnant and you won't be able to walk long distances. Conclude the conversation stating that you have always wanted to visit the White House. Let him know that you've been able to get a tour scheduled through your senator. We have this lined up for the day after you arrive. Fortunately, the delay in the hospital did not cause a problem.

"Find out where you would need to go to be a part of the tour. Taking the vials into the White House is going to be tricky. You'll need to figure out a way to slip them in, since handbags and lotions are not allowed.

"Before arriving in Washington, DC, you'll need to put on disguises. We need you to change your appearances completely. I would suggest that you add a mustache and maybe a goatee or beard. Put on those glasses that you have. Susan should wear a wig, becoming a blonde; use a lot of makeup; and try to disguise the pregnancy as best she can. She could use sunglasses to further change her face appearance, or better yet, wear glasses as well. I know that you have disguises with you that you have used in the past very successfully."

Frank nodded. "We had planned to do this all along. So, the target is the White House?"

"Yes," Samuel confirmed. "If that changes, I will notify you. We will have an escape plan for you, as I've told you. Before you leave to deploy the package, I'll get you details for the escape plan. I would leave your bags in your car the day of the event and take an Uber to the area.

"Oh, and by the way, we want you to stop at Johnny's Used Cars and swap out cars. He'll be happy to take over yours for one of his, believe me. We've worked with him before, and he will be discreet and keep you anonymous. He'll probably try to negotiate the price, but he knows that there's a limit to his price-gouging. We've made that clear to him before. I'm going to text you the directions how to get there."

Maggie and Mack made it to the airport after gathering clothes to take on the trip. The other agents were staying behind, pursuing any information they could find on the Lees and Jason Turley. The FBI agents from the Cleveland office and a hazmat team were being assembled, and they would be helping Mack when he arrived at the Choice Hotel. The flight was quick, and after gathering their bags, they took a taxi to a Hampton Inn close to the Choice Hotel. After they had checked into their rooms, Maggie met Mack in his.

"Do we really need two rooms?" she enquired. "Maybe it's a waste of government money."

"We have to keep it this way for now," Mack said ruefully. "That is, until I get through all this case. Then we can move in a different direction."

"I understand," Maggie assured him. "I just enjoy being with you. You have turned my life upside down. I don't know if you even recognize that."

"I understand that completely because it has been the same for me. Why don't we have a glass of wine from the bar downstairs and discuss our strategy for tomorrow? I'm getting more and more concerned about the Lees. This isn't looking good to me. There are just too many coincidences."

"All right, party pooper. You know I like wine, and you're right we need to have a plan for tomorrow. How about I get the wine and get out a tablet so we can write down the steps we want to take?"

Maggie found her way to the elevator. On the lobby level was a small bar where you could purchase wine and charge it to the room. She picked out a Chardonnay for her and a Cabernet for Mack. As she was carrying the wine upstairs, Maggie began to wonder what the rationale for poisoning people would be. *Why would you give a deadly virus like Ebola to people you don't even know? Is there an intent to create pandemonium? Moreover, who are these people?*

Back at the room, she saw Mack at the table with papers spread out. He had placed headings at the top of each page.

"I didn't know you were so compulsive," she said.

"I thought that you would be surprised," he chuckled. "As an agent, I try to think of every scenario. It's best to take the emotion out of the project and look at the facts. That way, you don't cloud your thinking and miss something that is obvious. I've put down several pieces of paper to write on. Let's start with this one: how would someone spread the virus if they had an evil thought of infecting others?"

"Well, most of the time the virus is spread by bodily fluids of an infected patient, but here we don't have an infected individual lying out in broad daylight with oozing wounds teaming with the virus. So if you took serum that was super-concentrated with the virus—a virus that was particularly virulent—and managed to spread it throughout a room, it could deposit on surfaces. If the person touching that surface had any crack in their skin, maybe the virus could enter their body. I discussed this with Jamie, and she said there are a few reports that the virus might spread by droplets, but this isn't the usual method where another person gets the disease."

Mack mused, "It would seem if the people that we know were in this hotel and both got infected, they would have to have been in the same location to contract the illness. There were many other guests, yet we haven't heard of anyone else with the disease."

"True, but maybe they simply haven't been diagnosed as of yet."

"Sure, but this is a deadly disease. They don't just get the sniffles. They end up in an emergency room deathly ill and have all the hallmarks of this illness. With all the news channels talking about this, I suspect emergency rooms have a heightened awareness to look for it."

"You're probably right," said Maggie. "That's how we heard about these cases. So now we have to ask the question: Why only two people? Why not more?"

"I'm guessing it's because these people were in some space together."

"That makes sense," said Maggie. "Do you think they were having an affair?"

"I doubt it," Mack responded. "From your description of these people, it would seem they wouldn't really fit together at all, but who knows? I would suggest we try to identify a common space where they may have been. We can look at their rooms, but I wouldn't think that they would have acquired the infection in their room, since others in the hotel were spared from the disease."

"So, tomorrow, let's look at common spaces," said Maggie. "Well, we have a common space now, and I doubt that I will get infected. After all, I'm an infectious diseases specialist, and I look out for infections and avoid catching them myself."

With that, Maggie pulled off her blouse, removed her bra, and pushed Mack onto the bed. She had been blessed with her mother's full figure, which men had always admired. After thirty minutes of making love, they both decided that they should sleep in their own beds that night, even though many people knew of their close relationship. Maggie returned to her room content and sleepy, thinking, *I'm going to sleep great tonight.*

CHAPTER 22

The next morning, everyone gathered at the entrance to the Choice Hotel. There were signs on the door stating that the hotel was closed. The manager was there with a key, and the receptionist Mack had talked to had come as requested so they could ask any additional questions. The hazmat team began putting on their clothing.

Jamie had arrived late the night before, so she was the last to make it to the hotel. "Well, guys, what do you think we're going to find here?" she asked.

"That's a good question," Maggie replied. "Mack and I talked about this last night, and we concluded that for only two people to get infected and being in separate rooms, they must have been in some common space where the virus existed. We thought we should explore these spaces first, since this would make the most sense."

"I've got that," Jamie agreed. "I have some of our team members here, and they have the resources to obtain cultures. It's still not certain how lucky we will be in culturing the virus from an object. It isn't clear if it can spread in this way, but we'll find out."

Everyone put on protective gear and proceeded to enter the hotel. The manager and receptionist were instructed to remain outside and be available to answer questions. Before they entered the hotel, the manager mentioned that the fitness center had been closed for maintenance.

"Here is the reception area, obviously," Mack pointed out as he entered. "There appears to be a small dining room where breakfast is served." He turned to the others and said, "Maggie and I will check out the indoor pool and the fitness center on the second floor."

"This is going to be hit and miss, but we may be fortunate and find something," Jamie responded.

After arriving on the second floor, they inspected the pool area. "I wonder how often the pool would be used?" Maggie asked Mack.

"Probably not very often. Most of the guests likely stay only one or maybe two nights and are probably business travelers. If they are here more than one night, they may use these amenities. But they don't have time if they're here only for business," Mack answered. "The manager said that the fitness center was closed, but the receptionist mentioned that the gentleman had used the fitness center. He complained that he gained weight by being on the road all the time and not getting any exercise. We need to check this area out."

On entering, they could hear a noise in the ventilation fan. "I wonder if the problem was in the ventilation system. Hey, Joe, call down to the manager and ask him if the ventilation system was an issue," Mack asked of a fellow agent.

In a short time, the agent got back to him.

"He states there was a problem with the fan for the ventilation system, and it actually was around the time that your guests stayed here. That hadn't occurred to him until just now. He said they were going to have a heating and air-conditioning company check it out, but they hadn't been in to fix it, so they've kept the fitness center closed."

Mack and Maggie could hear the fan running, but there was an unusual sound, as if something were caught in a garbage disposal or maybe a rock was being thrown about. Mack directed the hazmat team to remove the grate over the vent. They found a switch on the thermostat to turn the fan off.

As the grate was removed, they shined flashlights into the area. There, lying at the base of the vent, were small pieces of glass that had obviously shattered. On the inside wall was a blackened area that had the appearance of soot or smoke.

"What do you make of it?" Mack enquired of an agent next to him. "Do you think that there was something made of glass in this area?"

"It looks like broken glass to us, and the blackened area may be from an explosive."

Mack turned to the other agents and asked them to take samples of the black material on the wall. He asked Maggie to get Jamie to come up to the second floor and look at this.

"She will need to bring her team," he advised.

In a short time, they arrived.

"Jamie, what do you think of this?" said Mack. "There are pieces of glass in this venting system, and there is a black discoloration on the inside wall. We're going to test this for explosive material. Maybe a vial exploded, threw the virus in liquid form into the air, and the fan directed it into this space."

"That makes some sense," Jamie responded. "We may have luck culturing inside this space, since it would likely have a dense collection of viruses, if that were the case."

Jamie's team diligently took samples in several areas in the ventilation duct. They also took samples from the handles of the equipment, but they were less confident that these cultures would provide an answer.

"Let's find out the room numbers of our two patients who stayed here," Mack said. "Jamie let's get samples from their rooms as well. How long do you think until we get the results?"

She replied, "It will likely take two or three days. I'll call Maggie with the results as soon as I know."

"Maggie," said Mack, "I think we're through here. Let's check out of our hotel and head home."

As they got into an Uber to go back to the hotel, Mack turned to Maggie and said, "I'm concerned that we need to be moving faster. If the Lees are releasing the virus intentionally, and if they plan to do this again somewhere else, we need to find them now and stop them. Without the ability to track their phone, we don't know where they may be going, and we're losing time waiting for the cultures. I think we have enough concern that we need to get an order to search their house. I'm going to get the central office to help with this. This also may be the time to meet the boyfriend. We have to find out his involvement in a plot if there is one."

Mack opened his cell phone and called Jamison. He got the man's secretary initially, but when he identified himself, he was immediately put through to the director.

"Johnson, what do you have?" Herb Jamison asked gruffly.

"Mr. Jamison, we have found possibly the source of the Ebola at the hotel in Cleveland. We won't know the results of the cultures or the testing for two or three days. But I have enough concern about the Lees that I believe we need to search their house. You probably remember they had stayed at this hotel at the same time the two latest infected people were also here. They're traveling east, but we don't know their final destination. If they are intending to spread the virus again, we need to track them down and stop them. Can you get me a search warrant for their house?"

"Absolutely. We need to get on this and now. You'll have the warrant in two hours. Have your agents send me their information and address."

"Perfect. We should be back to Chicago in about three hours, and I can arrange to get into their house then."

Susan had gotten dressed, and Frank had their bags packed. They didn't want to put on disguises until they got closer to Washington, DC—plus, when they checked out, they wanted their appearance to be no different than when they checked in.

Susan waited in the room while Frank got the luggage loaded in the car. After he came back to the room, he helped her to the elevator and to the car. He again had paid for the room with cash, so he simply turned in his key and thanked the receptionist for the great hospitality at the hotel. He had estimated that it was only going to take them about an hour to get to DC, but he knew that the traffic could be brutal, so he anticipated it would likely take longer. They were going to take their time.

As they were traveling, Frank turned to Susan and said, "So, what are you thinking now? We're getting close to the target and the date to deliver the final package."

"Which package?" she asked. "The virus or the baby?"

"The virus, of course. But I know that you have your mind on the baby."

"Wouldn't you if you looked like this?"

"Probably."

"I'm just wondering what is going to happen to the baby,"

she said. "What if we have to leave? Do I take the baby with me? Does Jason get the baby? Will we have time after the deployment of the package to get back home, or are we going to our real home? This is what's on my mind. I'm getting tired of what we do here. I have to admit that I've grown to like the United States. It is so different from China. People are nice. You're free to say what you want, do what you want, and go where you want. We haven't enjoyed these kinds of freedoms back home. Knowing what we do, we're supposed to find people to disclose secrets to us, or we are to snitch on our fellow Chinese who may be keeping something from the government. If that happens, we never see them again. Is that how you like to live?"

"I wouldn't talk like that, Huan," Frank warned her. "That could get you in trouble."

"That's my point," Susan replied. "Here, it doesn't get me in trouble, but in China I might disappear. Don't you see?"

"Yes," Frank said. "I get your point. But our society is controlled. Here, things can get out of control, especially if you let everyone say whatever they want."

"It doesn't seem out of control to me," Susan exclaimed. "In fact, people here are happier. If they have an idea and work hard, they succeed. In our country, they're discouraged from doing many things because they don't have the freedom to do them and don't enjoy the successes if they do."

"You're starting to talk like an American," Frank cautioned.

"Maybe I am. I guess I may have become an American, and I like their way of life."

"For now, that can't be," Frank instructed her. "We need to finish this job."

"I know. You're right. Doesn't mean I can't dream."

Maggie and Mack landed in Chicago and hurried to baggage claim. Mack got on his cell phone to contact his team. He had texted them about the search warrant.

"Do you have the warrant?" he asked. "As soon as I drop off my bags at home, I will get to the hospital, and we'll go to their house. They may have a security system, and if they do, it could alert them to an alarm. If so, we need to have a way to quickly disconnect it. Any ideas?"

Tim replied, "If they have a sign for ADT or one of the other security companies, we can call them and have it paused while we're in there. I think we should probably wear hazmat gear just in case."

"I agree," said Mack. "Get that ready so we can go there as soon as I arrive. Maggie will come along as well so she can identify any lab material that could be there."

Mack arranged for the driver to drop Maggie off first at her house and then take him to his hotel room. "I'll meet you at the hospital, Maggie," he told her. "Just go to our control center, and then we can head to the Lees' home."

"Sure, Mack. It won't take me long. I'll just freshen up a bit."

"Well, you look fresh to me right now, but whatever. See you then."

Maggie unloaded her clothes quickly, put them away, and applied some new makeup. She heard her cell phone chirp, indicating a message. It came from Dr. Perkins in Philadelphia. He told her the Zendenivir had arrived, and he had given it to Sally Schneider. She was apparently already showing some improvement, and he wanted Maggie to know. Maggie smiled as she read the message. *That feels good just to hear*

that. I hope this young girl can pull through. If anyone can, it would seem she could. She has been in excellent health.

Maggie jumped in her car and sped to the hospital, then hurried to the control center. Doing this investigative work had become fun. It really seemed, in a sense, like to trying to solve a patient's illness, but now finding an answer that could save many people's lives. When she got to the control room, all the agents were there and ready to go.

"Am I late?" she asked.

"Nope, just getting started," Mack assured her. "Grab your gear and we'll head out. This should be interesting going through their house."

The agents rode in a black van that the department had provided. Mack rode with Maggie in her car. The Lees' home was about five miles from the hospital in an upscale middle-income area. The house appeared very ordinary. It was partially brick and partially siding painted light blue. The house had about thirty-five hundred square feet of living space, with three bedrooms upstairs and a basement. There was a two-car garage.

The agents decided to go through the front door. There was no sign for a security system, so they hoped they wouldn't hear an alarm on entering. The lock was easily picked.

"Here we go, guys," Mack said as he opened the front door. Immediately, there was a high-decibel screech that felt like it would rupture their eardrums.

"Shit," Mack said as the alarm permeated the house. "Call the police and let them know what's going on. Now the question is whether the Lees will know that we're here. Let's hope this alarm stops soon. It could drive us all crazy." He grimaced. "Let's get started and go upstairs first."

The alarm finally stopped, and the agents went through every drawer looking for any sign of a conspiracy or information about Ebola virus, but nothing suspicious was found. After concluding there was nothing of interest, they moved to the main level and went through the kitchen and closets, looking again for any evidence of a plot to cause harm.

"So far, Mack, this looks like a normal household: food, clothes, books, but nothing that seems out of the ordinary," John noted.

"One last place to go," Mack pointed out. "The basement. Let's see if this reveals anything."

They found a light switch and cautiously moved down the stairs to a finished basement. There they found a recreation room with a pool table and a TV with a couch and soft chairs. But there was an adjoining room that was locked.

"Tim, we need you to pick this lock so we can get into this room. It's locked," Mack asked.

"Sure, Mack. No problem."

After several attempts, Tim was able to pick the lock and opened the door. It was dark and difficult to find a light switch, so Mack used his cell phone's light to look into the space.

"Oh my God," he exclaimed. "Look at this. There's a lab table, microscope, culture plates and media, a hood. Maggie, take a look."

"Holy cow, Mack. This is a full lab set-up. I think this gives you the answer you were seeking. They appear to have a full-service microbiology lab."

"There's a safe over here, Mack," Tim called out. "The door has been left open. It may have been used to store the virulent material. Maybe we should try to culture the surfaces."

"I suspect this is going to have a low yield," Maggie responded. "It has been days since they've left, and most likely the material was kept in a vial, not exposed to the space—unless, of course, they wanted to catch this disease themselves, which I think would be pretty unlikely."

"John, our next stop is going to be Jason Turley," said Mack. "He must know something about all this. Do you have his address? We need to bring him in for questioning."

"I can get it," John replied. "It's going to be interesting to talk to the boyfriend. I wonder what all he knows?"

CHAPTER 23

As Jason Turley arrived home, he noticed two black vans parked by the curb of his house. *Curious,* he thought. *I wonder who they are? I haven't seen these vehicles before.*

Pressing the garage-door opener, he maneuvered his BMW into the first garage slot. As he got out of the car, three men dressed in black suits approached.

"Can I help you?" he asked.

"Mr. Turley, I'm Agent Matthew Johnson with the FBI," Mack said as he flashed his credentials. "We need to speak to you about an issue that we are investigating. Would you like to talk at your home or at the FBI headquarters in Chicago?"

Nervously, Jason stuttered, "Well, I suppose here is fine. Can you tell me what this is about?"

"We will do that, but we need to ask you a few questions first. Why don't we go inside?"

Jason led the agents through his garage and into the kitchen to the living room. "Is this OK?" he asked.

"This is fine with us as long as you're comfortable."

Beads of sweat began to appear on Jason's forehead as he sat down. "So, am I in trouble?"

"We don't think so, but we need some information. Do you know the Lees?"

Jason squirmed in his chair, his face turned red, and he sheepishly answered, "I know Mrs. Lee."

"And how do you know her?"

"I met her in a bar about eight months ago."

"Are you more than just friends? Are you romantically involved?"

Looking at the floor with his head bowed, Jason nearly whispered, "Yes."

"What can you tell us about the Lees? Where did they come from? What do they do?"

"I don't know her husband very well," Jason admitted. "I just know who he is. I'm aware that they have a successful dry-cleaning and laundry business. They don't have children, but Susan, Mrs. Lee, is pregnant."

"Do you think that you are the father of the child?"

Again, with nervous agitation, Jason answered, "Yes."

"Has Mrs. Lee asked you to do anything for her?" Mack asked. "Has she ever discussed anything dealing with viruses?"

"Well," Jason said thoughtfully, "she was interested in my work at the Pentagon. We worked with bioweapons. I'm a financial guy, but I was familiar with the research going on, so she knew my connections with the federal government. She would ask me about my work there. She would ask about where in the government I worked. Did I have any contact with the bioweapon's investigators? What division did I work in? Things like that. She often would flatter me by telling me how I must have been very important. Why would you ask?"

"Are you aware that the Lees have a complete microbiology laboratory in their basement?"

"No," Jason replied. "I've never been in their house."

"Did Mrs. Lee ever mention an individual named Alex Williamson?"

"No. I don't believe I know that person. Wait a minute. Is he the young man who had Ebola?"

"Yes, that's him. We've been trying to find the source where he may have contracted this fatal virus. You're probably aware from news reports that he hadn't traveled to an endemic area where the virus exists, and he has had very few contacts with people in general, but we believe that he has had interactions with the Lees."

"Why would the Lees want to be connected with him?"

"That's what we would like to know," Mack replied. "Mr. Williamson was a viral lab technician; he died from Ebola, and he appeared to have frequent interactions with the Lees, who have a complete laboratory in their basement."

Puzzled, Jason looked straight ahead, trying to take all this information in.

Mack continued, "With your conversations with Mrs. Lee, did she ever ask you for anything?"

"Really, no," Jason began. "We have had a great relationship, and I'm in love with her. I've tried to convince her to leave her husband and marry me so we could raise the baby together, but she says it's too complicated right now for her to leave Frank."

"Has she asked you for any information of significance recently? Anything at all?"

"I can't think anything of importance. You probably know that they are on vacation right now."

"Yes, we are aware of that, but there has been some discrepancy about why they left. In one instance, they have told people that Susan's mother is desperately ill and on her deathbed. In other cases, they've simply said that they're vacationing. But many have thought that it would be a strange time to vacation at the end of a pregnancy."

"I had said the same thing," said Jason. "It didn't make much sense to me either. Because she is so pregnant, she asked if I had any access to the floor plans of the federal buildings in Washington, DC. I used to work in the Pentagon and have several friends in DC. I was able to get floor plans for many of the buildings for her so she could choose paths that would lessen the amount of walking that she would have to do."

"Could you tell us which buildings?" Mack asked.

"I can print them off again, because they were sent to me by my friend—but as I recall, they included the Smithsonian museums, the capitol, the Lincoln and Jefferson memorials, and the White House. Maybe a few more."

"Do you know where the Lees came from?" Mack asked.

"No, I don't, but China originally, of course. That's something we never talked about."

"Well, you have been very helpful. We would just ask that you don't leave town, because we may have more questions for you. And we would like to get the list of all the building floor plans that you gave them."

"I'll send them over to you as soon as you can give me an email address."

As the agents left Jason's house, Mack turned to the others.

"I think we can all see that the Lees are setting out to do something very destructive," he began. "They appear to have no issue with infecting anyone with the virus. I would assume they are close to Washington, DC, by now if not already there. Tim, we need images of both of them and the make and license plate of their car. I'll get ahold of the home office in DC. We need to post their pictures everywhere and stop them before they do something worse than they've already done."

"Got it, boss," Tim answered. "I'll get right on it, and I'll send you their pictures in the next hour. I can get their license plate number and car description."

"It's too bad we can't track them now," Mack said. "I would think they would be checking into another hotel. Once we have their pictures, we should send them to every hotel in DC so if they check in, we can identify them."

"I can do that once Tim gets me the pictures," John responded.

"I'll call the director and fill him in," said Mack. "He wants to know everything. I suspect that this should fire him up. They're going to be in his backyard."

After getting back to the control room at Deaconess, the agents started working. Mack dialed Herb Jamison.

"Mr. Jamison. I have an update on the Ebola situation."

"Great, Johnson. We need to know what's going on. Did you find the contact that may have given the young man the virus?"

"We believe so, but we don't think this contact was infected. It's actually more concerning. You see, we believe that there is a couple that has been modifying the virus in a laboratory in their basement. They appeared to be using Alex, the young man who was infected, to make the changes in the virus. We believe that he may have accidentally gotten infected, but we can't be sure. We believe the Lees, Frank and

Susan, may have intended to take this very virulent virus, modify it, and release it specifically to infect people.

"We've been trying to find some background on the Lees, but we have been hitting a dead end. We can't seem to track their history back from Chicago. They pay for everything in cash, use no credit, and have no past history that we have been able to find. Quite frankly, Director, I'm concerned that they have plans to deliver the virus even more broadly to cause major problems in our capital. That is your backyard.

"They have been very good at avoiding us, but we have reason to believe they will be going to one or more of the government buildings and are likely carrying the virus with them. They seem to know what they are doing. The one thing that is against them is that Mrs. Lee is very pregnant and due anytime. This is likely slowing them down or causing them concern that it may interfere with their plans."

"My God," said Jamison. "Get me their images and any information that you have on them. I'll get the office here working on identifying them. Plus, we will put out an all-points bulletin to find them. We can't let them do this. I'm going to contact the White House and let the president know the situation. He's been very concerned and has been calling me almost daily. He's noticed the markets getting nervous and falling, and you know that presidents depend on a strong economy for favorable reviews from their constituents."

"Yes sir. We'll get this to you as soon as possible."

CHAPTER 24

Frank drove a short distance from the hotel and found Johnny's Used Car lot, as Samuel had directed. As he pulled in, Johnny came running out, ready to do business.

"So, I see you have a very nice Toyota Camry," he said. "Are you looking for another car?"

"Yes," Frank replied. "As you can see, my wife is pregnant, and we believe that we are going to need a larger vehicle when the baby arrives. What do you have that would be better for a family?"

"You've come to the right place!" Johnny exclaimed. "Over here is a very low-mileage minivan. Only two years old. It would be perfect for you. Plenty of room to haul that little one around and prepare for the next three children that you'll have."

Frank grimaced for a moment and then asked, "How many miles are on the vehicle?"

"Only ten thousand miles," Johnny told him. "It'll be just right. It's immaculate and only one previous owner."

"What are you asking for it?"

"Fourteen thousand five hundred dollars," Johnny said, "but I can make you a great deal on a trade-in. How many miles on your Camry?"

"Forty-five thousand miles. It's four years old."

"Let me do some calculating, and I'll get back with you in a minute."

As Johnny ran back to his small shack, Frank could see him looking at a computer and running numbers on a calculator. Soon he returned with a piece of paper in his hand.

"I can let this go for only ten thousand dollars."

"So you're only giving me forty-five hundred for my car?" Frank asked.

"Well, you do have quite a few miles on the car," Johnny pointed out. "The minivan has only ten thousand and is newer."

"That still seems too little for my car," Frank objected. "I'll give you nine thousand dollars, and you've got a deal."

"I'd be robbed at that price," Johnny protested. "I tell you what: we'll split the difference. Ninety-five hundred dollars, and the minivan is yours."

"Hmm. I'm not sure that the price is that great, but it is a nice vehicle, so I'll take it."

"How do you want to pay?" asked Johnny.

"I'm going to give you cash."

"Cash?" a bewildered Johnny said. "Your friends who told me you were coming always seem to pay in cash as well. Sure, why not. Are you into gambling? I normally don't get paid this way, but cash will be great."

"No, I'm not a gambler," said Frank. "I just don't like using any credit. You know it's always better to pay in cash and have no debt to anyone else."

"Should I just switch the plates?"

"I wonder if you can give me a thirty-day tag instead for

now," Frank said. "I may want to get another car for myself and use this license plate on that car."

"Whatever works is fine with me," said Johnny. "I can sell you another car right now!"

"Sorry," Frank said. "We both can't be driving."

After paying for the minivan, Frank carefully moved their luggage and their special package to the new vehicle. He shook Johnny's hand and thanked him. He then found the entrance to the interstate and started driving toward DC.

After driving a short distance, he found an exit to a rest area and pulled off of the highway, parking a considerable distance from any other car. He got out of the minivan and opened the tailgate, from which he removed a duffle bag. When he got back into the van, he turned to Susan.

"So, Susan, I've always wanted to see you as a blonde. Now's my chance." He handed over the wig. He also found glasses for both of them, a mustache for himself, and a wig also. Together they began to change their appearance as much as possible. They used a mirror to assess their success and turned to one another to get approval.

"Didn't you have a dress to change into that is very full in the front, potentially hiding the pregnant bump?" Frank asked.

"Yes, it's in my bag," said Susan. "Once I finish with the makeup, I can go into the restroom and change. I think it may just make me look somewhat fat, but even so, it's going to be hard to hide the pregnancy."

"I understand," Frank said, "but do the best you can. The target is the White House. We have to behave like interested tourists visiting the White House for the first time. Our tour time is three o'clock. With the floor plans we've gotten through Jason and Samuel, I've identified several spots to deploy the package, but it's going to be tricky. I know there are guards throughout, so one of us will be the scout while the other delivers our surprise. Since time is limited, we will need to consider doing this toward the end of the tour. Do you think you're up to this?"

"Listen," Susan said, "I've been through much worse. I can handle it."

After finishing applying the disguises, they started down the highway toward Washington, DC.

Mack received the photos from Tim and immediately forwarded them to Jamison. He also sent copies to every hotel in the DC area and had the other agents call the managers of the hotels asking them to have their personnel watch for these individuals. Tim was put in charge of calling.

"Can I have the manager of the hotel?" Tim inquired.

After a pause, the manager of the Capital Hilton came on the line. "May I help you?"

"My name is Tim Scott. I'm an agent with the FBI. We expect a man and wife to check into some hotel in Washington, DC, and we're not certain which hotel. They are people of interest who we're concerned may conduct a terrorist attack. We've forwarded their picture to you. Their names are Susan and Frank Lee, but they may register under an alias.

"We don't know which day they may be checking into your hotel or another in the DC area. It is possible they are there already. We would appreciate having your personnel keep an eye out for them, and if they're seen, I'm going to give you an 800 number to call. We will want to know immediately if you identify them. We wouldn't want you to reach out to them. They could be dangerous."

Nervously, the manager responded, "I will talk to our employees and let them know the situation. I'll have them report to me immediately if they spot this couple, and then I will call you. Thank you, Agent Scott, for alerting us to this. We will do our best to keep an eye out."

After hanging up, the manager asked to have all his employees come to the small conference room in the hotel. The cleaning personnel, receptionists, dining employees, and maintenance men gathered around a conference table. The manager, with a serious look, began the conversation.

"Ladies and gentlemen, we have a situation here that could be a very big problem. I've been alerted by the FBI that there is a couple that will be checking into a DC hotel. This couple may have terrorist intentions. Although their names are Frank and Susan Lee, they may register under another name. I'm passing around their pictures so you will know what they look like. If you identify them, I want to be notified immediately. It is possible that they have already checked in. The agent who just called me wasn't sure if they were already here or not, so please be on the lookout, even with our current guests. They could be here or at another hotel. Thank you for your diligence. We're so fortunate to have great employees, and I know that if they are here, we will find them."

The manager concluded his remarks, and the employees began exiting the room. Many were talking amongst themselves as they left. Randy from maintenance looked at his fellow employee.

"I feel like I'm back in the Marines trying to find the

snipers in Afghanistan," he said. "You would never know who might be a suicide bomber. Maybe a young girl. This should be interesting if they decide to stay at our hotel."

Herb Jamison put together a series of FBI agents to provide additional surveillance of all the federal sites. Each agent had a copy of Frank's and Susan's pictures, and all knew to look for a red Toyota Camry with an Illinois license plate number 071-306. The agents were to be in plainclothes so as not to give an indication that they were FBI. He encouraged them for once not to wear the typical dark suit and sunglasses but to look more like a tourist.

"Gentlemen, we have a serious challenge here," he began. "These people are dangerous. We don't know their background, but they've already demonstrated a willingness to deliver a fatal virus to unsuspecting people, and we believe they will be here in DC with plans to do something even worse. We don't know their target and we don't know their background, but they are clearly skilled at what they do and appear to have the resources to carry out a significant attack."

Mark, one of the agents in the back, stood up. "Are they armed?" he asked.

"We don't know, but I think we have to treat them as if they are. We're not sure if they're working for another country, but we have to believe they are. They wouldn't have been able to pull together these kinds of resources without a network worldwide and money to back it. It's my understanding that they speak perfect English and may be Americans. They likely appear to be the all-American couple. And by the way, the lady is very pregnant. This is probably the most important thing in our favor. She isn't going to be moving fast. We think that could have been a slip on their part. If spotted, I would call in reinforcements before going after them. They are dangerous."

After a few more mundane questions, the group broke up. They were each given assignments as to where they would be stationed, and they had to work out their shifts to cover their area twenty-four hours a day.

As Susan and Frank entered Washington, DC, they found themselves in evening rush-hour traffic. *Just as I anticipated,* Frank thought. *Miserable bumper-to-bumper traffic. Not the best timing arriving at rush hour. At least we're going into the city and not leaving. We need to get to our hotel and rest up. We can plan our drop for tomorrow. It would have been nice to give Susan an additional day of rest, but we have the appointment already set for the tour.*

After fighting the traffic every bit of the way, Frank pulled into the entrance of the Capital Hilton and asked for valet parking.

"Welcome, Mr.?" the bellman asked.

"Adams, Jonathan Adams. And this is my wife, Julia."

"It is great to have you at our hotel. How long will you be staying?"

"We believe about three or four days," said Frank. "We want to take in the sights of our nation's capital. I know this isn't probably enough time to see everything. What would you suggest we try to see in three days?"

"Well, personally, I always enjoy the Lincoln Memorial, the Jefferson Memorial, the Smithsonian museums, and the White House," the bellman replied. "I suspect if you can cover all these, you'd have a good taste of DC. At the Smithsonian, you could spend three days alone, but if you take a tour you can catch many of the highlights."

"That sounds like good advice," Frank agreed. "How do we get these tours set up?"

"Our concierge just inside can do this for you. Can I help you with your bags?"

"Yes, please," he said. "But we are leaving one package in the car that I have to deliver to someone, so I'll get out the bags that will be with us here."

With that, Frank carefully removed the bags from the minivan, taking care to leave the vials, now hidden from view in a bag of their own, under the back seat of the vehicle. The bag had been specially created to maintain a constant temperature to avoid any destruction of the virus.

Frank handed the valet driver his keys and followed the bellman taking the bags as he made his way to reception.

"Good afternoon," the receptionist said. "Checking in?"

"Yes. Jonathan Adams."

"Thank you for choosing our hotel, Mr. Adams. I will need to see a form of identification, and I will need a credit card."

"Here is my driver's license," Frank responded as he handed over the new license that Samuel had provided. "I would like to pay in cash. Do I need to leave a deposit?"

"Yes, we will need a hundred-dollar deposit for any incidentals. You will receive this back when you leave if nothing is used in the minibar or in the fitness center."

"Thank you," Frank said politely as he handed over a hundred-dollar bill.

The bellman followed them to their room and spread out their luggage. He gave them an overview of the amenities at the hotel and showed them how to adjust the room temperature.

"Thank you," Frank responded, handing the bellman a tip. After the man left, Frank gave a long sigh. "Well, I'm glad we're through that."

"So am I," Susan responded. "I'm going to take a hot bath and relax. The tour is tomorrow at 3 P.M., right"

"Yes. I told them at the front desk that we would be here three days, but we may need to leave immediately after the deployment. Samuel has to give us the escape plan in case we run into problems."

"I think that's very important," Susan agreed. "Anyway, I need to rest up. This is going to be taxing whatever way you look at it. I may give Jason a call later. Tell him that we made it."

Mack met with his agents to find out the status of the search.

"John," he asked, "have we sent out a notice to look for their car?"

"Yes. State troopers and local police have the make of the car and the license plate. So far, they haven't found it."

"Tim, any luck with the hotels?"

"So far, nothing. But it may be early. They may not have arrived."

"These people can be very elusive," Mack said. "I'll give them that. But I think we're going to have a break here. Just you wait."

He added, "Guys, I want you to continue to work on trying to identify these people. I know that the home office is doing the same, but I believe we have more invested in this and may find out something sooner. I'm considering flying to DC and may take Maggie with me. She knows so much about this disease and could guide the agents in DC as to how to handle the infection."

There was snickering in the back as John popped up. "So, is it her knowledge or her looks?" he asked sarcastically.

"Well, I suppose a little of both," Mack shot back. "All right, I get it. Sure, I like being around her, but she is damn smart. You have to give her that."

"We understand," another agent said. "I think John's just jealous."

After leaving the control area, Mack texted Maggie.

Pack your bags again, babe. We're going to DC. You can help them if they discover the virus.

I'm not sure I'm completely unpacked from the last trip, so this shouldn't be a problem, she texted back. *When do we leave?*

Tonight. I'll get the flights lined up. I'm guessing that the director will want to meet with both of us.

Susan was tired after finishing her bath, but she felt the urge to call Jason. He had been so nice to her, so eager to become a father, and so concerned that she wanted to reach out to him. For once, she was letting her emotions take over where normally it was always about her duty and allegiance to her country. She dialed his number, and he answered after a few rings.

"Jason, it's Susan. I just wanted to let you know that we made it to DC safely. Frank went to the lobby to pick up a few snacks, so I thought I should give you a call."

There was a long pause where Jason said nothing, so Susan asked, "Are you there, Jason?"

"Yes, I am. I'm just trying to decide what to say. I guess

the first question is: Who are you? I thought I knew you, but I realize I don't. I wonder what your real name is. What are you planning? How did I get mixed up in all this?"

Flustered, Susan answered, "What do you mean? I don't know what you're talking about."

"Let's start with this," Jason said coldly. "Are you on vacation or are you visiting a dying mother or are you planning something deleterious and lethal?"

Susan mulled over in her mind what to say and slowly responded, "What do you mean? I have no idea what you're talking about," as she realized that he now knew more about her.

"FBI agents have questioned me," he snapped. "They tracked me from my conversations with you. They know that you have a microbiology lab in your basement. They think that you have some connection to the man who died from Ebola. So again, I'm asking—who are you really?"

"I'm Susan. The same person you've always known. I love you; I hope you realize that."

"I don't know what to believe. I want to believe you, but now I just don't know."

"When I return and the baby is born, we can work all this out," she assured him.

"We'll see. I'm somewhat doubtful." With that, he hung up the phone.

Susan was panicked and texted Frank to come back to the room immediately. Within minutes, she heard the lock open on the door, and Frank came flying in.

"What is it? Are you in labor?" he asked.

"No, this is worse. I called Jason. He was questioned by the FBI, and now he's questioning who we are. Apparently, the FBI has found the laboratory in our home. I suspect they know that we are in Washington, DC. They are going to be crawling all over this city looking for us."

"But they know you as a brunette, not a blonde," Frank reassured her. "They know me without a beard or mustache. I would have thought that we would have been recognized on checking in if they were so sure of our appearance. But you're right to be concerned. They're closing in."

CHAPTER 25

Mack and Maggie arrived at the airport terminal at five that evening and checked their bags. They made their way to the gate with a flight to Reagan Airport. Mack had made reservations at the Capital Hilton, anticipating this would be close to many of the Washington landmarks. Their flight was direct, so it didn't take long to get there. They gathered their bags as they walked to a taxi station.

"Maggie, what are you thinking? You seem lost in thought."

"I am. You would think I would be working as a physician right now and not as an agent's sidekick in trying to solve a crime. It has been fun. I'm just hoping that this won't all end, Mack. This is eventually going to come to an end with this Ebola thing, but I don't want us to come to an end when it does."

"I can assure you that it won't. It started as a simple investigation, but now it's a national crisis. It started as a simple working relationship, but now I can't live without you."

"You know just the right things to say. I love it just like I love you."

"And I love you. Together, we're going to solve this problem."

As they traveled to the center of DC, Mack said to Maggie, "Have you seen anything more beautiful than our nation's capital and its landmarks? I've always been impressed by the beauty of this city. I guess in many ways, I get more patriotic and nationalistic when I see these sites where our forefathers had the insight to forge the backbone of our great nation. It's why I went into the FBI. To preserve this heritage. To stop those people who would try to destroy it."

"I admire your conviction, Mack. I've probably had the same drive to care for my patients. Every one of them is special to me, and I feel a sense of loss if they pass away under my watch."

"See, we really aren't all that different, are we?" Mack observed. "We may come from completely different backgrounds, but our commitment to what we do is very similar. I must say that I think I'm turning you into an FBI agent. You're getting good at solving problems."

"Isn't that what I do every day when I try to find the cause of my patient's illness?" she asked. "You're right, we really aren't that different."

When they arrived at the Capital Hilton, it was nine o'clock at night. They checked into two different rooms, but before going upstairs, they stopped into the bar to have a drink together.

"Tonight, you can have your wine," he said. "I'm having a Scotch on the rocks. I've gotten to like Scotch."

"Fair enough," Maggie agreed. "Scotch seems like a man thing to me. I don't know if I could handle one of those. That's a lot of alcohol."

"Believe me, you could," Mack countered. "Your liver has been upregulated to process all that wine you drink."

"You know, you're probably right. Let me take a sip. Hey, this is pretty good, but I'll stick to my Cabernet."

After finishing their drinks, they headed to their rooms. They were on the same floor but a few doors down from each other.

Maggie gave Mack a kiss and said, "I'm giving you the night off. I'm beat and need some rest."

"OK, party pooper. I can understand that. I'll see you in the morning."

Frank called Samuel. "We've got problems. The FBI has talked with Jason. He knows about the laboratory in our basement. He was told that we have connections with Alex, and now Jason wonders who Susan really is. I'm sure he's told them that we are in Washington, DC."

"We've been concerned that they were getting close to you. We can't waste any time. Do you think that you were recognized when you checked in?"

"It doesn't seem like it. No sign that they were suspicious of us. The disguises make us look completely different."

"Good," replied Samuel. "I would plan to get to the tour of the White House as early as you can. We can't waste any more time. How is Susan feeling?"

"Fine," Frank reported. "No problems. I'm guessing the place will be crawling with FBI agents."

"You're probably right," Samuel agreed. "Be careful. Do you have the elixir in the room or your vehicle?"

"We've left it in the minivan that we just bought," Frank told him, "but I'm going to retrieve it in the morning. I didn't want the cleaning people to discover it and potentially open it."

"That's probably wise. It's kept cool, correct?"

"Yes, we've kept it in a special cooling bag."

Maggie was startled when her phone rang. Sleepily she answered.

"Hey, gorgeous," said Mack. "Are you awake?"

"Barely. Are you my alarm clock?"

"I guess so," he said cheerfully. "How about meeting in the lobby? There's a Starbucks where we can get coffee and maybe something to eat."

"Perfect but give me twenty minutes. I'm just getting up. I'll get showered and meet you down there. What are the plans today?"

"We're meeting with Herb Jamison, the FBI director," Mack told her. "He's eager to meet you, and we have to talk about the strategy to find these people. I've got our guys looking for their car, and every hotel has their pictures. We have to find them before they do something."

"I couldn't agree more. I'll be down in a short while. You can get me an American coffee. I don't tend to drink that fancy stuff. Black is fine."

"Will do. Want any pastries?"

"That would be great. I'll take a scone if they have one. See you soon."

Maggie showered and picked out a conservative dress

to wear, anticipating that when meeting the director of the FBI, it would be better to dress in this way. She applied some makeup and again tried to avoid overdoing this. She wanted to look as natural as possible. The reality was that she had natural beauty and didn't need a lot of makeup to look attractive.

She found her way to the lobby. Mack had found a small table for them and had the coffee and scone waiting.

"Who is this guy?" Maggie teased. "Somebody I know? Maybe he's available."

"All right, wise girl. You're lucky I beat you down here so you could have your coffee waiting."

"I am lucky. You're right. I'm lucky to be here with you. Let's hear about the plans for today."

"Finish this up, and then we head to the J. Edgar Hoover Building. Our appointment with the boss is at nine o'clock."

"Should I be frightened of this guy?" Maggie asked.

"No, he's fine," Mack reassured her. "Maybe a little rough around the edges. That's the way these agents tend to become."

"I'll run upstairs to grab a few things and meet you by the front door."

Back at the room, Maggie picked up her cell phone, purse, and a jacket. It was cool outside, and it looked like it could rain. As she went through the lobby, she noticed an attractive man talking with the concierge. He was tall, with dark-rimmed glasses and a goatee. *Hmm, he's looks familiar,* she thought. *I wonder where I would have met him. I'm never in DC. Probably just a coincidence.*

Mack was waiting for her and had already hailed a cab.

"Jump in, Maggie," he said as he opened the door. "I'll point out the sights as we go."

The ride through DC was beautiful. Traffic was heavy,

but because they had to go slow, Mack could tell Maggie about the buildings they passed. Maggie marveled at the Washington Monument, the Lincoln Memorial, the capitol. She had seen all these structures on TV, but she found them even more beautiful in person.

Eventually, they got to the FBI building. After showing his credentials, Mack directed Maggie to the elevator and the director's office. The secretary immediately recognized Mack.

"Mr. Johnson, the director is expecting you," she said. "Just follow me." She led them down a hallway and to a large office with a round table and four chairs. The director was behind a mammoth desk and stood up when they entered, extending his hand.

"Agent Johnson," he said to Mack. "Good to see you again. And who is this good-looking lady with you?"

"This is Dr. Margaret Hamilton," Mack said in introduction. "She has been instrumental in diagnosing these Ebola cases and treating them. Fortunately, some of the patients have survived, probably because of the care that she was able to give them."

"Very nice to meet you, Dr. Hamilton," said Jamison. "Now let's get down to business. I don't think we have much time here. Tell me what you know."

Mack began, "What started out as a rare infection that shouldn't have affected a person who never left Chicago has ended up in a race to find a possible terrorist whose intentions appear to be nefarious. We don't have all the answers, but Frank and Susan Lee—probably not their real names—have probably altered the Ebola virus and are planning to release this deadly infection somewhere in Washington, DC. Susan had an affair with a gentleman who had previously worked at the Pentagon. He was in bioweapons research, and we believe she tried to extract as much information as possible about germ warfare. He was so infatuated with her. She asked him repeatedly about bioweapons and where Americans stood regarding prevention of these diseases if they were used as a bioweapon. He thought that she was just interested in his job.

"She was a pro at extracting information without raising any red flags. He seems innocent of being complicit with them and was totally hoodwinked by her. She was definitely skilled at luring him in and finding information. He doesn't know where they may be going, but he has gotten them floor plans of the main federal buildings here in Washington, DC, so we believe they are here."

Jamison nodded and said, "We have agents stationed in all the main monuments, and they will be there around the clock."

"We provided the hotels with their pictures," Mack added, "but they may have changed their appearance. We don't know."

"I want the two of you to be available if they're spotted," Jamison said. "You may not recognize them, but you know how they think. If they're apprehended, you can help with the interrogation. In the meantime, I would suggest that you meet the agent in charge of the local operation so he can get your contact information. I've asked him to come here shortly."

About that time, Jamison's secretary called him on his desk phone to let him know that Agent Jeffries had arrived.

"Great, show him in."

A six-foot-four towering figure entered the room, dressed like every FBI agent in a plain black suit. He had a smile on his face on entering.

"Phillip Jeffries," he said, extending his hand. "It's great to meet you."

"Agent Jeffries has been with the agency for twenty-five years and has extensive experience in counterintelligence,"

Jamison remarked. "So I thought that he would be an excellent choice for this job."

"I think you're right," Mack responded. "We have provided his agents with what we know about the Lees. Have you been able to find out anything additional?"

"We believe they may be Chinese agents," Jeffries replied. "They seem to have broad connections. They've been very good at avoiding discovery, and to do that requires working for an adversarial country like China. We have known for some time that China's agents are in this country. They often come here disguised as man and wife, college students, or professors at universities, and they blend into the community. They can bury any past by avoiding taking out credit, paying in cash, and having very common names. They usually have legitimate businesses, which is a great front for what they do behind the scenes. I suspect the boyfriend was really duped. They use sex, force, and any other means to extract what they want, and they're very well trained to do what they do."

"I believe you're absolutely right," Maggie said. "But what do you think is their motive?"

"We're not sure, but it may be that they simply want to create a great disruption in the United States. Their relationship with our country hasn't been very good lately, and they want to get back at us. Their economy is doing poorly, while ours has been off the charts. They want to derail this."

"What would you like us to do?" Mack asked.

"How about join the others downstairs and we'll go over our plans."

"Perfect."

Frank made his way to the concierge desk and asked about tours of the White House. He noticed an attractive lady looking over at him as she walked through the lobby, but he didn't recognize her. He didn't think that she recognized him, because she gave no indication of any concern, so he turned back to the concierge.

"We are scheduled to go there at three o'clock," he said, "but I wasn't sure when we should be there."

The concierge thumbed through his book of contacts and made a call. After about ten minutes of talking, he set down the phone and looked up.

"You're in luck," the concierge told Frank. "They told me that your tour has been set up at three o'clock, as you said. You apparently arranged this through your senator or representative. You'll need to meet at the outside gate about fifteen minutes before it starts. Your tour guide's name is Shirley. She will be expecting you. As you've probably discovered, the traffic in DC is awful. You can walk there."

"My wife is pregnant so we may take a cab even though it is a short distance."

CHAPTER 26

Mack and Maggie met the team of agents in the second-floor conference room. Agent Jeffries projected images of the various buildings that potentially could be targets of the Lees.

"The problem we have now is that Mr. Turley provided them with plans that give them schematics of multiple buildings. There is no indication which building would be their target. Therefore, we have to be prepared for any of them being the target. We have agents stationed at these sites twenty-four hours a day. We dressed them like tourists, but obviously at night you wouldn't expect a tourist watching cars or other vehicles.

"I have special cell phones that I want to give you that will allow you to communicate with us directly. That way, if you are aware of anything, you can call us or vice versa—if we discover something and need your help, we will call you. If we apprehend them, I believe both of you can be beneficial in their questioning. If they are Chinese intelligence, they will be very skilled at avoiding giving any direct answers and will likely be very convincing."

After completing the meeting with Agent Jeffries, Mack and Maggie made the decision to return to the hotel and think through their own strategy while waiting for something to occur.

"Maggie, we're in a rather uncertain predicament right now. We have leads on these people, but we don't know if and when something may happen. I suppose we should catch a bite of lunch near the hotel and then talk through what we can do while we're waiting."

"I think that's a great idea, Mack. I may go for a run or work out in the fitness center to clear my mind a bit while we contemplate next steps. I need a break from all this."

They grabbed a cab at the entry of the FBI building. Mack asked the driver to take them around to many of the federal buildings as they returned to the hotel.

"It's amazing how beautiful all the structures are," said Maggie. "I would hate to see something happen to any of them."

"I agree. Ebola wouldn't destroy the buildings, but it would certainly destroy the people."

After arriving at the hotel, they found a small café nearby. Maggie ordered a salad with grilled chicken. Mack had a burger and a beer.

"So, Miss Smarty," Mack said. "What are you thinking?"

"I'm thinking that never in my lifetime would I have thought that I would leave my practice to be with an FBI agent trying to find a Chinese agent," Maggie marveled. "I feel like I'm in a spy movie!"

"Just another day in the life of an FBI agent!" said Mack.
"Yeah, right. I'm sure."

"Well, quite frankly, most of the time my life is rather boring, but you have made it special. Maybe today we can catch the bad guys. Who knows?"

After finishing their lunch, they walked back to the hotel. Mack reached down to hold Maggie's hand as they walked.

She turned and smiled at him as they strolled toward the hotel. "Like I said, I'm going to put on some exercise clothes and maybe go for a run. I'll catch up with you when I get back."

"I'm less energetic. I'm going to take a nap."

Frank made his way to the parking garage and found the van. He carefully removed the vials and placed them in a carrying pouch to transport them to the room. On arriving, he placed them on the counter, removing them from the cool storage.

"Susan, here's your favorite perfume," he smiled.

"Sure, it's just a killer," she remarked. "One vial should be enough. What should we do with the remainder?"

"I think we'll leave them in the van. We can take them with us, but we aren't going to be able to return to Chicago. They know where we live, and we can't go back. We're going to have to start over somewhere else. Let's pack our clothes," he suggested, "and I'll put them in the van along with the extra vials. The White House is close to the hotel, but in your condition, I think we should take a cab. Once the vial is deployed, we'll return here and leave immediately."

"That sounds just right," said Susan.

"I'll text Samuel and let him know we're ready to leave."

Maggie changed her clothes and headed out of the entrance to the hotel. She found that since she was close to the White House and other monuments, she could run by these, giving her something to look at as she jogged. It was cool outside but perfect for running. She found herself going farther than normal because she was distracted by all the sights and didn't pay attention to how far she had gone. By the time she returned to the hotel, she realized that she had outdone herself in running today.

After wiping the sweat from her brow, she headed to the elevator. When the elevator arrived, a couple exited that looked vaguely familiar. When the doors closed, she realized that the man was the same individual she had noticed talking to the concierge. As she rolled this over in her mind, she kept asking herself where she would have possibly met him, and she just couldn't place a location or situation.

As she showered, she couldn't get this out of her mind. As she was drying off, she thought to herself, *Wait a minute. What about the lady with him? I think she's pregnant. Could it be them? I've got to tell Mack.*

After dressing quickly, she ran to his room and knocked on the door frantically. He came to the door with sleepy eyes.

"I thought that you were trying to knock down the door," said Mack. "What's going on?"

"I may have seen them!" Maggie eagerly reported. "I saw them get out of the elevator. I had seen the man this morning talking to the concierge, and at the time I thought I recognized him, but I just couldn't place him. Now, when they stepped out of the elevator, it suddenly came to me that the girl with him was pregnant, and I put two and two together. I think it's them. We could talk with the concierge, and maybe we will find out where they were planning on going. He may give us the target."

"Fantastic, Maggie," Mack exclaimed, suddenly wide awake. "Let's go to the lobby now."

Maggie was pumped with adrenaline and decided to run down the stairs and not wait for an elevator. She felt time was of the essence. They found the concierge stand, but there was another couple getting information about local tours. Mack became impatient and interrupted the couple.

"Listen," he said, "I'm sorry to intrude, but we have a serious question that I need to ask this gentleman. Would you mind if I step in for a moment?"

"I guess it won't be a problem," the irritated husband responded.

"Actually," Mack clarified, "I'm an FBI agent, and this is regarding official business."

The man was suddenly less irritated and told Mack to go right ahead.

Mack spoke urgently to the concierge. "There was an individual who was talking to you this morning. My friend noticed him as she was going through the lobby. He had dark glasses, a goatee, and was dressed nicely according to the lady here. Can you tell us what he was asking about?"

The concierge smiled. "Oh, yes. I remember the gentleman. He was quite nice. He said that they had never been to DC, and they wanted to see the sights. They were particularly interested in the White House and had already set up a tour. Let's see. I believe it is supposed to start at three o'clock. Yes, that's correct."

"Thank you. You've been very helpful."

Mack picked up the cell phone Jeffries had provided him and immediately called. "Agent Jeffries," he began, "Maggie has likely identified the target. It appears to be the White House. Maggie saw a gentleman who she thought she recognized but couldn't place. When she saw him leave the hotel, he was with a lady who was pregnant. They fit the description even when they don't have the appearance of the photographs we've sent."

"I'll call now and make sure that we have agents stationed completely around the White House, and we'll try and cancel any tours," Jeffries responded.

Frank and Susan arrived early, as planned, before the tour was to begin. As they were waiting at the gate, ten other people gathered who were planning to take the same tour.

One older gentleman leaned over to Frank and said, "I've always wanted to see the White House. Despite all the travels my wife and I have made, we just never made it here, so finally this is going to happen. What about you?"

Frank said, "It's been a place that my wife and I have wanted to visit as well. We're excited about the opportunity. To think that this is where the President of the United States lives. It's exciting."

At that moment, Shirley, a white-haired lady with a striking appearance, arrived. She gave them general directions of where they could go with maps to use, but she then pointed out that these were self-guided tours. They were free to stroll through at their leisure, but she would be with them to answer questions.

They began walking and first had to go through a checkpoint to ensure that they had no guns or explosives. Susan had attached the elixir to a set of keys, suggesting it was simply a key holder, and it passed through the checkpoint.

As the tour progressed, Frank and Susan tried to lag behind. Frank kept going over in his mind each room from his recollection of the drawing that Jason had sent. He knew the exact room on the schematics where he had found a vent to deploy the elixir, and they would be approaching that area soon in the West Wing.

He turned to Susan and said, "Honey, don't you think we should slow down a bit to give you time to rest before we continue?"

"You're right, dear," said Susan. "Let me just stop for a moment."

Shirley, their guide, noticed that they had stopped and became concerned.

"Are you all right?" she asked of Susan.

"I'm fine," Susan assured her. "Just a little tired. I'm ready to get this pregnancy over with."

"I can certainly understand that," said Shirley. "You're brave to be out doing a tour when it appears you could deliver at any moment."

"Probably just a little crazy," Susan agreed, "but it's been on my bucket list for a long time to visit the White House, so I couldn't pass up the opportunity. We've had these tickets that we got through our senator, and I didn't want to give them up."

"Well, it really is spectacular," Shirley said. "Just rest up, and you can catch up on your own time."

As he glanced around, Frank found the vent that was on the schematics in the corner of the room. When the guide was out of sight and there appeared to be no guards around, he slipped into the enclave, inserted the elixir through the vent, pulled off the top cap to arm the device, and pressed the bottom button to deploy the charge. He returned to Susan, who was resting and watching for anyone who might approach.

"Well, dear, are you rested up now? I believe it's time for us to move on."

"I'm fine. We can go now."

With that, they began to hurry along to leave the building.

As they exited, they were told that all the tours had been canceled for the day.

That was close, Frank thought. *We just made it.*

As they were walking to the curb, Susan stopped.

"What is it, Susan?"

"Something happened, Frank. Look!"

When he glanced down at her dress, fluid was dripping from the hem and down her leg.

"Oh my gosh," he said. "Your water broke."

"I know, and now I'm getting contractions—big ones!"

"We need to get an ambulance to take you to the hospital."

Frank found one of the capitol police and told him what had happened. The policeman immediately placed a 911 call for an ambulance. Within minutes, Frank could hear the ambulance approaching the White House.

Secret Service agents and the FBI agents rushed into the White House. The head of the Secret Service began evacuating the building. The president was out of the country on this particular day, but the building was filled with White House personnel. A steady stream of people began leaving.

The agents had brought bomb-sniffing dogs into the building and began searching from one room to the next to try to find the vial of virus. Maggie and Mack had just arrived and found Jeffries directing his agents to look for a bomb or any suspicious package.

Maggie stopped him for a moment. "Listen," she said, "I don't know if this would be helpful, but at the hotel where the virus was deployed, it was placed in a vent for the heating and air-conditioning system. We found fragments of a glass vial, so you should keep this in mind."

"That's great information." Jeffries picked up his phone and immediately asked the agents to check all the vents. "This may be the location of the package, possibly a glass vial," he informed them.

A moment later, one of the agents radioed back. "We think we see it, sir. We're in the West Wing. Bring the bomb squad in here with the dogs."

In a short time, they found the glass vial and placed it in a special container for bombs that completely sealed it off. Ten minutes later, they heard it detonate.

"I think this answers your question," Mack responded. "The vial that was at the hotel venting system was exploded by a charge and here we see the same thing. The agents need to continue to search the remaining vents for other vials and now we have to find our subjects. Let's see if anyone noticed them when they left the building."

Mack and Maggie exited the building and decided they should ask the capitol police if they had seen anyone suspicious. Carl Green, the policeman located near the exit of the building, was the first person they found.

"Captain Green, my name is Matthew Johnson. I'm an FBI agent. We have been tracking a couple who we believe may have planted an explosive in the White House to spread a virus. Did you notice anything unusual of the people who left the tour recently?"

"No, not really," said Captain Green. "I did think I was going to have to deliver a baby. This very pregnant woman went into labor coming off the tour. I called an ambulance for her, and she was taken to George Washington University Hospital. I suspect she's delivered a baby by now."

Turning to Maggie, Mack said excitedly, "That's got to be them. Let's go."

CHAPTER 27

They found Jeffries and told him of the lady taken to the hospital.

"This has got to be them," Maggie said. "We need to get there now."

"Let's go in my car," Jeffries replied. "I have lights to enable us to speed through the traffic. I'll radio ahead and find what floor she may be on. I won't ask them to do anything. I don't want to spook our suspects."

"Good idea," Mack said as Jeffries made the call.

"She should be on the third floor where labor and delivery are located," Jeffries noted. "We can get there in a few minutes."

After finding his car, Jeffries placed the light on the roof, and everyone jumped in. As he accelerated, the tires squealed, and he sped toward the hospital. On arrival, he put the car in the emergency room parking lot, and they entered the through the ER access door. Jeffries flashed his creds, and they were immediately escorted in.

"How can we help you?" the doctor in charge inquired.

"You had a young woman brought here only a short time

ago from outside the White House, and she was in labor. Do you know where she is now?"

"Well, she was in full labor when she arrived and was taken immediately to the obstetrics floor," the doctor replied. "She has surely delivered by now. She was already complete when she arrived, and we had her doing transitional breathing to slow things down."

"What's the fastest way to get there?" Mack asked.

"You can take the elevator just outside the exit from the emergency room, and it will take you to that floor. It was set up just for those women who come in ready to have the baby."

"Perfect," Jeffries said. "Let's go, people. No time to waste."

They raced to the elevator and escorted out anyone inside. After arriving on the third floor, they again showed their credentials.

"You had a lady that was brought here from the emergency room only a short time ago, and she was in advanced labor. Where is she now?"

"That must be Mrs. Adams," said the nurse. "Julia Adams. Yes, she arrived here having major contractions. She delivered an eight-pound fourteen-ounce boy shortly after arrival. It was amazing that she was able to deliver the baby with almost no anesthesia. She's a tough person. Usually, they're screaming in pain, especially with a large child. Mrs. Adams barely made a peep. I'd say she was one of the toughest women I've seen go through the labor and delivery so heroically. Hardly a sound."

"Where is she now?" Maggie asked.

"She should be in her room. The baby would be in the nursery getting some attention and evaluation but will be returned to her after."

"May we see her?" Mack requested.

"Yes, but only because you're Feds. Normally we wouldn't allow visitors at this time who aren't family."

The charge nurse led them down the hall to room 3233 and opened the door. There was the bed, a crib, bedsheets pulled back, and a hospital gown lying on the unmade bed—but no patient.

"I wonder where she is," said the nurse. "Let me check the bathroom and the halls. She may have gone for a walk, but I haven't seen her out of the room."

Agent Jeffries looked at Mack. "I'm guessing she's out of here."

"I'm guessing you're right."

Maggie looked at both inquisitively. "So what's going on?"

"We both think they're gone. They likely had an escape plan in case this happened."

"And just leave the baby?" Maggie asked.

"Most likely. They couldn't handle taking a newborn child with them now."

The flustered nurse returned. "We can't find her anywhere, nor her husband. They seemed to have disappeared."

Frank and Susan walked down the flights of stairs to the back exit of the hospital. Frank opened the door, and a black SUV was parked waiting for them. A sullen-faced man in a black leather coat got out of the passenger seat and opened the door of the SUV, never cracking a smile.

Susan remained at the exit to the hospital. She was pale and weak from the delivery. As she mulled over in her mind what to do, she turned to Frank and said, "Frank, I can't just leave."

"What do you mean you can't leave? You have to. There is no choice."

"I can't leave the baby," Susan said quietly. "Maybe you're right. I've become an American. I think I'm in love with Jason. I just can't do it."

"You must," Frank insisted. "You know too much."

The man holding the door reached inside his jacket and pulled out a Glock, pointing it directly at Susan's head.

"See, Susan?" said Frank. "No choice." He put his hand in front of the gun and directed the barrel toward the ground. "Let me talk to her," he said to the man dressed in black holding the gun.

Turning back to Susan, he said, "Susan, you have to be reasonable. We must go back. The FBI is likely here. You'll end up in prison. You see, there really is no choice for you."

"There is always a choice, Frank. If I go to prison, then I go to prison. It's either prison here or back home. I view that as a prison for me. It is not a life that I want to live. Here I have a child and someone who loves me."

With that, she darted back into the hospital, slamming the door just as a gunshot rang out and ricocheted off the metal.

Frank tried to open the door, but it was locked with no handle.

"Do we risk going through the front entrance to find her?" Frank asked as he turned to the man in the black jacket.

"Too risky," the man said. "FBI is here. They'll catch all of us."

With that, the men jumped back into the vehicle and sped off.

Susan, feeling faint, found her way to the elevator and chose the button to the third floor. She thought they wouldn't likely kill her around other people in a hospital elevator. But then again, she knew her country would kill people for much less than this. After exiting, she turned away from the hallway toward her room.

"Can we look at the surveillance video, since you have cameras everywhere in the hospital?" Jeffries asked.

"I'm sure security can help you with that." The nurse directed them to the main level. When the agents arrived at the security office, they again showed their creds. The security officer was staring at a bank of video monitors showing images throughout the hospital.

"Can you show us the video from the cameras on the labor and delivery floor, in particular the last two hours?" Jeffries asked.

"Sure," the officer replied as he rewound a tape that was recording that camera's video. "Here it is," he answered.

The agents scrolled the video slowly. The camera pointing down the hall from the Lee's room showed nursing staff and orderlies going back and forth. Then there was a lull in activity. The door to the Lee's room was opened slightly, and it appeared that someone was peering out. Soon, Mr. and Mrs. Lee were seen moving quickly to the exit and the stairs. The time of the recording was six o'clock, which was close to the shift change for the nurses. Mack asked to see the video on the perimeter of the building.

"Which side of the building do you want to see?" asked the guard.

"Can you show us the potential exit from the stairway coming down from labor and delivery?" said Mack.

"Sure, here it is."

"We need it from about six o'clock to six-fifteen"

After adjusting the video back and forth, the officer found the exact time. As the video was slowly advanced, two people stepped out of the door to the stairwell in the back of the hospital. They could see Susan remain at the door, and she appeared to be arguing with the men. Then the gun was drawn and fired as she slammed the door shut. The men climbed back into the vehicle sped off. The license plate was covered, so it wasn't possible to identify a number.

"I always knew women were the stronger sex, but carrying out a terrorist attack, delivering a baby, then being shot at—now that's a tough lady!" Mack said.

"I'm guessing she couldn't leave the baby," Maggie said. "She may be a Chinese agent, but now she's a mother. That became more important to her." She turned to Mack and said, "I know where to find her. Try the nursery. She couldn't leave."

As they went down the hall to the nursery, they cleared away any visitors. They didn't know what to expect if they found her there. Maggie was right: Susan was standing at the window, staring at her baby, whose crib had been pulled close to the window so she could she see her new son.

"Susan Lee?" Mack asked.

Susan turned slowly and answered with a soft voice, "Yes."

"You're under arrest. You have the right to remain silent," Mack began, reading her the Miranda rights.

She said nothing, simply turned to gaze at the baby with a smile on her face. She was escorted back to her room, and guards were left outside to prevent her from escaping.

—◁▥▶—

"What are we going to do with the baby?" Maggie inquired.

"We know who the father is," Mack said. "How about we let Jason know that he is a father? He can tell us what he would like to do with his new son."

Mack had Jason's number and dialed him using his cell phone.

"Is this Jason?" he asked when he heard the person on the other line.

"Yes, it is. Who is this?"

"This is Agent Johnson. I met you at your house. We have tracked the Lees to Washington, DC, thanks to your help. They attempted to plant a vial of Ebola in the White House, but we were fortunate in that we stopped this before it got deployed. We discovered that Mrs. Lee went into labor and ultimately delivered the baby, a boy, at George Washington University Hospital. When we went to the hospital to question them, we found the baby in the nursery. He is a healthy eight-pound fourteen-ounce boy."

Jason sighed. "I'm thrilled to be a father, just not under these circumstances. I wanted Susan to leave her husband and marry me, but I came to realize that this was never going to happen. I know you may think this strange, but I still love her."

Mack said, "We found that Susan started to leave, and they tried to take her with them, but she ran back into the hospital. She's here and under arrest. She wants to talk to you."

"So she didn't abandon her baby?" said Jason, confused. "Wait a minute, I keep forgetting, I'm a father. I'm half of this creation. Our baby. I'll catch a flight tonight and be there tomorrow. Can I talk to her now?"

"I'll hand her the cell phone," said Mack.

When Susan was on the line, Jason said, "Susan, you're a mother! I'm a father! And now we have a Henry. I know what happened. I'm not sure what's going to happen to you now, but I want you to know that I love you. We will find a way to work this out, and I will be with you through all this. I'll be there tomorrow for you."

"I love you too, Jason," she said. "I can't wait to see you."

Mack took the phone back from Susan and found Maggie in the hall.

"What do you think will happen to Susan?" Maggie asked.

"She will likely have prison time, but I suspect she knows a lot, and there is a good chance she may get a plea bargain and not spend long behind bars. It's likely she'll get a new identity with a witness protection plan, because the Chinese will be furious."

"Well, Mack. This has been quite a trip. I would have never believed that my life as a physician would have gone down this path—or that I would ever have met someone who could make me so happy. I just don't want this all to end."

"It isn't going to end," Mack said. "Our next stop will be a trip to Indiana. I want my family to meet the love of my life."

"I can't wait," replied Maggie. "I want to meet the mother and father who created such a great guy. But if I meet your family, then you have to meet mine. My family is going to fall in love with you as much as I have."

At that moment, Phillip Jeffries found them in the hall. "I've been told that the Capital Hilton ballroom is packed with media, and you two should be the ones to address them, since you've been with this from the very beginning. You might let the press them know we've found a van that belonged to our couple and discovered more vials of elixir under the back seat. We've disposed of these as well. Oh, sorry if I've interrupted a special moment," he said with a smile. "Agent Johnson, you've done a great job. I'm sure this is going to lead to a promotion for you. The big boss has told me how proud he is of your accomplishments. You've prevented potentially many fatalities and pandemonium in our country. The president also wants to meet with you at the White House and thank you both personally. But I want to also thank you for finding the lethal elixir."

Turning to Maggie, Mack looked into her eyes. "It wouldn't have been possible without this special person here. I believe that I'm going to get more than a promotion. I believe that I'm going to get a wife."

Jeffries said smiling, "I'd say that this has been quite a trip for both of you. I want to be the first to congratulate you."

With that, Maggie began to cry.

CPSIA information can be obtained
at www.ICGtesting.com
Printed in the USA
LVHW010051031021
699331LV00003B/3